MW01041427

of mine is —

my favorite.

CIRCUS ON THE SQUARE

Dennis Lanny

11/2. / 18

ook

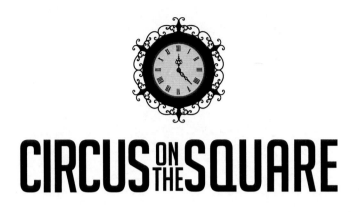

CIRCUS ON THE SQUARE

DENNIS LANNING

TATE PUBLISHING
AND ENTERPRISES, LLC

Published by Tate Publishing & Enterprises, LLC
127 E. Trade Center Terrace | Mustang, Oklahoma 73064 USA
1.888.361.9473 | www.tatepublishing.com

Tate Publishing is committed to excellence in the publishing industry. The company reflects the philosophy established by the founders, based on Psalm 68:11,
"The Lord gave the word and great was the company of those who published it."

Book design copyright © 2015 by Tate Publishing, LLC. All rights reserved.
Cover design by Nino Carlo Suico
Interior design by Jomar Ouano

Published in the United States of America

ISBN: 978-1-68142-929-8
Fiction / Christian / General
15.05.05

To the churches I've served as pastor,
Thank you for shaping my life.

ACKNOWLEDGMENTS

Thank you to Professor Thom Brucie, Jeffery Jackson, Kelly Arnold Roark, Donna Beall, Meghan Jackson, and Crystal Seagle (deceased). Enrolling in that English 350 evening class at Brewton-Parker College was a big step for me. You encouraged me as I started this book. You'll recognize the first few chapters.

Thanks to Pat Jones and Debbi McCarthy for reading through my first draft. I took your advice!

Every pastor needs good friends to lend support in the good times and bad. I've got "K5": Barry Giddens, Thad Harvey, Craig Hutto, Tucker Lewis, and Rodney Porter. Thanks, guys!

As always, my biggest support comes from the love of my life, Joy Lanning. You are always just what I need.

CHAPTER 1

"Circus on the Square," the headline shouted. It still irritated Ernie.

Who gave this Cindy Martin the right to call my store a circus? he thought. *Call it a variety store, a mercantile, even perhaps a department store, but not a circus. This is my source of income you're talking about.* The article appeared in the Saturday, March 21, 2009 issue of the *Columbus* paper, in a regular feature about area businesses. Nearly two weeks later, Ernie Bostwick still kept a copy of the article tucked under the counter by the cash register. He had circled the many instances of words like *different* and *strange* and *old-fashioned*. He disgustedly slid it back into its place.

The shop that displayed the name *Ernie's* over the door certainly was unique, but not a circus.

To the left, upon entering, the shopper encountered the lamp section. Lamps like these could not be bought anywhere else in Barkley. In fact, the whole United

States of America did not contain another collection like the one on display.

In the middle of the area, a former skateboard, now a lamp, proudly pointed its toe in the air. To the right, about three-feet distant, a pressure cooker sported a silver lampshade hat and light from a sixty-watt bulb. A pole lamp at the back of the section had obviously had a previous career as a hockey stick. Irons, wig stands, teddy bears, bowling balls, wine bottles—all did their share to light up the room, for all had been equipped with plugs, bulbs, and everything else needed to proudly join the light-fixture family.

The clock section behind the lamps was bereft of cords or plugs. Every clock had the same small black box in the back equipped with an AA battery that operated the hands. However, there the similarities ended. Baseball bats, football trophies, flowerpots, and cast-iron fry pans had all acquired the ability to keep time. An old phone book, forever glued shut, was now a clock. A dartboard had lost its darts, but had found an hour hand and a minute hand.

The section to the right of the front door had toys and games. All were classics, all could have been found in a toy store in 1950. Board games included checkers, Life, chess, Parcheesi, Monopoly. Toys like pop guns and sling shots were also on display in quantities that indicated they sold well. Ernie's had cap guns and bows with arrows that had suction cup tips. Bags of marbles could be bought in different sizes—different-sized bags or different-sized marbles.

There was much more in the store, including newspapers, magazines, a coffee shop, juggling supplies, and used books. "Circus?" Ernie said to himself. "This store can please anyone with something. It is criminally negligent to portray it as odd."

In reality, the newspaper story had been a boon for Ernie Bostwick's store. Within a half day, new customers appeared, looking for special lamps and clocks they'd read about. Coffee sales were up as visitors lingered. A few beginning jugglers were proud to find a store that carried clubs and rings. In fact, every department in the store showed a significant increase in sales. Though the proprietor still burned about the word *circus*, revenue had increased.

Ernie picked up a news magazine and sat in one of the comfortable stuffed chairs in the coffee shop, waiting for Melissa Rhodes to arrive from school. He wondered if her hair would be colorful today, or still its normal shade of blonde. Once she was here to handle the register, he could work on a couple lighting fixtures back in his workshop.

The bell over the front door jingled as a tall, well-dressed lady entered. The brown-haired woman looked slightly familiar, but she was not one of his regulars.

"Can I help you?" he offered, putting his reading down.

"I'm not really sure what I'm looking for," she said. "I know you have some very unique lamps. I need something for a particular corner of my den, and you probably have something that would do. Let me look just a minute."

"Let me know if I can help," Ernie replied, resuming his reading. "Sometimes I can build a custom lamp, if you don't see it on display." Actually, he already had enough orders for one-of-a-kind lights to keep him busy for several days.

The door jingled again, and Ernie recognized Melissa arriving for work, though she wasn't pink-haired or blonde. Today, his high school worker had an Irish look with flaming red hair.

"Hey, Mr. Bostwick. I'm *so* glad to be here. I thought the school week would never end." Melissa always liked Friday.

Smiling broadly, Ernie kidded her, "I'm glad you're here too. I should give you a raise. I think some young men do business with us just to enjoy the varying hues of your hair."

In mock seriousness, she shot back, "Wow! How about a quarter an hour more for each new hair color?"

"Let me think about it," he said, "for the better part of a year."

Ernie had temporarily forgotten about the customer in the lamp section. "Find anything, ma'am?" he called in her direction.

She stood still, frowning back and forth at two floor lamps. "It seems a shame to settle for one of these fairly ordinary floor lamps. I don't need anything to read by, just something to brighten up the corner of the room. Do you have anything else?"

"Maybe I've got something in the storeroom that you can use to decorate that corner," he ventured. "Melissa, we'll be right back." Ernie led the tall lady toward the back, heading for the door on the right.

"Okay, Mr. Bostwick."

~

"This is my storeroom, Miss...?" Ernie paused.

"My name is Cynthia, Mr. Bostwick," she said, extending her hand.

"Please call me Ernie, Cynthia," he said as he shook her hand. "These are items I've acquired from estate sales, yard sales, going-out-of-business sales, and so forth that I thought had potential for becoming a lamp or a clock one day. It's amazing how many lamps have started in this room from items that someone else had given up on."

Ernie's customer looked over the odd collection. There were kitchen utensils, bicycle parts, hat racks, just to name a few of the items. He could see a truckload of doubt in her visage. Shortly, though, Cynthia's eyes fairly jumped out of her head.

"That's it!" she cried.

Ernie tried to guess which item had gotten her so excited. "I'm not sure I see it," he tendered. Then he saw what she was staring at. "Do you mean you'd like a lamp to be made out of that artificial ficus tree?"

Cynthia looked at Ernie doubtfully. "Am I being ridiculous?" she asked.

Ernie dragged the four-foot-tall tree forward into better light. He rubbed his head of gray hair, looked at the plant from every imaginable angle, then took off his glasses and stroked his gray moustache. After the better part of a minute, Ernie's face sprouted a smile.

"Yes, Cynthia, I can do it. The bulb and shade will look great nestled in the middle of the foliage, and I've got an idea of how I might camouflage the cord. This is going to be fun. I guarantee that you'll like the final product." Ernie turned toward the door; Cynthia understood this meant they were heading back to the front of the store, and she walked in that direction.

"Would it be possible," she said, "to have the lamp as early as Monday? I'm having company then, and I'd really be proud to show off my new floor lamp."

"Yes, ma'am," the store owner said. "I'll have it ready Monday afternoon. Does thirty dollars sound reasonable?" Actually, Ernie was going to insist on that amount.

Cynthia smiled and nodded.

"Melissa will get your name and phone number. We appreciate your business."

A few minutes later, Melissa found Ernie in his workshop, carefully putting the finishing touches on a cutting board wall clock. "I knew that lady looked familiar," she said. "I see her picture on her column in the paper every Wednesday and Saturday."

"Really?" Ernie replied. "I did have the feeling that I'd seen this Cynthia before."

Melissa was suddenly grinning impishly. "Mr. Bostwick, that Cynthia is the one who wrote that article two weeks ago that you've been complaining about. That was Cindy Martin!"

Ernie's face paled a little bit.

His helper asked, "Do you want me to add twenty dollars to the price of the lamp?"

Saturday morning, sunshine yanked the city of Barkley out of bed. Temperatures normal for June were occurring on April 4.

When Melissa arrived at Ernie's at 8:00 a.m. to help open the store, she found the boss had already brewed two flavors of coffee and sat in the coffee shop in the middle of the store, reading the morning paper.

"What time did you get here, Mr. Bostwick?" she queried. "I'm not late, am I?"

"No, you're not late. It seemed like too nice a day for an old bachelor to just sit at home," he answered. "I guess I got here about half an hour ago."

"Who told you that fifty-five is old? My dad is forty-two, and you are in better shape than he is. And you've still got all your hair." Melissa headed for the lighting fixture part of the store; Ernie liked to have about half the lamps turned on.

"Mr. B, you remember that this is the first weekend of the month, don't you?" Melissa finished turning on lamps. "Are you going to hit the yard sales this morning, or skip a month?"

Surprise blossomed on his face. Ernie stated the obvious: "I forgot that this was the first Saturday." The best yard sales in Barkley always seemed to be on the first Saturday of the month; they were Ernie's primary source of unusual lamp and clock material. Spring cleaning made April and May yard sales especially bountiful.

"Whew, I don't know," said Ernie. "I've got Mike coming in at ten to work until one, but I've got that crazy lady's ficus tree lamp to put together. I thought that I could probably finish it today." Since Ernie had learned Cindy Martin was the Cynthia who had ordered the special lamp, he had been referring to her as "that crazy lady."

Just last night before closing at five, Ernie had looked through his storage room. Lately, business had been brisk. The assortment of items that he used as materials for making unusual clocks and lamps was at an all-time low. There were a number of skateboards, but Ernie had made dozens of skateboard clocks and lamps. Candlesticks of all sizes littered the room, easy starters for lamps. Ernie was actually a little tired of making lamps from candlesticks. There were several sports-related items, and many kitchen utensils and pots and pans. Ernie needed some new ideas, and just the things he needed were going to be in yard sales all over town today.

He had to put that lamp together today though. He couldn't really depend on having time Monday. *How many times have I told somebody*, he thought, *that Mondays are dependably undependable?* He needed to be at the yard sales, and he also needed to be here at the store; it was the age-old problem of not being able to be in two places at once.

But first Ernie would finish his coffee.

A well-dressed lady in her forties was today's first customer. "Good morning, Melissa. Love your hair! Did you do the color yourself?" It was Gloria.

"It's just a rinse, Ms. Smith," replied the cashier. "I thought I'd try it a few days."

Gloria pretended to be offended. "Please, Melissa, would you call me Gloria? Don't make me ask again. 'Ms. Smith' makes me feel so old!"

Melissa giggled. "I'm sorry, Gloria. I guess my parents brought me up too well. Going some place special today? You look great!"

Actually, Gloria always looked like she was headed for a special appointment. She always wore jewelry, always wore makeup, including lipstick. She never had a hair out of place.

"Is Ernie somewhere amongst all this?" Gloria asked Melissa.

"Mr. Bostwick is in his workshop, I think, Gloria," she replied.

Ernie stuck his head out of his workshop door. "Good morning, Ms. Smith!" he called out, grinning from sideburn to sideburn.

Gloria frowned and called back, "All right, Mr. Bostwick."

Gloria found the workshop in the midst of a planning phase. Lamp parts were neatly laid out on the floor, including a small green lampshade, a socket, green floral tape, another sand-colored roll of tape, a small roll of electrical cord, and various tools. In the midst of it all was an artificial ficus tree; Ernie stood with one hand on the tree and the other stroking his chin in contemplation.

"You would have more room if you'd move that tree," she said.

"It's not a tree," he said, not looking up. "It's a lamp."

Gloria wasn't sure how to respond, so she changed the subject. "Got your check in the mail for the store rent Wednesday. Ernie, I wish my other shops were as timely. I thought you'd be getting ready to go to yard sales today. There are signs at every corner," she said.

"It's a shame I can't go," he responded. "I really need some fresh ideas, and my storeroom is looking too reasonable."

Ernie started rummaging through bins for a few more parts. He found a plug and placed it on the floor. He considered two small metal pipes with threads at one end and, after standing each one next to the ficus, decided on the longer of the two.

"I'll go to the sales for you," Gloria said brightly.

Ernie stopped what he was doing and stared at his lady landlord. She had on an expensive blue suit, paisley blouse, and medium black heels. *She wouldn't know a yard sale from a garden club meeting*, he thought to himself, but instead said in response, "Oh, thanks, but I'll just get by for another month. It'll be all right."

"I guess you don't think I can handle it," she said. "Too bad."

"No, no," he quickly replied. "I'm sure you are a good shopper, but yard sales are…different. You've got to be a real cheapskate. You've got to dicker about prices and be tough."

Gloria didn't say anything. She was obviously miffed.

On the other hand, Ernie thought, *yard sales might do my landlady a lot of good. She'd meet some people she'd never cross paths with otherwise.*

"All right, Gloria Smith," he said. "I'll let you be my buyer today. Find me some strange things to make lamps and clocks out of, but make sure they are in good shape."

Ernie stepped to the workshop door. "Melissa, Gloria is going shopping for me. Give her twenty dollars out of the cash register and leave a note under the drawer."

"Yes sir, Mr. B," Melissa called back.

Gloria looked very surprised. "Aren't you being a little cheap, Ernie?"

Ernie went back to his work. "If it were me doing the shopping, I'd come back with six or eight things. Just do the best you can."

Something inside Gloria started to simmer. She loved a challenge.

❧

The morning eased into afternoon. The bell over the door welcomed a steady flow of customers. Warm spring weather was drawing people outside and into the downtown shopping district, like grizzly bears drawn to honey. At this rate, the ficus would have to wait another day for its transformation into a floor lamp.

CHAPTER 2

About a block from the square in downtown Barkley where Ernie's was located, Gloria ran into her first yard sale. She didn't get out of the car right away but just watched. She hadn't been to a yard sale since going with her mom to one about thirty years ago.

Gloria was about to get out of the car, but suddenly froze. *Lord, help!* she thought. *I can't get out of the car dressed like this! What was I thinking?* She pulled her car back into the street and rushed home.

Gloria lived in an older middle-class neighborhood, mainly two- and three-bedroom brick two-story homes on half-acre lots. She could afford much better. She really didn't need a bigger house though.

Pulling into the carport, she burst into her house and ran for the bathroom. Gloria turned on the lights over the mirror and quickly removed all her makeup. She dug in the back of the closet and found a sweat suit she hadn't worn in a decade. It looked too neat.

Taking her heels off, she jumped up and down on the garments for several seconds until they looked as if she had already worn them a day or two. *Great yard sale look!* she thought. She put on the gray sweat suit, ran her fingers through her hair for a few minutes until it looked sufficiently wild, then found a plastic visor with the name of a plumbing company on it. "Where in the world did I get this thing from?" she wondered. She put on her old gardening shoes to complete the look. She stuck Ernie's twenty dollars in the sweat pant's pocket, grabbed her purse to place in the trunk, and headed back to the yard sales.

At the end of her street, Gloria's newest neighbors were having a yard sale. She hadn't visited them yet. The moving van had just left two days ago. Evidently they had some things that didn't make the grade for inclusion in their new home.

She pulled her white Grand Marquis up to the curb and got out. There was only one other car parked. The owner, who looked like the world's grumpiest old man, was getting in with no purchases in hand.

A young couple sat in lawn chairs behind two six-foot folding tables full of things Gloria would never want. She reminded herself that she was shopping for her tenant, not herself, and Ernie had said he particularly wanted *strange* things. She wondered if anything in the array in front of her could ever be his raw materials.

The man behind the first table said, "Let us know if we can help you."

"Thank you," Gloria replied. "I'll know what I'm looking for when I see it. It will just have to grab me."

The young man glanced at his wife with a look that said, *This ought to be easy.*

To Gloria, he said, "Let me show you something I've been looking for a good home for since we moved here." He rummaged around in a box a few feet away, producing a yellow and purple porcelain lamp.

"Oh no, I'm sorry," Gloria said. "I've got too many lamps already."

She noticed an old ukulele lying on the ground next to the man's chair. It had two broken strings and one fret was missing.

"Do you play that ukulele?" she asked.

"My dad bought it for me when I was ten. I tried to play it for a week or two, but it's been in storage ever since. I'm afraid I let it get too hot sometime, and now it's useless to me. I do have a guitar though," he offered.

"It's kind of pretty," Gloria replied. "Can I have it? I don't know what I'd do with it, but I'd hate to see it thrown away."

"Oh, sure," the owner said. "It's no good to me." He stepped back to pick up the ukulele off the ground then handed it to Gloria.

"Where in the world did you get that big red piggy bank?" she said as she accepted the musical instrument. "I saw one like that in a Sears commercial, years ago, advertising how much a person who shopped with them would save."

The man started to answer, but the wife spoke first. "Tom and everyone else in the world got one for shopping in Sears on the day that commercial first ran. I used to love it, but we really don't have a place for it. Do you have a grandson that could use it? It's only fifty cents." The husband frowned at his wife, but she didn't seem to notice.

"I've got just the person for it," Gloria said brightly. "And I'd also like to get this old wooden walking stick, if it's not too much."

"Just make it fifty cents too," the young wife said. "You owe us a dollar."

Gloria handed her Ernie's twenty, got her change, and took her purchases to the car. She had spent a dollar and got three items. *Good start*, she thought.

Driving another block in the general direction of Barkley's downtown, Gloria found a second yard sale. The sign announced in big letters, "5-Family Yard Sale," and it was drawing quite a crowd. She counted at least ten vehicles parked near the sale with more folks milling around than could fit in twice that many cars. She had to parallel park to get a space at all.

Joining the crowd, Gloria hurried past the clothing and shoes. Nothing in housewares or hardware made an immediate impression. She wondered if she was too late—at 9:00 a.m.—for the best items but then found herself face to face with a strange and wonderful hubcap. It was as if it had *clock* written all over it. She picked it up to take a closer look.

"Need a Chrysler hubcap, ma'am?" the older gentleman queried.

"Oh, is this for a Chrysler?" Gloria asked.

"Yes, ma'am," he said. "I found it between boxes in my garage yesterday. It's the only one I've got. Sold that car years ago." The man looked at Gloria quizzically, wondering why she had any interest in the metal disk.

"Um, I knew it was special. It just kind of reached out and grabbed me. If somebody else needs it, I really don't have to have it." Gloria started to put the hubcap back on the table.

"Well, now, if it appeals to you, ma'am, I want you to have it," he said. "I sure don't want it to end up back in my garage. You just keep it, no charge." The older man took the hubcap from Gloria's hand, put it in a plastic bag, and handed it back to her. He nodded and smiled.

Gloria moved on to the other tables. Behind one of the back tables, she saw five or six bamboo poles. She reached to lift one up but found it didn't move. She grabbed a shorter one, but it also would not budge. That puzzled her. After trying to pick up two more with the same result, Gloria stopped, stepped behind the table, and took a hard look at the collection. Now she could see that the six bamboo pipes of varying lengths were embedded in a cedar planter, like hollow pool cues awaiting the next billiard game. A red sticker on the longest pole had "$1" written on it.

A blonde lady, slightly older than Gloria, saw her puzzling at the strange item and stopped by to explain. "That was my youngest son's first attempt at art when he was taking a course at college," she said with a chuckle.

Gloria immediately thought of her daughter Sharon's first attempt at art in college, a six-foot flower made from aluminum soda cans. It sat in the garage for five years. Two different years, birds had built a nest in it.

"The professor couldn't figure it out, so he gave him an A," the blonde lady said. The two ladies simultaneously laughed. Sharon had gotten an A too! Soon both ladies were giggling, and for some odd reason, they couldn't seem to stop. One would almost get control of her laughter then would look at the other and would start giggling more. Then the other would almost stop, but would see her neighbor out of control and would launch her laughter with new vigor. The commotion went on for two full minutes.

A man that looked to be in his eighties walked up and took the blonde lady by both hands and turned her away so that she couldn't look at Gloria. Slowly, ever slowly, the two females got their hilarity under control. Finally, Gloria gave the other lady a serious look and said, "Thank you so much. I haven't laughed that well in years."

This set them off again, but they only laughed for a few seconds this time. The other lady said, "I'm so glad to meet you. My name is Patty Johnson, and I live in the blue house across the street. Please stop by anytime. I feel like I've made a new friend."

"And so do I," said Gloria. "My name is Gloria Smith. I live at the end of the next street. Please let me buy that bamboo sculpture. I'll have to smile now whenever I look at it." She gave Patty a one-dollar bill.

The bamboo thingamajig was actually lighter than Gloria first thought. She was able to carry it in two hands to the car, while hooking the bag with the Chrysler hubcap on one finger. She carefully placed them in the trunk.

She had spent two dollars so far for five items.

After four more stops, the Grand Marquis trunk was full. The dashboard clock read 11:30. Gloria decided to head for home and lunch; there was no hurry in getting her purchases back to the store on the square. Thoughts of leftover quiche, her Savory Succotash, sweet tea, and her feet up on the ottoman made the two-mile trip home seem nearly instant.

Gloria was greeted by the beep of the answering machine when she walked in the door. "You'll just have to wait a minute," she told it firmly. The last piece of Quiche Lorraine was eased onto a pure white Mikasa plate and inserted into the microwave for a forty-second pick-me-up, to be followed shortly by a generous serving of the succotash. By the time Gloria had her iced tea poured, the rest was ready.

Guess I'd better listen to the answering machine before I settle down to lunch, she thought. Stepping to the corner of the den, Gloria hit the play button and immediately recognized Sharon's voice.

"Mom, Grandma called and wants us to go out for Italian next Thursday for our monthly 'girls' night out.' Call me when you get a chance. Love you." Gloria made a mental note to call her daughter later in the day.

Retrieving her meal and putting it together on one plate, Gloria walked to the den. Before taking a bite, she thanked God for the food and her successful shopping then took off her shoes and rested her feet on the old brown leather footstool. "Ahhh" escaped from her lips without a fight.

What a morning! she thought. *Why in the world did I volunteer to go to all those yard sales? Was I bored and looking for something different to do? Actually, I enjoyed the challenge. Mostly, though, I was just helping out a friend. Ernie is a decent man, but he tries to do a little too much sometimes.*

The shopping had gone miraculously well, but the only prayer she could remember praying was one "Lord, help!" before she really got started. God had certainly done a lot with a little.

It occurred to Gloria that she had not seen any of those small suitcases with the telescoping handle and little wheels at any of the yard sales. They certainly had become popular. Probably no one wanted to get rid of theirs, and everyone just wore his or hers so completely out that it wasn't even fit for a yard sale. She liked that thought. Her deceased husband, Van, had come up with several patents for that piece of luggage then sold the patents. She was living quite comfortably now on the proceeds of his sharp thinking.

"As far as I can tell, you haven't moved since I was here five hours ago," Gloria kidded Ernie. She was back in her makeup and nice clothes. "You'll never get anything done like that." The workshop still had lamp parts neatly arranged on the floor, around the ficus tree.

Ernie smiled faintly. "It's been a busy day. Melissa has been in the store all day, except for lunch, and even with Mike here for three hours, all of us had all we could do to wait on customers. I may have to finish that crazy lady's lamp on Monday."

"Business has been pretty good lately, hasn't it?" Gloria said.

"It certainly has. I may have to think about getting some more help," he said. "I'm having a little trouble getting everything done."

A dark thought slipped in uninvited: *What would Cindy Martin write in her Wednesday column if he didn't finish her lamp on time?*

"Let me see. Ernie, your business started booming just after Cindy Martin's column about your store appeared in the paper, didn't it?" Gloria said.

Ernie could tell where his landlady's conversation was leading, but he wasn't going to jump to the end until she pushed him there. "Yes," he said. "It's kind of ironic that her article had a critical tone, yet it did my place a lot of good."

"Remember that line from our Bible study, right here in your coffee shop last Thursday? The one Joseph said to the brothers that sold him into slavery?" Gloria said, waiting patiently for Ernie to respond. When he didn't answer after several seconds, she filled in the missing

Bible verse. "You meant it for evil, but God meant it for good. Remember that verse?"

He nodded, without saying anything. As much good as Cindy Martin had done for his business, maybe it was time to stop calling her "that crazy lady."

∽

"So, Gloria, I see that you didn't bring any yard sale items in with you when you got back. No luck?" Ernie felt a little smug. Not everybody could do well at yard sales.

Gloria quickly replied, "Actually, I need some help to carry it all in. Can you lend me a hand?"

Ernie looked a little surprised. *Then again*, he thought, *it's probably some heavy monstrosity that won't be any good for me or anyone else.* He followed Gloria to her '96 Grand Marquis.

Gloria popped the trunk open. "We'll probably have to make two trips," she said.

It was a big trunk, and it was full.

Ernie Bostwick nearly fell over. What a collection! "Look at this stuff!" he exclaimed. "Where did you get this old tabletop juke box? Hey, a red piggy bank! Man alive, would you look at that Uncle Sam statue?" One by one, he picked up each item, sixteen in all. There was a ukulele with a fret missing, a foot-tall ceramic Winnie the Pooh, a hubcap, a catcher's mask, and a multitude of other items, including a bamboo whatever you call it.

"Oh, I almost forgot," Gloria said, as she dug in her purse. Pulling her hand out of her pocketbook, she deposited a quarter and a dollar bill in Ernie's hand. "Your change."

It took three trips for the two of them to unload the car trunk and carry all the new treasures to the storeroom at the back of the store. Ernie did his best to thank Gloria, but he was still a bit dumbfounded, so he didn't do it very well. As she drove off, he stood, staring out the plateglass window. *Now that is a special lady*, he thought.

Five o'clock arrived quickly. Not as much had been accomplished in the workshop as Ernie had hoped, but it had been a good day. Melissa clicked off all the lamps, checked that all the appliances in the coffee shop were turned off, and met Ernie at the cash register for her pay.

"Melissa, your pay is a little different this time," Ernie started.

Melissa worried a little when he said this. Had she broken something this week? Had she made a mistake by giving someone too much change? She usually received nine dollars an hour for the four afternoons and Saturday she worked, sixteen hours in all. She had to pay her daddy a hundred dollars for car insurance this week, and she was saving all she could for college.

"You've been working here a year now," her boss said. "I decided that this would be a good time to start giving you ten dollars an hour. You've done a good job."

Melissa reached out to receive her paycheck and immediately turned her back. She looked at her check and froze. Ernie got a confused look on his face, wondering if he'd done something wrong.

Suddenly whirling around, Melissa gave her boss a huge hug, a bigger smile, and hurried out the door.

In just a few minutes, Ernie finished putting the store in order. He went out the front door and locked it, trying the knob to be sure it was locked. "See you Monday," he said out loud to the building. It had been a tiring week.

Thank God for Sunday. Life was starting to unravel.

CHAPTER 3

Ernie stared inside the refrigerator. The grated sharp cheddar stared back.

With Sunday morning breakfast preparation well underway, change cast a flirtatious smile his way. The whole wheat bagel, split and ready for action, waited patiently in the toaster. The cream cheese was on the table in the small breakfast nook that adjoined the kitchen. A twelve-ounce glass stood stalwart on the gray formica countertop and looked forward to a flood of orange juice, filling it nearly to the brim. Two beaten eggs sat on the kitchen island in a cup next to a frying pan on the stove. And now grated cheese wanted to intrude.

"Why not?" Ernie thought out loud.

He rummaged in the Frigidaire's vegetable drawer and found remnants of a chopped onion and put it in the frying pan. In the pantry, Ernie found an unopened jar of sliced jalapeno peppers and added about a dozen slices to the pan. He sautéed the vegetables in a tablespoon of olive oil then added the eggs.

After a couple minutes, Ernie loosened the edges of the mixture in the pan and deftly flipped it. He sprinkled a quarter cup of the grated cheese on the omelet, folded it in half, and sprinkled more cheese on top. When it began to melt, he slid his creation onto a plate.

"Don't forget the bagel," he reminded himself and pushed down the slide on the toaster.

At nine thirty sharp, Ernie Bostwick began leisurely eating the best breakfast he'd made in a month.

Somewhere in Barkley, church bells sang the arrival of eleven o'clock, beckoning all that would to come to worship. On 212 Elm Street, Ernie slid back his chair from the table, put down the Sunday paper, picked up his old red Bible, and headed for the back porch. He settled into one of the two white rockers and bowed his head in prayer, rocking his way to God's throne.

After thirty minutes or so of smiles, frowns, wrinkling of the brow, and chuckles with his Best Friend, Ernie opened his eyes and began to sing an old favorite praise song:

Each day You make me better, more than yesterday could dream.

Each week my burden's lighter. Lord, it's You alone I seek.

Jesus, lead me.

Savior, guide me.

Spirit, bring Your light to me.

Four more verses followed. In a dogwood at the back of Ernie's half-acre backyard, a crow did its best to disrupt the man's mellow tenor with a flat-pitched "Caw!" thrown in at irregular intervals.

Ernie spent the next few minutes reading from Luke, chapter 4, especially noting verse 14: "A report about him spread through all the surrounding country." That caught his attention, because of the report (Cindy Martin's newspaper column) that had been bringing his store so much business lately. Maybe he should go back and read her article again. It probably wasn't as critical as he had originally thought.

Who was this columnist? Ernie had met her briefly as a customer, but now he wondered about her personal life. How old was she? She looked about forty, maybe forty-five. Did she have a husband and children? He detected a slight northern accent, perhaps more New England than Illinois or Ohio. Just as Jesus had a history and family in Luke 4, so Ernie needed to think of Cindy Martin as a real person, not just a customer or a face in the newspaper. "Thanks, Lord, I needed that," he breathed to himself.

The aroma of grilled steaks slithered through the morning air from Frank Garborrow's house a quarter mile away. Frank always tried to have lunch ready for his family when they got home from Trinity Presbyterian.

Ernie fought the distraction and continued reading into chapter 5 of Luke, which reinforced the idea of blessings from listening to and heeding God's guidance. The listening was easier than the other part.

Church bells signaled twelve o'clock. Church was over. Ernie went inside.

As usual, Ernie was invited to join Jack and Tina Rhodes and their daughter, Melissa, for lunch at the Ranch at the east end of Barkley at one o'clock. Reserving ten minutes for the drive, Ernie grabbed the last section of newspaper he had yet to read.

On another side of the city of Barkley, Mike Bruce laughed at how normal a noon breakfast had become.

His first couple weeks of night stocking at Sneed's Grocery had been exhausting. Now three months later, his sixty-year-old body had made the adjustment. Two mornings working at Ernie's for the past three weeks were no problem at all.

Mike spooned up the last few flakes of raisin bran then reached for the box of corn flakes. He poured just enough of the corn flakes into his bowl to use up the last of the milk. Before taking a bite, he grabbed the notepad that clung to the refrigerator and jotted down *milk*.

Man, this would be a great day for tennis, he thought. Since watching the Australian Open in January, he yearned to get back to the sport. *If I can run three miles a day, I ought to be able to still play singles*, he surmised. *I think I'll go hit a few against the wall at the middle school. I might get lucky and find somebody there to play against.*

Mike polished off his cereal and apple then rinsed his bowl and spoon and placed them in the dishwasher. He gathered the Sunday paper from the front steps and placed it in the center of the coffee table's clear glass top.

The hobby room, as Mike referred to the spare bedroom, would be the obvious place to hunt for his tennis racquets and, hopefully, an unopened can of tennis balls. Looking first in the closet, he found them standing in the front corner. He grabbed two racquets and two cans of balls and stood them next to the back door then went off to change.

&

"Somebody was asking about you in West Point this week, Ernie," said Jack. He lifted a forkful of blueberry pie toward his mouth.

"I hope you don't mean Freddy Owens." Ernie laughed. "He was seventy when I left there in '92. And he didn't look a day over fifty."

"Actually, I did see Freddy working in Best-Mart from a distance," Jack replied. "No, it was his granddaughter, Kate, from the photo studio who was asking about you. She said you were the best manager they ever had. She still appreciates your giving her a chance to manage that department when she was fresh out of high school."

Jack's wife, Tina, returned to the table after walking her daughter to the door. Melissa had to meet a girlfriend at one forty-five at the public library.

"Well, Jack, I knew that Kate was polite and intelligent, and I'd seen her in church enough to know that she sincerely cared about people." Ernie returned his gaze to his apple cobbler, one of the specialties of the Ranch. No one was sure what made it so good; Ernie suspected a touch of almond extract lurked somewhere between the apples and the crust. "I'm not surprised that she did well."

"Jack is always telling me about somebody in West Point or Perry that measures store managers by how you handled those Best-Marts," said Tina. It always amazed Ernie how much Tina and Melissa looked like twins, except that Tina's hair color was normal.

"Are you ever sorry you left the chain?" Jack asked.

"No, I'm really not. When upper management starts calling you *Store 83* instead of your real name, it's time to get out." Ernie took another bite of cobbler. He reached for his coffee cup, but it moved quickly out of his reach. The waitress poured coffee to its brim then returned it. "Thank you, Janice."

"Do you miss church?" Tina asked.

Ernie frowned. He took a long drink of coffee.

"I'm sorry, Ernie. That was rude of me. But you mentioned that you went to the same church as Kate," Tina said, blushing slightly.

"That's all right, Tina," he said. "I've never stopped worshiping God every Sunday morning. And West Point Community Church made my spirit sing until they started bickering about whether to build a new youth building or not. Churches can drive people away as fast as they bring them in."

"Jack," Tina said, "did something not agree with you? That was an antacid just now, wasn't it?"

"It was. I seem to be having a little more heartburn lately," Jack said. "Maybe I'll try to keep track of what I eat this week. Either that, or buy us some stock in whatever company makes Tums."

Jack finished off his pie then pulled back his chair and turned to Ernie. "We'd better be going, I guess. I've got to pack for a three-day swing to Savannah and Valdosta. I need to leave by about five tomorrow morning. You know how store managers look forward to Jack Rhodes bringing in those new summer displays."

Ernie smiled back at Jack. "Nobody else brings such a wide variety of hot-selling items. You always made me look good, friend. Have a nice trip."

Jack and Ernie left generous tips for Janice then went to the cashier to pay for lunch. Ernie exchanged hugs with Tina and Jack before heading for their cars.

Flip, flip, klunk. It always sounded like this on Sunday afternoon. It took a few minutes for the treasured Sunday nap to wear off.

He picked up the errant beanbag and restarted his juggling. Ernie tossed with the left hand then the right then the left, over and over—this time without mishap. After a full two minutes, he caught all three bags, laid them in the basket, and chose four baseballs. After a few drops, the rhythm of juggling four items nestled in, and Ernie felt himself shedding the stress of a busy week.

Slipping out of the laundry room, Ernie returned soon with a beautiful red apple ready for consumption. This time he picked up three tennis balls and the apple and began a juggling cycle that included a slight pause with every fourth item. When he felt ready, Ernie began taking a quick bite out of the apple each time it came around. Soon there remained but two bites of apple, at which point he caught the apple and let the tennis balls fall to the floor and skitter in three ridiculously dissimilar directions.

Chomp, chomp. It was a very good apple.

Practice continued another fifteen minutes, alternately with scarves, Indian clubs, and rubber knives.

Who would sell juggling supplies without being able to demonstrate them?

☙

Ernie did not usually work on Sundays, but today he decided to spend some time working on Cindy Martin's lamp. He suspected that he had not tried very hard to make progress on it on Saturday because he still held a grudge against her for her newspaper column. God needled Ernie about the situation. *Love your neighbor as yourself* kept running through his mind, as well as *Forgive, and you shall be forgiven.* The only way to quiet his conscience was to work on the lamp.

He found all the materials for it still laid out in an orderly manner. The first task was to thread an electrical cord through the five-foot section of pipe that would, along with the tree trunk, be the vertical support for the lamp. Ernie cut eleven feet of brown cord then pushed it through the length of pipe. Stripping a half inch of the two leads at one end of the cord, he attached them behind the screws inside the socket he had chosen then screwed the socket onto the end of the pipe.

Ernie had to remind himself what the inside of the tree's base looked like. The ficus was planted in a two-inch layer of concrete in the bottom of an octagonal cedar planter. On top of the concrete were two semicircular pieces of polystyrene foam, coming to within three inches of the top of the planter, covered with a layer of artificial Spanish moss.

Removing the polystyrene, Ernie drilled a half-inch hole in the side of the cedar container, just above the concrete, into which he inserted a black rubber stopper that had a hole in the middle big enough for the electrical cord to run through. He secured the pipe to the tree trunk with plastic tension ties, with the bottom of the pipe an inch above the concrete, then ran the cord from the bottom of the pipe out through the rubber stopper. He attached the electrical plug to the end of the cord.

At this point, the lamp should be functional. Ernie put a 40-watt bulb into the socket and plugged the cord into the wall. The lamp did not come on.

He rubbed his head, took off his glasses, and stroked his moustache. What could be wrong? He carefully examined the lamp, starting at the wall plug. When he reached the socket, he immediately saw the problem. He pulled the string that dangled from the socket, and light came forth.

The lamp worked, but it was far from being finished. Ernie replaced the polystyrene in the planter. Because of the pipe, it was a tighter fit, but he was able to put it back in its place without any cutting. Finding the roll of sand-colored floral tape, he carefully wrapped it around the tree trunk and pipe all the way to the socket, which Ernie wrapped with green floral tape. He then replaced the Spanish moss atop the polystyrene, clipped a small green lampshade onto the bulb, and took a few steps back for a final visual inspection.

As expected, the socket and shade blended in well with the leaves of the ficus. The pipe and tree trunk were covered by the sand-colored tape and matched the color of the branches. He wondered whether to try to change the color of the white pull string but decided that would make it too hard to find.

He wanted to try one more thing. Closing the door of his workshop, he turned off the overhead fluorescent lights. The tree emitted a pleasant green glow from somewhere in the midst of its foliage. "Beautiful!" Ernie said softly.

The lamp had only cost Ernie an hour of his Sabbath day. He was glad to have the project finished. He was home before his regular suppertime at six.

Nine o'clock caught Ernie by surprise. "Wasn't there something I was supposed to do before going to bed tonight?" he asked himself. "Was I supposed to wash something? Was I supposed to call somebody?" Ah! He had planned on picking up some bagels at Sneed's for breakfast. He grabbed the keys for his black Jeep Cherokee.

❧

"Hey, Mike. How's Sunday night treating you?" Ernie called out to Mike Bruce, who was stocking shelves, just as he always was when Ernie had to shop late at night.

Mike wanted to tell Ernie the truth, but he decided nobody wants to hear about somebody else's aches and pains. Tennis for the first time in years produced numerous grumpy places in his arms and legs. Who would have thought that some skinny middle schooler would run him so ragged? Slowly rising from his knees, he responded, "Great, Ernie. People keep buying, and I keep filling the shelves back up. There's nothing like regular work to keep an old bachelor out of trouble."

Ernie flashed his big grin. "I can tell you from personal experience, you're one hundred percent correct! If everybody worked as hard as you and I, nobody would have time to get into trouble." He was glad he'd already picked up the bagels he needed; he had a bad habit of forgetting what he was doing if somebody engaged him in conversation.

"Ernie, did you get that lamp done for the newspaper lady after I left yesterday afternoon?" Mike asked the storekeeper. "I know you didn't get any time to work on it while I was there."

"You know, I rarely work on Sundays," Ernie said, "but God kept that lamp on my mind this afternoon until I finally decided to go work on it. I've got it all done and ready for the lady to pick up."

"Look," Mike said, "if you ever need me to help in the store a few extra hours, I'd be glad to. I'm here nine at night to five in the morning, every night, but Tuesday and Friday, but I'm usually free otherwise."

"I've been really busy lately, Mike, but I think it should slow down a little soon," Ernie said. "If it doesn't, I certainly might give you a call. Thanks."

Ernie felt in his shirt pocket for a grocery list but found nothing. Hopefully these bagels were all he came in for.

CHAPTER 4

"This is ridiculous," Ernie said. "I can't believe I'm trying to get another shave out of this old razor blade."

Ernie ejected the Gillette Sensor blade into the bathroom waste basket. He hunted for the next package of blades. Only the left side of his face had been touched.

For some reason, he had not put the spare blades in the top drawer of the maple cabinet that surrounded the sink. They were always there. "Why did I put them someplace else?" he wondered. He looked in the other three drawers. He checked in the built-in linen cabinet in the outer bathroom and through all the drawers beneath that double sink. He plundered through the cabinet above the toilet. Ernie couldn't find the blades anywhere.

On some mornings, a dose of reality can awaken an adult better than coffee. This was one of those mornings. Ernie Bostwick was out of razor blades and could only face the world smoothly if it approached him from the left.

He dug around in the nearly full waste basket for a few seconds but decided he did not want to find the old blade by sense of touch. Even a dull razor blade has a tendency to draw blood. He would just have to go by the drug store on the way to work and finish shaving in the restroom at the store before he opened for business.

The vintage black Ford Mustang nearly pushed Ernie's Jeep Cherokee off the street as he began to pull into a parking space in front of his store, then it veered into the next space and stopped suddenly. A tall, shapely brunette with short hair stepped out of the vehicle. Nothing about her manner was apologetic for nearly running over the store proprietor.

Ernie fought back the urge to yell at the lady, quickly recognizing that this was a customer.

"Good morning, Ernie! I've just got to have some coffee. I thought you might be open by now, and I remembered that you had some Cinnamon Blueberry fixed when I was in here last week. That would certainly get my Monday off to a good start." Cynthia Martin quickly made her way to the front door of the shop and seemed surprised to find that the door was locked.

Oh, great! he thought. *The lady tries to kill me with her Mustang then wants to tell me what kind of coffee to brew. Lord, are you sure you want me to love my neighbor?* He jingled through the coins and keys in his left front pocket until the front door key hit the palm of his hand, then he quickly unlocked the door.

"Please come in, Ms. Martin. I'll have some coffee ready in just a couple minutes."

"Aren't we on a first-name basis anymore, Mr. Bostwick?" she retorted with a radiant smile.

"Excuse me…Cynthia. Would you mind turning on a few of the lamps?" Ernie decided that he might as well put his customer to work a little while she was waiting.

Ernie measured out three quarters of a cup of ground coffee, placed it in a paper filter, and put it in the brewmaster. He poured a half gallon of water in the top and turned the machine on. It immediately sputtered to life. Ernie turned his attention to putting money into the cash register from the old green bank bag—one twenty-dollar bill, two tens, three fives, twenty ones, a roll each of each kind of change——$92.50. It was always $92.50.

He looked around the store for Cynthia, but the fragrant aroma of brewing coffee found her first, and she was following her nose to the source. She helped herself to a large mug of "liquid alarm clock" and slid into an upholstered chair.

Ernie brewed Aloha Dark and Seattle Sunrise to complement the Cinnamon Blueberry that Cynthia Martin had requested. He poured himself some of the Aloha and sat in a straight chair a few feet from the lanky brunette.

"Cynthia, do you get up early to get a head start on the rest of the world, like I do? Or do you have to get your husband and kids off to work and school?" Ernie winced inside; he hadn't meant to sound so nosey.

"I guess I want to enjoy my first cup of coffee without worrying about being behind the crowd," she said. "This is as good as the aroma, Ernie. Why haven't I discovered your coffee before now? By the way, there is no husband. It's just me. Did your wife see what a lousy job you did shaving this morning?" She couldn't help but laugh as she saw his face reddening behind his stubbly face.

Feeling a bit chastened, he raised his hands in surrender. "Sorry about the bad shave. I ran out of blades. If I had a wife, she would have never let me out of the door like this. I meant to finish shaving before any customers came in. Please excuse me for a couple minutes."

When he returned, Cynthia was sitting in a different chair, sipping her coffee and reading *Newsweek*. He took a stroll around the store, reminding himself of things he needed to order from suppliers that week. After a couple minutes, he found his coffee right where he had left it and settled down in a more comfortable chair.

After several minutes, Ernie got up, suddenly excited. "I want to show you something." Ernie hurriedly walked around the room, turning off all the lamps Cynthia had turned on earlier. Running back to his workroom, he quickly returned with the ficus tree he had made into a lamp for her. He sat it down about six feet in front of where she was seated, plugged it in, turned it on, and returned to his chair.

"What do you think?" he asked.

She couldn't help it. She tried to keep it in, and was successful at first, but soon she burst out with a hyena-like laugh.

"I didn't know what in the *world* had gotten into you," she said. She suddenly turned solemn, examining the glowing light fixture carefully. She rose from her chair and slowly circled the lamp. After completely circumnavigating the ficus, she eased back into her chair and picked up her coffee mug. Cynthia focused her eyes on the producer of the object in question and quietly purred, "It is every bit as lovely as I had imagined it could be. Well done, my friend."

Ernie and Cynthia sat quietly, sipping coffee for a few minutes, by the jade glow of a single bulb. The mood was rudely interrupted by the ringing of the bell over the front door, announcing the arrival of the store's second customer of the day.

"Good morning! Are you open? It's so dark in here." It was Gloria. She suddenly noticed Ernie and Cynthia Martin sitting in the dimly lit coffee shop. "Oh. Excuse me. Am I intruding?"

Cynthia immediately jumped up. "I've got to be going, Ernie. Let me pay for my lamp and coffee."

As Ernie got up and moved to the cash register, Gloria went around the store, turning on lights. When she got to the ficus lamp, she hesitated as she looked it over from top to bottom then turned it off and unplugged it.

"Cynthia, I'll carry your lamp to your car for you," Ernie said as he closed the register. He picked up the ficus lamp, wrapping the cord loosely around his wrist.

Gloria was looking over the coffees that Ernie had prepared, and was pleased that he had fixed some Aloha Dark.

"You need to call me Cindy, Ernie. That's what my friends use," Cynthia said, as she and Ernie headed out the door. Gloria's eyebrows rose.

Gloria got her coffee, though she couldn't have her usual mug, the one that said, "I'm #1." It had already been used today by the previous customer. She settled for a plain burgundy mug. She sat down in her favorite chair, still warm from Cynthia's use of it.

When Ernie returned, he came back to the coffee shop area and retrieved his near-empty cup. Filling it back up to the brim, he sat in the chair next to Gloria. "I hope you brought some of your wonderful muffins and cookies this morning. I'd be glad to buy a dozen of each. Customers are really beginning to ask for them, especially the blueberry muffins."

Gloria could see that the four large glass jars lined up on a nearby shelf were nearly empty. There were two bran muffins left, two or three of the four-inch sugar cookies, one molasses cookie, and no blueberry muffins.

"I was going to bake this morning, Ernie, but I wanted to see what you needed first. I'll have them back here before lunch."

"Did you get a chance to see that lamp I just sold to Cindy Martin? It really turned out well. I might try to make another of those soon," Ernie said. "I'm nearly caught up with orders now with just a couple more clocks that a guy from Columbus wants by the end of this week. I really would like to start working on some of those things you bought for me last Saturday."

Gloria was fidgeting in her chair. Ernie could tell something had her a little nervous.

"Have you ever done much bowling, Ernie? I used to bowl a lot with my dad when I was a teenager, and I was thinking about brushing up on it a little." Gloria picked up her coffee mug, taking several sizeable sips.

"Well, actually, I used to bowl every week when I was in my twenties. I even thought about joining a league," he said. "But I guess I haven't been to the alley in a long time."

"Would you care to join me for some bowling tomorrow night? Bowling is not the kind of thing you do by yourself," Gloria said.

Ernie mentally paged through his calendar and found no commitments for Tuesday night. "Sure, why not?" he said. "Could we go about seven? That would give me time to get home and have a little supper."

Gloria finished her coffee and stood up. "That sounds fine. Listen, I'll be back in a little while with the muffins and cookies, and you can take my coffee out of what you owe me." She headed for the door. "Bye!"

"I'll see you soon, Gloria. Take care," said Ernie.

It was nearly eight forty-five. Glen and Sam would probably wander in anytime, so he'd better see if the Ledger-Inquirers had been tossed on the doorstep yet. Ernie grabbed a legal pad to jot down things he needed to order today from Smith Distributing.

§

"What's this, Ernie?" The tall, balding man was staring at a cheap picture frame leaning against the cash register. A yellow piece of paper tried unsuccessfully to fill the space within the frame.

"Read it, Jack," said Ernie. "What a day!"

"You'll still have to explain. 'Best H and C Sub ever, 4-8-09 2:28'" Jack Rhodes looked like he was trying to read a Chinese cookbook.

Ernie just had to laugh at Melissa's father. "All right, I'll clear it up for you. I finally got a chance for lunch about two o'clock, so I called Glen's sandwich shop and asked if he could deliver me a ham and cheese sub." Ernie pointed at the framed paper. "That's H and C Sub. Best one I ever had. And I took my first bite at two twenty-eight. It was so good that I just had to commemorate it somehow."

Jack started to laugh but suddenly frowned. He pulled a bottle of antacid tablets out of his suit pants pocket and chewed a couple quickly. "Man, I should have had what you had for lunch. This jalapeno chili is killing me."

"Actually, the two together would be outstanding," said Ernie. "I can eat just about anything without any trouble from heartburn."

"Me too, usually," said Jack. "Lately, heartburn sneaks up on me when I least expect it. Hey, Ernie, that was sure nice of you to give my daughter a raise last week. She loves this place."

Ernie smiled broadly and replied, "When Melissa came in here with you last year to buy your wife a birthday present, I knew right away she was a quality person. When I realized shortly after that, that I needed to hire some afternoon help, she immediately came to mind. She's done a really good job."

Jack looked carefully at Ernie to see if he was serious. "That's amazing. If I'm not mistaken, she had bright green hair that day, and she was carrying a taxi-yellow purse." Jack wandered over to the clock section. "Ernie, my Melissa has a birthday coming up. Has she mentioned anything in here that she wishes she had?"

Ernie pondered the question a minute. He took off his glasses and rubbed his head a little. Then he snapped his fingers. "Yes! Jack, last Saturday I was helping Gloria carry in some odd things she'd bought at yard sales. I had commissioned her to use her imagination and find me some raw materials for making lamps and clocks. I remember that Melissa really admired a big red piggy bank and said, 'Mr. B, if you ever figure out a way to make a clock out of *that*, I want it!'"

"Hmm." Jack pulled on his right ear lobe, lost in thought. He loosened his pink tie a little then tightened it back.

"Can you have it ready for me to pick up on Friday about two o'clock?" he asked.

❧

"Was that my dad's car that I saw leaving when I was coming in?" asked the girl with purple hair.

Ernie had learned to never be surprised at the color of Melissa's hair. "Sure was. We were just chatting about jalapenos and banks."

Melissa looked at her boss quizzically then shrugged. She wondered why Ernie and her dad never talked about anything important.

"Guess I'll work on those clocks for the man in Columbus, Melissa. If you need me, just yell." Ernie started toward his workshop in the back.

"Mr. B, did the newspaper lady pick up her lamp yet?" she said.

"Yes, she got it first thing this morning. I think it turned out quite well," said Ernie, now twenty feet away.

"Darn! I was hoping to see how it turned out. Mr. B, you can make a lamp or a clock out of anything," she called back at him. Melissa noticed the framed yellow paper next to the cash register and opened her mouth to speak. Her boss beat her to it.

"Ask your father!"

It was strange how the blue color of these books triggered the beginnings of a memory in Ernie. Where had he seen books this color before?

About a week ago, Mr. Winton had brought Ernie the two volumes. Could he make matching clocks out of them? Mr. Winton planned to place them on matching bookshelves in his home. Ernie assured him that he had made clocks out of books several times before. It took a little time to do the drilling and gluing, but it was a straightforward process. He could have them in about ten days.

Since receiving the order, Ernie had been puzzled by the color. It was a deep, dark blue, almost navy blue but not quite. It was close to the color of encyclopedias, but that was not quite it.

Today the memory was trying harder than ever to break through. It had something to do with college.

Becky. Becky Nottingham. She was the last girl he had seriously dated.

CHAPTER 5

The congregation stood as the piano and organ finished the introduction and nearly two hundred voices combined in the Charles Wesley hymn, "O for a Thousand Tongues to Sing."

Becky and her parents, Frank and Betty Nottingham, occupied the same pew they'd sat in for nearly every Sunday of the past twenty years. At the other end of the pew were Mavis and Opal Carollton, leaving room for the college classmate that accompanied Becky the past few weeks, Ernie Bostwick.

Ernie had no church background, but he learned quickly to follow the lead of the people around him. He noticed the very first week that an asterisk next to an item in the order of worship meant everyone stood up. When the offering plate was passed, only folding money or checks seemed acceptable. When the organ played a prelude at the beginning of the service, everyone was expected to stop talking and act prayerful. And no matter how excellent a vocal solo or choir presentation, no applause was the rule, unless the performance was by a child.

It occurred to Ernie today that he had never before seen the exact shade of navy blue of the hymnals. It nearly mimicked the blue of his *Webster's Dictionary*, almost copied his parents' set of Encyclopedia Britannica, but neither matched perfectly. The hymnals exhibited a blue that was deeper but not darker. Ernie pronounced them "Methodist Hymnal blue."

Becky nudged Ernie a little and smiled. She could see that his mind was wandering a bit. She needed him to continue making a good impression on her parents. She knew that her dad, especially, scrutinized her dates carefully, looking for some small way they might not be good enough for his daughter.

Ernie stifled a giggle, which brought a harder nudge from Becky. He wiped the grin off his face, doing his best to match the sober look of everyone around him. *I'll have to tell Becky later*, he thought. He had overheard one of the teen boys telling a friend, after church last Sunday, "I heard the old Carollton ladies used to sing Off-Broadway. That's why they always sing off-key!" He wouldn't be able to look at the dark-haired sisters today without a giggle.

A few minutes later, Tom Brown launched into an energetic sermon on Luke 16:1–9, "the dishonest manager." The thirty-five-year-old minister had an engaging style, using few, if any, notes and maintaining eye contact with nearly the entire audience. "Why would God hold up such a loser as the hero in this passage? We're told immediately that he's stealing from the boss!" said the preacher with a mischievous smile. The ensuing silence made the congregation hold its breath in anticipation. "Because God wants you to look that manager in the eye and see who it really is…it's you!"

A few in the congregation began to fidget, including Ernie. "We've been receiving God's blessings, enjoying His provision, embracing His love, and keeping it all for ourselves. That was never the Master's intention. We're supposed to be spreading His love, spreading His blessings, bringing people to know the goodness of our Lord so that they might recognize God wants to forgive their trespasses against Him. We make salvation so difficult. We seem to require the sinner to be perfect before he can darken God's doorstep. But salvation is free! Just accept that Jesus's death on the cross recompensed God for everything. Look at how God commends the dishonest manager for making it easy for debtors to get out of debt."

Reverend Brown followed with stories about Billy Graham, Billy Sunday, Ronald Reagan, and an unnamed woman in a local drug rehabilitation clinic.

It was a short sermon, but it was a great sermon, at least to a college boy named Ernie. When the preacher asked anyone who wanted to accept Jesus's death on the cross as payment for their sins, to come forward during the last song, Ernie stood and began moving at the very beginning of the first stanza. He made his way to the center aisle, and as he slipped clumsily by Mavis and Opal Carollton, the sisters patted him gently on the back. He stepped quickly to Reverend Brown at the altar rail.

"Do you want to accept Jesus as your Savior?" the pastor quietly asked.

"Yes, please," was all Ernie could manage to say. The two of them knelt at the altar, and Reverend Tom Brown put Ernie's hand in the hand of Jesus.

"Hey, I'm sorry I called after nine, Becky. Hope your dad doesn't get upset. I got the job! Best-Mart called a little while ago from Houston. Becky, it was Jack Best himself!" Ernie took a deep breath to calm himself.

"That's wonderful, Ernie!" said Becky. "When do you start?"

"The Monday after graduation, Becky, sixteen days from now. The manager training program starts with four weeks in Houston, then they'll put me in one of their 'super' stores as an assistant manager. Mr. Best said they expect great things from me! Can you imagine that?" Ernie was still talking too fast and still needing more breath.

"Well, Ernie," Becky replied, "I hate to bring you back to earth, but I'll bet Mr. Best tells every new management trainee that he expects great things from them. It's probably a psychological thing."

"You're probably right," he conceded. "Still, I'm one of twenty that were picked from over a thousand applicants. I feel like this is the company I'll be with for the rest of my life. I want to be the best at Best-Mart."

"That probably means you'll live in a new city every two or three years. You can't get promoted by staying in one place," she reminded him.

"That's okay," he said. "We're the kind of people that can adjust to new places pretty easily, I think. This country is full of good people we've never met. I'm just excited about the future. Well, I'd better let you go. I can tell you the rest after church tomorrow."

"My dad is starting to frown," she said. "Ernie, we're skipping church tomorrow. We're going to get up late and then go visit Uncle Fred and Aunt Esther. I'll see you before media marketing class on Monday."

Ernie couldn't find words to say. He couldn't fathom that a family would agree together to not worship God. It was a full five seconds before he clumsily replied, "Uh, yeah…Monday. Good night. I love you."

"Good night, Ernie. I love you too."

Houston boggled Ernie's mind, both the city and the Best-Mart headquarters, but Becky was irritated that Ernie's calls always started with a description of a big Houston church he had attended. "You'd love the music, Becky," Ernie said. "There's not an organ in sight. The songs are like rock music. People put their whole heart into worship. I wish you could be here." As far as Becky could tell, every church in Houston had gone to electric guitars, drums, and keyboards.

"Have they told you yet where you'll be going as an assistant manager?" she asked after the third week of his training.

"As a matter of fact," he replied, "that was going to be my next sentence. They told me today I'm going to

Montgomery, Alabama. I'll get a week between Houston and Montgomery. That'll give me time to pack and then get there a few days early to find an apartment."

"How far is that from Savannah?" Becky asked. "It doesn't sound all that far."

"It looks like about seven hours. It might have been a lot worse. Becky, I'll be home Saturday. We've got a lot to talk about. Would you go to Bennigan's with me for dinner Saturday night?"

જી

The waiter came by for about the twentieth time, this time to remove the empty dessert plates. Allen gave the impression of either being very attentive to his customers or working hard to get a big tip.

"How was your chocolate cheesecake, Becky?" said Ernie. "It looked incredible."

"It tasted even better than it looked," she answered. "I'm going to learn how to make that one day. And then I'll become very, very fat."

"I'd love you anyway, you know," he replied. "If we couldn't walk hand in hand, I'd be glad to push you in a wheelbarrow."

He yelped suddenly as the toe of her right shoe connected with his left shin. She laughed, then he grimaced, then she laughed, then he frowned, and then finally they laughed together. "I deserved that. Thank you for caring enough to straighten me out," Ernie said with a substantial smile.

For a minute or so, neither spoke. Becky was the first to restart the conversation.

"Ernie, you're not the same man I fell in love with a couple months ago," she said. Her smile looked forced.

"I know, Becky," Ernie said. "Life just came alive for me since then. I've discovered a new way of looking at the world."

"You're just not you anymore. I don't feel comfortable in your arms anymore," she said, a tear starting to slide from the corner of her eye. "I'm a Christian, but not like you."

"Becky, I thought it would rub off on you. Jesus is all the world to me," he said.

Crash!

Something out in the store shattered. Ernie leaped back into Barkley's present day.

"Mr. Bostwick, we need some help out here!" Melissa called out.

Ernie trotted over to the toy and juggling supply section of his store. A slender teen boy and Melissa were scrambling like two overcaffeinated spiders to pick up the last pieces of a ruined lamp.

"What happened?" Ernie asked.

The young man stood and held out a club used for juggling. "I'm sorry, sir. I'll pay for the damage. I've been juggling two years, but I've never seen a real juggling club, except on TV. I was just tossing it a few times to see what it feels like, and I kind of made a bad catch. I'm so sorry. I wish I'd never picked it up."

Ernie looked at him then at Melissa.

"Mr. Bostwick, he didn't mean it. Teddy's a great juggler. I've seen him juggling a few times just before school. He can juggle anything. He just hasn't done Indian clubs before."

Ernie frowned. He looked at the two teens then focused on the demolished lamp. He actually hated that lamp. He had made it in about fifteen minutes five years ago from an ugly brown jug. It just wouldn't sell. He had tried five different shades on the lamp, hoping one would strike a chord with somebody. Ernie had moved it out of the lamp section two months ago to help the aesthetics of the lamp department.

Scanning the mess, he could see that the basic parts he had added were still intact. "Is the shade still in good shape, Melissa?" Ernie asked his employee.

"Yes, sir," she said. "It's here on top of the checkers table."

"Sir, how much can I pay you for the lamp I broke?" Teddy eked out. He shifted his weight from one foot to the other then back again.

Ernie asked, "What do you juggle besides balls and oranges? Melissa said that you can juggle anything."

Teddy's face lit up. "Oh, I can do baseballs, softballs. I have trouble with footballs. I'm good with earrings and little things like pink erasers and ping-pong balls. One of my favorites is athletic shoes."

The bell over the door announced the arrival of another customer. Melissa headed back to the center of the store, sneaking a look back over her shoulder every few steps she took.

"Teddy," Ernie said, "I'll make you a deal. If you will come back this Saturday morning at ten and juggle out in front of my store for fifteen minutes, we'll consider the lamp paid for. Don't bring any balls. I want you to use things I sell in this part of my store. Does that sound fair?"

"Oh, yes, sir! Thank you, sir! I'll see you Saturday, Mr. Bostwick." Teddy shook Ernie's hand and headed for the door, giving Melissa a thumbs-up as he left.

☙

No steam rose from the soup. Ernie decided it wouldn't burn his lip, so he slipped into his kitchen chair. Oops, wait a minute. Last time, hot sauce took this soup to a higher level.

He took a spoonful, then another. "Ernie, you have achieved chef status in the soup category," he told himself. He smiled as his taste buds did a happy dance. Another dash of hot sauce launched them into a rumba.

Ring!

He frowned at being interrupted but quickly realized that second Monday, 7:00 p.m., had slipped up on him again.

"Hello?"

"Hey, how's the old bachelor doing tonight?" the voice at the other end chimed in.

"Life rolls on. If I had more fun, it would be illegal. Are you and Dad still outrunning Arthur Itis?" Ernie asked.

A male voice joined the conversation, evidently on another extension. "Some days I can tell old Arthur is gaining on us, but we're running as fast as we can," Ernie's father said.

Nancy and Bob Bostwick, seventy-nine and eighty respectively, stayed incredibly active, playing tennis, bowling in a league, dancing every Saturday night, and walking three miles each morning. The second Monday night of each month was the only time they knew they'd always have free.

"Say, Ernie," said Dad, "I've got a new clock idea for you. I just made one for Uncle John out of an old Chrysler hubcap. The workings tuck into the back of it just perfectly. And if you drill the hole for the stem just right, the word *Chrysler* is perfectly underlined by the hands four times every day."

"Amazing you should say that, Dad. I just got a Chrysler hubcap from a yard sale last Saturday. I'll try that. I'm always glad for your advice. You taught me everything I know."

"While we're at it," Mom said, "you ought to see what I did with my old plaid bowling bag. You remember it? I believe it's sixty years old now. Prettiest lamp you ever saw. I've got it in your old room."

"Every time you tell me about a new lamp, Mom," Ernie said, "you say it's in my room. Is it officially designated a lamp museum? You might have to have a license for that. By the way, I'm going bowling tomorrow night. It's been a long, long time. Hope I can start out on the right foot."

"Left foot, son," Dad put in. "You always started with your left foot."

"One of the guys in your Bible study group?" Mom asked.

"What?" Ernie was confused.

"Who are you going bowling with? One of the guys in your Thursday morning Bible study?" Mom clarified her question.

"Gloria, my landlady, asked me to go with her," Ernie replied. "She said she wanted to get back into bowling and didn't want to go alone."

In harmony, the elder Bostwicks cooed, "Oooh!"

"Oh, come on, you two, it's not a date," said Ernie. "We're just going bowling."

Mom added, "If it's just the two of you, it's a date. Let us know how it goes."

CHAPTER 6

"Lane fourteen, folks. Have a good time." The attendant brought the scoreboard and lights of the designated lane to life, leaving a six-foot darkened buffer between Gloria and Ernie and the Tuesday Night League.

"Oh, I love these seats," said Gloria, easing onto the leather-covered cushion of the blue plastic chair.

"I'd forgotten how colorful bowling alleys are," said Ernie. He worked at the zipper of his red and black bowling bag, unzipping a few inches then back a few inches, then a little more open, then back.

Gloria lifted her swirled light blue ball from its matching bag and took it to the ball return. Two lanes away, a gray-haired woman wearing an oxygen canister stood with ball in hand, concentrating on the array of pins sixty feet away. Slowly, step by step, the slim woman moved forward and dropped her ball onto the twelfth board with a klunk. The ball inched forward as its owner turned and headed back to her seat. Five seconds later, the shining black ball with red flame design nestled between the three pin and the head pin, toppling one pin then another in a lethargic chain reaction that left no survivors.

Gloria looked at Ernie and said with astonishment, "Did you see that?" He obviously had not.

Ernie had just extricated his ball from its bag, and Gloria barely stifled a laugh. "Ernie, I have never seen a bowling ball quite like yours."

"Oh, this was the height of style when I bought it," Ernie replied. "Everybody and his sister-in-law had a checkered ball. Red and black were my high school colors."

Two lanes away, a red-haired masculine mound of muscle fired an emerald sphere at the pins and left only one shivering sentinel erect. Another attempt still left the wooden soldier standing guard over the gutter.

Gloria looked to see if Ernie had been watching, but he obviously had not.

"I don't see any pencil and paper for keeping score," said Ernie. "Is the lane supposed to magically keep score by itself?"

"You really haven't bowled in a while," said Gloria. "All you have to do is type in your name, and the rest is done automatically."

"Oh. Sure. I knew that," he said.

Gloria bowled first. Her four-step approach concluded with a smooth release aimed at the second arrow from the right. Halfway down the lane, the ball got its legs under it and started easing to the left, barely missing the head pin. Five pins remained standing; her next ball put them to rest.

Ernie took his ball in hand. "I'll just throw the first one down the middle," he told Gloria. "I don't remember what kind of curve I've got."

Pushing the ball forward as he stepped with his left foot, Ernie's five-step approach launched the checkered ball straight toward the head pin, veering just in time to hit it solidly on the left. Every pin clattered to the hardwood.

Two lanes away, the oxygen-challenged lady was bowling her fourth straight strike. She and her partner were thirty pins ahead of the red-haired man and his female mate.

In the ensuing nine frames, Gloria's game gained consistency, while Ernie's was the epitome of random order. She bowled 165; he bowled 149.

"I love your curves," Ernie said.

"Why, thank you!" Gloria replied. "I didn't know you noticed."

He suddenly realized what he'd said and turned apple red. "I meant how it looks when you're delivering the ball down the alley. I mean, the gentle curves I see looking from behind you. No, no, you know, the ball." Ernie was totally flustered. Gloria erupted in laughter.

Forgetting his embarrassment, Ernie joined the hilarity. No one should laugh alone.

"Have you decided which guide arrow to aim at," said Gloria, "or are you trying to lay the ball on a certain board?"

"Actually, I'm thinking bigger than that." Ernie laughed. "I'm just trying to hit on the right side of the head pin. I keep moving my aim a little further to the right. Pretty soon I'll have to aim to miss the head pin completely if I'm going to hit it at all."

Gloria stared at Ernie, looking totally confused, then shook her head and chuckled.

The second and third games evidenced more consistency for both bowlers. Gloria was careful not to mention that she'd averaged a few pins more per game. They paid for their games, and Gloria asked the man behind the desk, "Did you see that lady with the oxygen tank bowling? She's incredible!"

"Yeah, that's my mom," the attendant replied. "She loves to bowl. I think she rolled a 260 tonight."

"I believe it was a 263," said Ernie. "They beat the other team by 19 pins even after the handicap."

"I thought you weren't watching," said Gloria.

"Who told you that?" Ernie questioned.

As they loaded their bowling bags in Ernie's Jeep, Gloria asked Ernie, "Can we stop for a milk shake on the way home? I've always done that after bowling since I was a little girl. We don't have to, of course, if you need to get home."

"I'd love to," he replied. "Dairy Barn is right on our way."

As they approached a small shopping center on the right, Ernie blurted out, "Look!" and slowed to a crawl.

"What is it?" Gloria asked.

"There's a leg sticking out of that box by the dumpster!"

He slowed the car to the speed of a lawn mower and eased up to the dumpster, just as a man of Asian descent was rounding the corner with two trash bags.

"Gloria, roll down your window and ask him about the leg," Ernie insisted.

She nervously eased down the window.

"Oh, sir! Sir!" Gloria waved her hand frantically.

The black-haired man with a black waxed moustache looked up and smiled. He tossed the trash bags into the dumpster and stepped quickly over to the Jeep. "Can I help you, ma'am?"

"Uh…," she began, "is that your leg sticking out of that box?"

The man turned and looked in the direction of the dumpster then lifted his head toward the sky and laughed for all he was worth. Ernie also couldn't help but laugh at the way Gloria had phrased her question.

When the Asian man regained control of his vocal cords, he turned to Gloria and answered, "Well, yes and no. I'm actually standing on the two legs I was born with. That's a mannequin I'm disposing of, that I inherited when I bought this former men's clothing store. My wife and I are opening a Chinese restaurant here in less than a month, and we had to clear things out for renovation."

Ernie quickly turned off the car and got out. "I'm Ernie Bostwick, and this is my friend, Gloria Smith." Gloria also hopped out and joined Ernie and their new acquaintance.

"I'm Dan-O Tang. You'll have to come to our grand opening on May 1." The restaurant owner shook Gloria's hand and turned to Ernie but found that he was pulling the mannequin out of the box of trash. The model was obviously male, though its naked form had no defining features. It was clean and about six feet tall.

Ernie ventured, "Dan-O, you don't really want this, do you? I mean, it was in the trash and all. Can I have it? I've never owned anything like this before."

Mr. Tang laughed heartily then walked over and shook his new friend's hand. "Ernie, it's yours. You're actually helping me out. What if the police had come by and seen that leg sticking out? Well, I've got to get back to work. Remember, we open on May 1." He turned and walked back to his restaurant.

Gloria whispered, "Ernie, are you crazy? What are you going to do, make a lamp out of it? What do you want with a mannequin?"

"I'm not sure," he answered. "I'm going on instinct. I know it will be some good somewhere down the line. Here, help me get it in the car."

Gloria dutifully helped carry the figure to Ernie's Jeep. "I never thought I'd be helping throw a naked man in your backseat tonight. I guess this cuts out stopping at Dairy Barn."

As they settled their guest into his seat in the back behind the driver, Ernie suddenly had an idea. He opened the tailgate and dug around a little, finally producing an old red flannel shirt. He tossed it to Gloria then plundered some more until he found a baseball cap and a blanket.

"If we can get this shirt and cap on Henry and cover his bottom half with the blanket," Ernie said, "he can just wait in the car while we drink our shakes. We can just say he didn't want to come in."

After another minute, Henry looked respectable. Gloria fastened his seat belt and got back in the front passenger's seat. Ernie closed Henry's door for him, returned to the driver's seat, and the three friends were off to the Dairy Barn.

"Gloria, I thought you would be a strawberry shake person," Ernie said, as they sat in a booth by the window. "Have you ever had a peppermint swirl shake before?"

"It's my favorite," she replied, "although I guess I've settled for vanilla a lot lately. I'm not surprised you're drinking a blue mint banana shake."

"You mean because I'm the adventurous type?" he said with a wry smile.

Gloria said, "Not really. It's because I really don't know what you'll do next. Like picking up Henry. Do you know that four people have waved to him so far?"

The couple glanced out the window at their mannequin friend just as a policeman walked by the Jeep and waved. The policeman called out a greeting, but as expected, the mannequin made no effort to reply. The cop tapped on the window and said, "You all right?" Still there was no answer. He stared at Henry in the backseat for a couple more seconds, shrugged his shoulders, and turned toward the Dairy Barn.

By this time, Ernie and Gloria were laughing so hard that tears ran down their faces. The cop saw their tears and came inside the building.

"Is that your friend sitting in the backseat of that Jeep, folks?" the policeman asked Ernie and Gloria.

Ernie got control of himself as quickly as he could and replied, "Yes, sir. He didn't want to come in. He's had a hard night and didn't want to talk to anyone."

Gloria added, "He's been thrown out of his home and doesn't know where he'll be next."

"Oh. I'm sorry. Hope things turn out okay for him. You folks have a nice night."

Nearly in chorus, Ernie and Gloria replied, "Thank you, officer."

In a few minutes, both shakes emitted that horrendous sound that signals the failure of a straw to find fluid. Ernie and Gloria went jointly to the cashier, where his wallet was much faster than her purse.

"Listen, folks," said the cashier whose tag identified her as Nancy, "I heard what you were telling the officer about your friend. If he needs any help finding a place to live, or getting groceries or anything, I know my church would be glad to lend a hand. It's First Assembly of God, just around the corner."

Gloria gave Ernie an uncomfortable glance.

"Thanks, Nancy," Ernie said. "He'll be fine. I'm taking Henry to my place, and he can stay as long as he wants. But listen, your church would do that? We're not members of your church. We haven't even attended."

Nancy quickly replied, "God doesn't care about all that. Jesus never walked by a person in need without helping, and we're trying to live like Jesus. Have a good night. Come back soon."

Ernie and Gloria headed back to his store, where Gloria had left her car. They were silent for a couple minutes. She was thinking about how they were going to get the mannequin into Ernie's store without any more commotion. He was thinking about a church that would help people without knowing any of their background.

"Have you thought about how to get Henry in the store?" Gloria asked. "He certainly seems to draw attention. And he doesn't have any pants."

"Well, I think I'll just leave him in the backseat in my garage tonight," Ernie responded. "I'll think about taking him into the store tomorrow. Henry has made us enough memories for one day, don't you think?"

"It's been a lot of fun," Gloria said. "You've been a lot of fun," she quickly added. "Thank you so much. By the way, we owe Dan-O Tang the pleasure of our company at his grand opening on May 1. That's a Friday. I'll remind you."

"It wouldn't hurt me to go bowling again that night, or sometime. I was pretty rusty. I'd like to get comfortable with my game again," he said.

Ernie parked next to Gloria's car in front of his store. He walked her to her car and held the door open as she got in.

"Good night, Ernie. See you tomorrow. And," she said as she waved, "good night, Henry."

Ernie closed her door and watched as she drove away.

"Where do you want to go now, Henry?"

No reply. Ernie drove home.

CHAPTER 7

"Sorry I'm late," beamed Cindy Martin. She looked through the coffee mugs on the racks near Ernie's three coffee urns and quickly chose the one that read "What a Day!"

"Late?" questioned Ernie. "You're still the first customer of the day."

She filled her cup with Java Jamaica and headed for the comfortable seating nearby. Henry startled her, sitting erect in one of the straight chairs, properly attired now in a blue polo shirt and navy slacks. "Oh! Excuse me! I didn't see you there." Cindy's subconscious esteem for the coffee kept her from sloshing out even a drop.

"Meet Henry," said Ernie.

"How do you...Ernie! He's a dummy!" She put her mug down and began a short, crazy combination of giggles and laughs, ending with a giggle.

Ernie settled into his favorite forest-green upholstered vinyl chair. A mug of Reggae Blend sat next to it on a platter-sized table. "I rescued him last night from a sure trip to the landfill. I expect Henry to be a fixture here."

"You mean a lamp?" asked Cindy. "Don't just shove a pole up his back."

"How cruel!" replied Ernie, "I'd rather think of him as a sales associate. Henry has a lot of potential, really."

Cindy settled back in the burgundy chair but never took her eyes off Henry. She noted the straight-ahead blue eyes and the lack of eyebrows or lip color. Was he looking at her? Now which old boyfriend did Henry most resemble, she wondered. Kurt had that same weak smile. Eddie's hair was the same light brown. Allen was a bit more.

"Cindy, how do you like your new lamp now that you've had it at home a couple days?" Ernie asked, intruding on her mannequin analysis. Henry didn't look a bit like Ernie. "Did your houseguests on Monday like it?"

"Oh, yes, they loved it!" declared Cindy. "My friend Sheila asked if you had another just like it. You don't, do you? I told her that your lamps are usually one of a kind."

"I doubt I could match it, at least at that price," replied Ernie. "I could try. She might do better if she came in and looked around the store at what I've already made."

"Well," said Cindy, "I doubt she is ready to buy something right away. She was just impressed at what I'd acquired."

"Do you live near here, Cindy?" Ernie ventured. "I'm sorry that it took you so long to run across my coffee shop. My coffee varieties seem to be just what you're looking for."

"I did live in an apartment in Barkley for a couple years. I moved to Midland three years ago when I got a bargain on a two-bedroom brick home. A sergeant at Fort Benning got shipped out and had to sell it cheap. When did you open this store? I swear this town didn't have decent coffee three years ago."

"I must have opened about the time you moved away," said Ernie. "Too bad. You might have stayed."

Cindy looked at Ernie quizzically then grabbed a section of the *Ledger-Inquirer* that he wasn't reading. They sat in silence for a couple minutes, perusing the *Columbus* paper and sipping coffee.

Abruptly, Cindy asked, "Do you go to church?"

Ernie looked a little surprised but managed, "Used to. What brought that up?"

"Oh," she said. "There's an obituary in here for a lady that was a member of her church for over eighty years.

That knocks me out. She must have stayed stuck in the same neighborhood her whole life. I couldn't stand that."

"Hmm." After a pause, Ernie asked, "Do you go to church?"

Cindy grinned. "I guess that's a fair question. I never have. My parents didn't go to church or send me. Sometimes I'm curious about it but not enough to go by myself."

After a few more minutes spent reading the newspaper, Cindy got up. "I guess I'd better get to work. This may turn out to be the only chance I get to relax all day."

Ernie headed for the cash register, took Cindy's five-dollar bill, and then handed her three ones in change. "See you Friday."

"You've already got me figured out after two coffees? See you Friday," Cindy said, and eased out the front door.

Mike had agreed to come in to work today at ten, so this would be a great day for Ernie to finish the piggy bank clock for Melissa's birthday. Jack would pick it up Friday.

The next hour and a half zipped by. The usual dozen or so customers came by for their *Ledger-Inquirer*,

New York Times, *Wall Street Journal*, *Atlanta Journal-Constitution*, or *Savannah Morning News*. Most of them bought coffee plus perhaps a muffin or cookie; some stayed to read. Ernie had a phone order for a lamp; it took a while to narrow down exactly what was wanted and what he had the materials to make.

The bell over the door jingled yet again. "Hey, Ernie. Glad to be here," said Mike.

"I'm so glad to see you, Mike," said Ernie. He glanced at his watch. "What! It's ten o'clock already? Well, I'll be."

Mike glanced at the customers reading in the coffee shop. There was Glen, the retired history professor, tall and thin, and always wearing a sweater vest. Next to him sat Sam, a plump and congenial fellow who lived off his inheritance. Two seats away was a new guy, not reading, just sitting quietly.

"Hey, Mike," called out Sam, "come over and meet Henry. He's new here."

Glen looked up from his paper to observe the introductions.

"Pleased to meet you, Henry," offered Mike, extending his hand toward Henry. Mike was surprised to see no response from the visitor. He held his hand extended for about ten seconds. Suddenly realizing what was going on, he turned to Sam with mock rage. In response, Sam burst into laughter, joined by Glen and Ernie.

Turning to the mannequin, Mike spat out, "You dummy!" And he laughed at the joke they'd pulled.

Now that help had arrived, Ernie excused himself to his workshop. "I've got a clock I need to make some serious headway on, Mike. Call me if you need me." He retrieved the eighteen-inch-long red piggy bank from the storeroom and placed it in the middle of his favorite worktable.

Sliding a tall stool over to the table, Ernie spent the next few minutes studying the pig. Should he put the clock in the snout or on a side? Looks like the snout wouldn't be big enough to hold the movement. As for the side, one was probably as good as the other.

Ernie picked up the red porker to see if the clock workings could be put in from the bottom. The standard clock movement was two and a quarter inches square and five-eighths of an inch thick.

"Well, would you look at that!" he exclaimed. The red piggy bank had a very large plug covering a very large opening in the bottom. Why would a bank have such a large hole for extricating coins?

After removing the rubber plug, Ernie measured the orifice and found it to be two and three quarters inches in diameter. Taking a clock movement from a nearby drawer, he tried slipping it inside the pig. No problem. "Thank you, Lord," he breathed.

Now Ernie was ready to lay out the parts he needed. First, the red glass piggy bank that Gloria had found for him at a yard sale. Next, he would need a clock movement that had plastic tabs to help him glue it to the inside of the pig. He picked out a four-and-a-half-inch metal dial with bold red numbers. Ernie placed an AA battery on the table, so he would remember to plug it into the movement before it got inside the piggy bank. Finally, he added a set of solid hands with antique black finish.

The only hard step in making Melissa's clock would be in drilling the hole for the shaft. He certainly had the appropriate bit, and experience had given Ernie many insights into how to secure odd-shaped pieces before drilling. "Just allow plenty of time," he told himself. "Slow and steady. This is only Wednesday morning."

This project, Ernie assured himself, was under control. Time for another cup of coffee.

Ernie poured himself the last cup of Seattle Sunrise, grabbed the Orders file from the shelf under the cash register, and sat in the platform rocker next to Henry.

Mike and a red-haired lady peered at tall shelves of classic books that occupied the wall at the lamp end of the store.

After a long sip, Ernie sat his mug down and opened the file. Alice Miller, the mayor's wife, wanted a lamp made from a two foot-tall elegant green vase she'd bought at an estate sale. "Please don't put any holes in it, Mr. Bostwick, in case I change my mind one day," she squeaked at him when she called in the order a little while ago.

Abe Lansing needed clock workings integrated into a frying pan to hang on the kitchen wall. His wife's birthday was still a week away.

The next order in the file showed a drawing of a plunger with a lampshade. Ernie would finish it this afternoon. The base of the plunger now hid solid concrete sealed within its suction cup; he needed only to attach the socket and cord to the top of the handle. The local plumbing company wanted a distinctive desk lamp.

The only other order, besides Melissa's birthday clock, involved replacing all the electrical parts in an ancient lamp a Mrs. Clark had found in her deceased grandmother's attic.

All in all, it was plenty to do. Then again, with Mike here to handle most of the customers, Ernie might get most of these orders done today. He definitely had to get Melissa's clock done since this was her day off.

"Excuse me, Ernie," said Mike. The red-haired lady was right behind him. "Do we have any *Guidepost* books? This is our new friend, Elsie, and she and I have looked high and low through the shelves for a book that is something like a *Guidepost* magazine."

"So nice to meet you, Elsie," said Ernie. "Can you tell me, maybe in a different way, what you're hoping to find?"

"Well," she began, "I want something that gives testimony to how God is active in our daily lives. It doesn't have to be a compilation of miracle stories, maybe just 'God sightings.' Do you know what I mean?"

Ernie thought for only a second or two then replied, "How about some chicken soup? That sounds like exactly what you need."

Mike looked at his boss like he'd flipped his lid, wondering how Ernie thought food would substitute for a book. Elsie frowned then suddenly brightened. "Oh! I know what you mean," she said. "I've heard of those books. They're all 'chicken soup for so-and-so,' or something like that."

"Yes, that's right. Mike, you'll find a few of those up on the second shelf near the back corner." Ernie pointed in the direction indicated. "Elsie, I'm glad I got to meet you. Come back soon."

A few minutes later, after Mike had found and sold the appropriate book, he took a seat next to Ernie in the coffee shop. "That kind of book seems pretty popular over the last few years," he said. "Some people just need a little encouragement. If they think God helps them with every little thing, they can find a way to cope."

Ernie twisted in his chair to face Mike directly. "Don't you think God works in the lives of ordinary people, Mike?" Ernie asked.

"Oh, I kind of doubt it," Mike replied. "There are a lot of people in the world, and really, God put things together pretty well in the first place. I think we're on our own. God has already done His part. We've got to use the brains we were born with."

Ernie grinned. "That may be all right for you, but I'm pretty mistake-prone," he said. "I think God is always ready to forgive. He's big enough to clean up the mistakes of the whole world, if we let Him."

Mike shrugged and changed the subject. "Got any big projects going on in the back? I've seen some pretty unique lamps and clocks go out the door lately. People get some wild ideas."

"Oh," Ernie replied, "I have really enjoyed accommodating them. Keeps me sharp. I was just looking at the orders again. There are three lamps and two clocks to work on. I'd better get to work on them. Maybe I can polish off a couple before your lunch hour at one."

Ernie headed for his workshop. "I finished off the Seattle Sunrise, Mike. How about replacing it with After Hours? It's late enough for decaf."

Mike nodded and went to work on the empty urn.

∾

By half past three, four of the five lamp and clock orders had been completed. Ernie decided to take a break before rejuvenating Mrs. Clark's antique lamp.

"Mike, you've been great," he complimented his employee. "Because you're here, I've gotten an amazing amount of work done. I appreciate you."

"Thanks, Ernie," Mike replied. "There's been plenty to do but not enough to be overwhelming. Any time you need me to work a few extra hours like this, just let me know."

Walking around the store, Ernie could tell that Mike had dusted and straightened here and there, and the coffee shop was immaculate. "Way to go, fella!" he said to himself.

In the games section, a blonde boy, probably about ten years old, sat at the checkers table. He picked up a black piece then a red one, examined them carefully, and restored them to their original position.

"Do you play checkers?" Ernie asked.

"No, sir," the boy replied. "I don't know how."

"Let me show you," the proprietor replied. "Call me Ernie. I've played checkers lots of times."

"That's great," said the boy. "I'm Daniel, sir. My parents won't let me call you Ernie, but I do want to learn how to play chesters."

"Checkers. Just call me Mr. B then. I think your parents would like that all right," Ernie said, sitting down in the wooden chair opposite his young customer. "One person has the black checkers and one has the red. We only use the black spaces."

"They're like frogs, and the water is red. Right, Mr. B?" Daniel asked, looking at Ernie.

"That's right, and they are trying to get to the other side of the pond. But your red frogs don't want my black frogs to get across, and my black frogs don't want your red frogs to get across," Ernie explained.

"Maybe they call it checkers because that's what they called frogs in the country that made up this game," offered Daniel.

"Maybe so," said Ernie. "The checkers slide one space at a time, unless they come to a checker of another kind with a space behind it, and then they jump."

"Frogs love to jump," Daniel said excitedly. "When they see a chance, they just have to. Right, Mr. B?"

"You're right, Daniel," said his teacher. "You're learning fast."

"I've got to meet my grandmother in front of the store at four thirty. By then, I'll know how to play checkers, won't I?" the boy said.

At four twenty-five, Daniel had just won his first game from Ernie. "What time is it, Mr. B?" he inquired. Looking at his watch, the straw-haired boy answered his own question.

"I'd better go, sir. Checkers sure beats my Nintendo. I'll come back sometime, and maybe you can beat me."

"Okay," said Ernie. "I'll try. Enjoyed it, Daniel."

Ernie wandered back to the coffee shop. The *Columbus* paper lay on the green chair, opened to the obituaries. *What was it that Cindy said about an eighty-year church member?* he wondered. Scanning the page, he quickly found the person she had referred to.

"Mavis Carollton," he read aloud. "Age ninety-six. Survived by a sister, Opal, also of Savannah, Georgia, and a niece, Betty Carollton, of Midland, Georgia."

Mike looked over at Ernie in time to see a shocked look capture his face. "Hey," he said, "what did you find? Something new for the store?"

"No, nothing like that," Ernie replied. "Just a time machine."

CHAPTER 8

At five thirty Wednesday afternoon, the Midland phone number rang twice before she answered.

"Hello? Betty Carollton's home. Can I help you?" The lady sounded very elderly.

"Is Betty there?" said Ernie Bostwick. "I saw in the paper that her mother died, and I wanted to offer my condolences. Betty doesn't know me, but I knew Mavis years ago."

"This is Opal, Betty's aunt. Who is speaking?"

Ernie hesitated. Would she remember him? "Miss Opal, do you remember a young man who came to church with Becky Nottingham and her parents? It was over thirty years ago now, and I guess it's unfair to even—"

Opal practically jumped through the phone line. "Ernie! Ernie Bostwick! Of course I remember you! And I remember, clear as anything, the day you took Jesus as your Lord. Hallelujah! There hadn't been anyone saved in that church in ten years."

"Miss Opal," said Ernie, "you amaze me. Yes, it's Ernie Bostwick, and I'm so sorry to hear about Ms. Mavis dying."

"Oh, don't worry about that," said Opal. "She's been off her rocker for ten years. Crazy as a loon. She's in heaven now and living it up."

Ernie followed with the obvious question, "And how are you? You sound great."

Opal tried to sound indignant. "Well, I'm not half cracked, if that's what you mean. I'm still sharp as an ice pick. I'm ninety now, and my doctor says I'm as healthy as a sixty-year-old. I should say so. Most sixty-year-olds sit around and get fat. Please tell me you're not three hundred pounds, young man!"

"No, I'm just the same weight I was the last time you saw me," said Ernie. "And thank you for calling me a young man. How long will you be staying with your niece?"

"This is permanent," she replied. "Oh, Betty acts like she's doing me a favor, taking the old lady in. Truth is, she's lonely since that skunk of a husband ran off with a young floozie. Betty had her mother nearby in an old folks home, but since her brain went for a walk, Mavis wasn't any company."

"Miss Opal," said Ernie, "I own a little store in downtown Barkley. I ought to be able to come see you some time, maybe on a Sunday."

"Don't you go to church?" she said with a definite bite. "I thought you might be a preacher by now. I'm surprised at you. Seriously, you don't go to church?"

Ernie tried not to squirm in his chair enough for her to hear. "No, actually I haven't been in a while. I spend an hour or more on my back porch on Sunday mornings, reading my Bible and praying and singing to God."

"That's not church," snapped Opal. "Ernie, you know better. Call me back when you get yourself back into church. Well, Betty just got home, so she'll wonder what man I've been talking to. Remember what I said!"

It was 8:00 a.m. on Thursday, and Ernie leisurely prepared for his first customers. He always began by preparing three urns of coffee then loading the cash register, getting the morning papers in, and turning on some lamps.

What a difference! he thought. *Best-Mart never closed, day or night. Every morning, I walked into some degree of chaos. Thank you, Lord. I don't deserve this, but I love it.*

Nothing compared to that time each day, about quarter after eight, when he poured his first cup of coffee and eased into the green chair. Ten minutes would pass, usually, before a customer invaded his peaceful kingdom. Cindy, of course, was not an invader; she was more of a fellow citizen of the kingdom.

About half past eight, the bell over the door jingled.

"Hey, Jack, how was Valdosta?" Ernie called from across the room. "Glad you're back."

"It went really well," replied Jack. "The weather lately has put stores in the mood to buy summer displays, and I am your one stop source for summer fun. Tell you what though. The past three days did a number on me. I'm glad I'm just going as far as Perry today."

Jack grabbed a white mug and filled it from the middle urn, containing Hearth Roast. He took a long sip as his eyes scanned the right side of the store through the assortment of clocks and games.

"Ernie," he whispered, "who's the guy playing checkers this morning?"

"That's Henry, Jack," Ernie whispered back. "He's new here. He's been at the table all night."

Jack's eyes got as big as half dollars. "All night? By himself?" Jack craned his neck to try to make out more of Henry's features but had little luck. He moved around the cash register to the game section and quietly walked up to Henry.

"He's a mannequin," declared Ernie, a little louder than he intended, and Jack jumped two inches off the floor.

"Man, Ernie! You made my heart jump. What's a mannequin doing in here?"

Ernie looked at Jack and grinned. Before he could answer his friend's question, Jack held up his hand to stop him. "I know, I know, right now he's playing checkers." Ernie and Jack broke out in laughter.

"I saw somebody about to throw it away," Ernie said, "and I decided I wanted it. It just had possibilities."

"You always had an eye for gimmicks," replied Jack. "Best-Mart lost a great one when you retired early. Too bad you're not managing their Perry store. That place is in big trouble."

"That Best-Mart is in a great location," said Ernie. "What do you think their problem is?"

"It's the General. That's what everybody calls the manager down there," said Jack. "He's got no people skills. Treats everybody like they owe him their undying allegiance. Morale is in the pits."

"They'll replace him soon, I'll bet. Jack Best won't stand for that very long," said Ernie.

"I don't know," replied Jack. "The guy has been manager there for two years."

Jack headed back to the coffee area to leave his empty mug with Ernie trailing him. "I used to love to stop by that store when you managed it, Ernie. The place was full of love. The cashiers, the department heads, even the ladies in the Returns Department were all smiling and upbeat. Now I get in and out of there as quick as I can. That place gives me heartburn."

Jack reached in his pants pocket and pulled out a roll of antacids. "I'm ready for him today."

Ernie rang up his friend's coffee at the cash register and gave him change for his five dollar bill. "Hey, Jack, before you go, how about having a look at Melissa's birthday present? I think I've got it done, but I want to make sure you're satisfied."

Ernie led Jack back to the workshop. The red piggy bank with attached clock was sitting in the middle of one of the tables.

"Yeah, yeah, looks good, Ernie," Jack said, circling the table. After a few seconds, Jack stopped. He stroked his chin as he studied the clock's dial.

"What is it?" said Ernie. "Anything need changing?"

"Well, maybe. You may not be able to do anything about it," he said, "but I wish the dial had more than just the numbers three, six, nine, and twelve. But I don't know. If it had all twelve numbers, that would be jumbled, I guess."

Ernie's face brightened. "How about," he said, "if I add lines where the other numbers would be? I could easily mark the distance and paint in lines. It wouldn't take long at all."

"That's great. Red lines, right? To match the numbers," Jack said.

Ernie nodded. "You got it. I'll get it done today before she comes to work. Thanks, Jack. Have a good day, buddy." He watched Jack walk across the street to his car.

Just before ten, the regular Bible study crowd would begin to arrive. If they all showed up, which was rare, there would be seven in the coffee shop area. There were six comfortable chairs.

❧

Gloria paused when she finished reading the forty-sixth verse of Matthew's chapter 26. Sam took the opportunity to speak.

"So Jesus prayed in the Garden of Gethsemane," he said. "What kind of garden are we talking about here? Peas and broccoli? Sweet potatoes?" The green recliner was not only Ernie's favorite chair. Sam Myers always stretched it out at full length.

"Jesus was called the Lily of the Valley. It was a flower garden." Marietta said it as if she were trying to sell them a new car.

Glen lightly tapped his forefinger on his thick, blue King James Bible. "No, my study Bible says it was a grove of olive trees. Of course, there may have been flowers too. Flowers are everywhere in the Holy Land." The former math professor always found a way to make reference to his 1987 trip to Israel.

"Everybody got enough coffee?" inquired Ernie. All six of the others in attendance nodded or made some positive gesture. (Sam grunted.) Ernie enjoyed the weekly study but always had to tend to customers during the hour. He folded out a metal chair that had been leaning against a floor lamp.

"Jesus prayed at this crucial point in His ministry," Gloria said. "Why did he need to pray?" As the founder and leader of the group, Gloria did her best to nudge discussion along, though it didn't take much to provoke an avalanche with this group.

"He needed to talk to God," Mack, the Pentecostal, answered quickly.

Mandy, the newest Christian of the group, shot back, "He *was* God!" A bit of fire appeared in her eyes.

"Look," Mack answered, "he talked to God a lot. If he was talking to himself all the time, he wouldn't have had hundreds of followers."

Ernie jumped in. "Jesus was both God and human. I think it was the human Jesus that needed conversation with God at this point." Both the tall blonde and the stocky gray-haired gentleman visibly relaxed at Ernie's intervention.

"All right then," Gloria said, "why *do* people need to pray?"

For some reason, none of the seven spoke for a few seconds. Ernie gladly responded to the entrance of another customer.

When Ernie returned from selling his last copy of John Bunyan's *A Pilgrim's Progress*, he was ready to answer the prayer question, but the conversation had traveled a good bit further down the road.

Sam stroked his chin as he asked Gloria, "So was it the God part or the human part that needed friends?"

"I wouldn't think that God needed anything," Glen interrupted.

Mandy responded, "It's not that God needs anything from us. He just likes having us around."

"Sounds to me like it was more than that in this situation," said Sam. "He needed his close friends."

"I agree," said Gloria.

Marietta tossed her red ponytail back over her shoulder. She whispered, "I'm looking for friends like that, who can stand by me in tough times."

The grandfather in Glen smiled and said quietly, "You might find one in a lifetime."

After an uncomfortable pause of several seconds, Mandy said, "That's depressing!"

Mack added, "My church is full of good folks like that!"

Sam wisecracked, "Friends that fall asleep?" He touched his index finger to his tongue and reached high as if tallying a new score for himself on an imaginary board.

"All church members are supposed to be friends who will be there for you," said Gloria, giving Marietta a motherly look.

"But they're not," said Ernie.

"I guess you've got to be willing to reach out first," said Marietta.

Sam responded, "Some people aren't lovable."

Mack got up to refill his coffee mug. "Those people you've got to take on faith even before they prove themselves to you."

Glen added, "You've got to love them even if you don't like them."

"I certainly agree with that," Mandy answered. "I doubt Jesus liked everything about his disciples. But having them there that night got him through a tough time."

"Yeah," said Mack, "you need church friends. You can be a Christian alone, but you can't be a growing Christian."

❧

Jan Carter, her daughter, and granddaughter rarely missed getting together for a meal on the second Thursday each month. Tonight made seventeen months in a row.

The aroma sneaking through the building, table to table, was definitely Italian. Jan suspected Romeo Fellini imported it from Venice and somehow pumped it into the restaurant's air-conditioning system before the restaurant opened each day.

"I love this place, Mom," said Gloria. "How did you ever find it? I thought I knew the north side of Columbus fairly well."

Sharon looked down at the table to keep from laughing. Jan had an open door to make up some wild tale to fool her daughter, and she could never pass it up.

"You may not believe this," Jan started, "but I was driving north on the Manchester Expressway one day and smelled an incredibly intoxicating aroma. As I pulled onto the exit ramp, it got stronger and stronger. I couldn't help but turn right and into this parking lot. You can literally follow your nose to this restaurant."

"Really?" said Gloria. "That's amazing."

Sharon burst out laughing. Jan tried to keep a straight face but couldn't help adding her own prolonged giggle.

Gloria's face started to redden as she slapped Jan playfully on the shoulder. "Oh, Mom! You got me again."

"You're too trusting, dear," Jan Carter responded with a smile. "I've got to get you over that. Especially if you're dating now."

"What!" exclaimed Sharon. "Mom, that's great! Who's the lucky guy?"

"Now who said I was dating?" Gloria queried.

"Oh, a little bird told me," said Jan, "an older two-legged bird that wears an oxygen canister and likes to bowl."

The waiter arrived with three plates of lasagna, steaming hot. The conversation quickly switched to food, punctuated by periods of silence and the miscellaneous clacking of forks. Gloria gladly left the previous conversation behind.

"Sharon," Jan said to her granddaughter, "Daniel asked me on the phone today if I'm any good at checkers. What's that all about?"

"He just learned to play this week, I guess from one of his friends," Sharon answered. "He's already passed my level of expertise. Maybe he was looking for better competition."

"Your mom was always the expert at that," Jan said. "Gloria could beat every kid at school at checkers."

"I'll dig out my checkers set and be ready when he visits Sunday," said Gloria. "I was getting a little tired of Chutes N' Ladders anyway."

The waiter returned to refill their iced tea and check on their progress with the entrée. "Please save room for tiramisu," he suggested. "Our customers tell me that it is especially good today." The waiter glided away to another table.

"I love tiramisu," said Sharon. "I'll make room for it even if there is no room!"

"Me too," added Jan. "I think that tiny bit of liqueur makes the cake absolutely irresistible."

"I think I'll leave it off," said Gloria. "This meal is plenty without dessert."

"Now, Gloria, you don't have to worry about the tiramisu getting you drunk," said Jan. "Or are you worried that someone will think you've gained weight?" Jan added a wink to Sharon, who responded with a broad smile.

CHAPTER 9

Twenty-nine years of married life were habit-forming. Certainly after ten or so, nobody thought about being single anymore. Gloria was now five years into *widowing*. It seemed like forever since she'd felt a man slip his arm around her waist, or plant a kiss on her lips instead of politely touching his lips to her cheek.

Van's love should have been enough to last me a lifetime, Gloria thought.

Ernie's moustache drooped more than it usually did at 8:00 a.m. He felt like a man trying to put on a four-fingered glove. More precisely, he had four flavors of coffee he wanted to sell today but had the same three urns as always.

Cindy Martin would rush in any moment now, looking for Cinnamon Blueberry. It was ready as was his personal favorite, Seattle Sunrise. His newest flavor,

American in Paris, arrived by UPS yesterday afternoon and begged to be opened. Gloria could be depended on to stop by at least four days out of the week and would prefer Aloha Dark.

He decided to brew the new flavor for urn number three. If Gloria had not come by yet when one urn was used up, he'd brew Aloha Dark next.

☙

The bell over the door announced the arrival of Ernie's first customer. The height and build were all wrong. It wasn't Cynthia.

"Hey, Ernie," said Glen. "I grabbed the *Ledger-Inquirers* on the way in. Don't I smell a new flavor of coffee?"

"Man! What a sniffer you've got. It's called American in Paris, Glen," replied Ernie. "It's got a real classy name. I suspect we won't have many of the regular crowd trying that flavor."

"What!" exclaimed Glen. "We don't have any class? Let me at it. As long as it's got a flavor that lives up to its name, I bet it'll sell."

Ernie felt a little guilty about taking advantage of Glen's natural pride, but maybe it would be the coffee love of Glen's life.

"Where's my buddy Henry today?" said Glen. "Last time I was in, he'd been playing checkers all night."

"I've got him reading a book for me over in the lamp section," said Ernie. "I'm trying to get people interested in the classics, so I thought perhaps he'd be an inspiration by holding *A Tale of Two Cities* in his lap for a day or two."

"So you got the mannequin as an advertising gimmick?" asked Glen. "That's pretty clever. It's kind of like the old wooden Indian that used to be in front of tobacco stores. You see the Indian, you think of smoke signals and peace pipes."

"Henry is still good for a chuckle when customers start talking to him," said Ernie. "I'm amazed at the number of adults who think Henry is a real person. Kids talk to him even after they know he's a mannequin."

"Ernie," said Glen, "if you want to keep fooling folks, you're going to have to change his clothes once in a while. Henry has been wearing the same outfit since he got here. Even a retired professor wears something different once in a while."

Ernie had to laugh. Glen had two favorite sweater vests, and two only, that he wore in turn for weeks at a time. Every-other-day friends never saw vest number two.

"Henry and I share the same wardrobe, Glen, but he's a little taller than me," said Ernie. "I'll have to find somebody's clothes other than my own to put on him. One of these days, I'll do some Henry shopping."

"I saw a book about that," replied Glen.

"About what?" Ernie asked.

"Shopping for dummies," Glen said, with a grin. "Gotcha."

Ernie wondered what was in the bag Gloria was taking out of her car. Usually, a customer had a return item when they brought a bag into a store, but Ernie couldn't remember the last time someone had been dissatisfied with a purchase. It looked too big to be the refill on sugar cookies she'd promised for later today.

He suddenly remembered the coffee. His wristwatch pointed its shorter hand directly at the ten. Cindy had never stopped by for her usual Cinnamon Blueberry, and that urn was nearly full. The Seattle Sunrise measured around half full. The new flavor, American in Paris, was down to a cup or two; should he dump it out and brew Gloria's Aloha Dark?

Gloria burst through the door and beamed from ear to ear. "Good morning, guys! I've got a wonderful present for the best-looking man I know!"

Mack put down the newspaper he was reading and smiled pleasantly. Glen perked up noticeably. Ernie's face turned slightly red.

Gloria walked by all of them.

"Please excuse me, gentlemen. Henry and I will be in the storeroom if you need us. Ernie, whatever that new aroma is, I'd like a cup, please." Gloria threw her arm around Henry's waist and carried him and his present to the back.

Mack went back to his paper. Glen looked slightly indignant. Ernie poured American in Paris.

A few minutes later, Henry was again staring out the front window with the same Dickens's novel in his lap as before. However, now he wore a bright red shirt with yellow pinstripes, black pants, a black belt, a bright yellow driver's cap, and a black bowtie.

Gloria sat next to Ernie, enjoying twelve ounces of American in Paris in her favorite mug. "I don't know why I never got rid of Van's clothes," she said. "At first, I couldn't even touch them without being blinded with tears. I suppose that, after a while, I simply forgot I had them. I recognized yesterday that Henry might be close to Van's size. Who would have thought a dummy could replace Van?" Gloria began to giggle, almost losing control.

Ernie frowned. He didn't know what to think of her last sentence.

❧

The familiar black Ford Mustang zipped into a parking space across the street from Ernie's. The proprietor, looking out the front window, hurried away to pour Cindy some Cinnamon Blueberry. He had nearly disposed of it a few minutes ago, thinking no one would want it after four thirty.

"Wow! What a day! And it's not nearly over yet," exuded Cindy. "Melissa! Oh, that's great! What a gorgeous shade of blue!" Cindy certainly had a lot of bounce for Friday afternoon.

Melissa Rhodes glowed at the compliment. "Wow, thanks, I've never tried blue before. I like how it turned out too."

"Variety gives life some pop," said Cindy. "It's fun to keep the world a little bit crazy."

Ernie chuckled to himself. *Yet she always wants the same flavor coffee*, he thought.

Carrying the mug of coffee he'd poured for Cindy Martin, Ernie made his way to the comfortable chairs in the coffee shop area. Before he could put the mug down, Cindy had taken Ernie's hands in hers and dexfully transferred the coffee to her own possession.

"I thought I'd stop for my usual 8:00 a.m. brew this morning," said Cindy, "but I was running late. I virtually dragged myself through the morning. I had to get a cup of gas station coffee at lunch time, which was a big mistake."

"You were lucky to catch me here at all," said Ernie. "I thought about closing early for Good Friday."

"What's that?" questioned Cindy. "I saw it on the calendar this morning, and I said to myself, 'Good Friday for what?'"

"That's when Jesus died for our sins," the blue-haired girl called out from the register.

At that moment, the bell above the front door announced the arrival of Jack Rhodes with a large incompletely-wrapped box under his right arm. Seeing his daughter, Jack made an elaborate pretense of trying to keep the present out of her sight, first behind himself, then behind a pole lamp. Expanding his repertoire, Jack snatched off his sport coat and threw it over the box then quickly stepped between it and his daughter.

"Oh! Hi, Melissa!" fumbled Jack. "Just thought I'd stop by to see my old friend Ernie. I forgot you were here today. Have a good day at school? So what's new?" He quietly fidgeted in front of the present.

By this time, Melissa could hardly keep from giggling.

"Daddy, what's in that box you're hiding?" she asked. "I don't suppose it's a present for me, is it?"

"Aw, shucks," he said. "You caught me." Jack looked at Cindy Martin and Ernie and said, "Will you join me?"

At this, Jack started singing happy birthday to his daughter, accompanied by a surprisingly good pair of backup singers. At the end of the song, Ernie grabbed three empty coffee mugs, tossing them into the air in turn and singing to the same tune:

> I juggle for you.
>
> I don't have a clue.
>
> We all love your blue hair.
>
> Happy birthday, you, you."

Luckily, not a mug was shattered. The crowd applauded wildly, especially the girl with the blue hair.

"Daddy, can I open my present now?" Melissa asked Jack Rhodes.

Jack smiled. "No, dear, let's do it at home so that the rest of the family can see it. But I can understand your impatience. You're gonna love it! And besides, I've got one more thing to put in the box." At that, he grabbed the box and ran to the workroom at the back of the store.

"Oh, what time is it?" said a startled Cindy. "I've got to get going. Glad I got to see everybody." She handed Melissa a five-dollar bill and rushed out the door. "The change is yours. Happy birthday!"

Jack reappeared in a couple minutes with the box under his arm and a big grin on his face. He kept himself between Melissa and her present and made his way to the door. "See you soon, dear."

Ernie looked at his watch. "Melissa, I'll close up," he said to his helper. "It's ten 'til five. Why don't you take off a little early? Happy birthday."

Melissa grabbed her purse and called out, "Thanks, Mr. B!" as she headed out the door.

Twenty minutes later, as he turned out the last of the lamps, Ernie noticed something under a chair. Reaching down, he retrieved a navy blue plastic name badge, imprinted with "Cindy." Below the name, in cursive, was simply "French's."

❧

She waved gaily toward the fifty-five-year old merchant, looking over his head at an imaginary friend. She held her pose with ease, intent on showing off the latest in ladies' fashions. Her identical twin stood next to her in the store window, also stuck in a pose and also looking at some distant acquaintance.

"I wonder if they're Henry's sisters?" Ernie wondered silently.

Judging by the number of cars in the parking lot, French's was not overly busy this Good Friday evening. Name badge in hand, Ernie ventured into the boutique.

"Looking for an Easter gift for your wife, sir? We've got incredible sale prices on nearly everything in the store." The twentysomething blonde, tagged Diane, smiled demurely. She obviously enjoyed an employee discount. Her taste in fashion mimicked that of Henry's sisters in the front window.

"Wonderful," replied Ernie. "Diane, do you happen to know if Cindy Martin is working tonight?"

"Why, yes," said Diane, smile slightly fading, "You'll find her in lingerie."

Ernie's face turned a medium shade of red. "Excuse me, I didn't know. I've caught her at a bad time." Suddenly realizing what she meant, Ernie added one more shade of color.

Diane just pointed to the back of the store and eased away. He moved in the direction she pointed, looking for some indication he was nearing feminine undergarments.

"Shouldn't you have an escort, sir?" Cindy suddenly touched Ernie's elbow, causing him to jump. "I'm surprised to see you here. Are you looking for anything in particular?"

"Actually, I'm looking for you," he replied. "I found your name badge in my coffee shop and thought you might need it tonight." He opened his hand to reveal Cindy.

"Thank you so much, Ernie," she said. "A replacement would have cost me ten dollars. I didn't know where it could be."

Ernie took a fresh look at his surroundings. "You never mentioned having a second job. This looks like a really nice store."

"I've been here six months. Money got a little tight, and my weekend nights were free anyway," Cindy said, looking away. "It's been okay."

"Well, I'd better be going," said Ernie. "Have you had a lot of Easter customers?"

"More last weekend than tonight," she replied. Cindy paused a little then said, "Would you go to church with me Sunday?"

Church? He did his best to hide his shock. "What church do you go to?" he managed.

"I don't *go* to church. You know that," Cindy replied. "I've just been kind of curious. People all around me are talking about going to church for Easter. So I thought I would. But I don't want to go by myself. I've never been to a church before. Would you go with me?"

He thought of Opal Carollton's admonishment: "Call me back when you get yourself back in church!" For these two ladies, he would go.

"It's a date, Cindy. Which church should we go to?" he replied.

CHAPTER 10

The boy could juggle.

Teddy Jarvis added a fourth bean bag to the three already hovering above his slender hands. The bag quickly made a home for itself equidistant between two others.

For downtown Barkley, at ten fifteen on a Saturday morning, the crowd standing spellbound in front of Ernie's was huge. Two mothers, with three small children, had been the first to pause to watch. A couple vacationing from New York had tried to stroll by but couldn't. Three elderly ladies, headed for a dollar store three shops down, stood amazed. Two of Ernie's regulars, Glenn and Jack, had come for coffee ten minutes ago but had not yet made it inside.

"Just takes practice, friends," Teddy interjected, never taking his eyes off a point of focus just above eye level. "I started two years ago with my mom's scarves. They float, so I had more time to catch them, and they didn't break if I dropped them. Then I moved on to softballs, but the juggling balls sold inside will fit your hand better. Rings like the ones I'm doing next are about six inches across. They really take practice, because you catch them and toss them differently."

The three children watching never took their eyes off the objects Teddy juggled. The adults did but only momentarily; they had to prove to themselves they could actually look away.

Every time Ernie glanced out the front window from inside the store, Teddy's crowd had increased in number. When he stepped outside with three Indian clubs, he counted eighteen spectators.

"Teddy's a great juggler, isn't he?" Ernie asked in a loud voice. Energetic applause blossomed all around. "And he's a quick learner. Teddy, let me show you how to juggle these clubs. We usually call them Indian clubs."

The crowd, including Teddy, focused on the shopkeeper. "First, toss one club from one hand to the other so that it makes exactly one revolution." Ernie tossed the implement a couple times successfully then gently passed a club the six feet to Teddy Jarvis.

The first time Teddy tried, the club made slightly less than a complete turn, and he grabbed it clumsily. His second toss was perfect.

"Now, Teddy," said Ernie, "try two." Ernie demonstrated for about thirty seconds then stopped and handed the teen a second club.

Teddy held a club in each hand, moving them up and down a little to feel the weight and balance then started juggling the two flawlessly. People started clapping, while a grin started to spread across his face.

"Teddy, you're amazing," said Ernie. "Ready for three?"

"I think so, Mr. B," he replied. He was visibly trembling with excitement. The multitude watching, now numbering in the midtwenties, oozed anticipation.

Ernie passed Teddy the third Indian club. "Want me to demonstrate? Just a time or two?"

Teddy quickly replied, "No, sir. I think I've got this."

The boy grasped two clubs in his right hand and one in his left. He pumped his arms up and down, forehead wrinkled in concentration, and tried to imagine how the pattern would go. Quickly he started juggling the clubs, and quickly they fell at his feet. Somehow he had not decided how to toss a club from his right hand while holding one in reserve.

"Show me one time, please, sir," he said to Ernie.

Ernie Bostwick grasped one club in his left hand by its throat and two in his right hand in like fashion. Teddy watched intently as Ernie smoothly released one club after the other into an eye-level arc from one hand to the other. Tentative applause broke out. Ten seconds into the routine, Teddy called out, "Okay, I can do it now."

Ernie deftly caught the clubs and handed them to Teddy, who was eagerly awaiting his chance.

"You should all learn how to juggle," Teddy said. "It's incredibly fun, and you can buy all these things, the balls, the rings, and even the Indian clubs, right inside. I don't know if he sells scarves."

"As a matter of fact," Ernie said, "I have scarves made especially for beginner jugglers."

Suddenly all eyes were on Teddy Jarvis. He began juggling three clubs as if he'd been doing it for years. Whistles, cheers, clapping, and all forms of excited encouragement rose from the bystanders. Cameras and cell phones clicked to record the event. Teddy looked like he'd just received a million dollars.

Mike Bruce found his boss, Ernie Bostwick, in the coffee shop late in the morning, enjoying a well-deserved cup of java.

"Ernie, you're going to have to order a few things for the juggling area of the store as soon as you can.

That Teddy really put a charge in the sales over there," said Mike.

"You know, Mike," said Ernie, "those twenty minutes he juggled were supposed to be a way for him to pay for a lamp he accidentally broke in here a few days back. Instead of a penalty, it turned out to be a real thrill for him. And now he wants to come by once a week for me to teach him more tosses."

"Mr. B," called Melissa from the cash register. "I think we must have sold more than a dozen of those beginner kits with the instruction booklet and three rubber balls. Oh, and Teddy just used his last dollar to buy three clubs."

Before anything more could be added to the conversation, two ladies entered the store and headed for the lamps. "You've just got to see this one he made out of a walking stick," said Gloria. "I bought it for the store from a yard sale, the same day I first met you."

Patty Johnson stooped down to look at the gnarled three-foot pole, polished to a high gloss. The base was made of plaster of Paris, painted an appropriate shade of brown. The socket was attached to the top of the walking stick with a brown cord winding tightly from the socket to the base.

"That is wonderful," Patty said to Gloria. "Let me just claim it right now. Oh, and look at this! I've never seen a lamp made from a pressure cooker. That is just unreal."

Mike hurried over to assist the shoppers and was quickly put to work, carrying lamps to Melissa's register. Ernie sat watching, pleased at first, but soon overwhelmed.

"Patty," Gloria said, "if you see something you like, you'd better get it now. I can tell you from experience, a lamp you think you'd like to come back for next week will end up being sold before you get back."

"Every lamp I see looks like the perfect gift for one of my relatives or a friend," said Patty. "If I buy a lamp for one person's birthday, their brother or sister will feel slighted if I don't get them one too."

As Ernie approached Gloria Smith and her friend, Patty, he could see that his stock of lamps had taken a hard hit.

"Ernie, please meet my friend, Patty Johnson," said Gloria. "I've been telling her about your lamps, and she just had to see them for herself."

Turning to Patty, Gloria said, "I told you they were one of a kind. Was I right?"

With an incredibly wide smile, Patty replied, "I'm simply amazed. So good to meet you, Ernie. Gloria speaks highly of you. Where in the world do you get these lamps?"

"Each one is my own creation," he replied. "I just take a fresh look at items other people discard and bring light to them. You'll have to look at my clocks. Each one had a previous life whose time ran out. Now they keep our time on schedule."

"I'd better look at the clocks another time," Patty replied. "I would like to try your coffee, though."

Ernie turned and motioned for the ladies to follow him. "Right over here. And I'd recommend one of the world's best molasses cookies to go with it."

❧

What a dumb idea, he thought. Black-and-white checkered floor tiles must have looked absolutely hideous in somebody's kitchen fifty years ago.

Today, though, these leftover tiles Ernie got at an estate sale at a bargain price were going to make a wonderful checkerboard for a blonde boy named Daniel.

Wait, that's not right, thought Ernie. *These tiles weren't just a bargain. They didn't cost me a cent. They begged me to take them away.* He chuckled at the memory of an elderly lady grabbing his elbow as he turned away from the half box of flooring squares.

His new young friend, Daniel, had been in the store yesterday afternoon, eager to play checkers. He beat Ernie the last game they played on Wednesday, so he just assumed he'd win every game from now on. He soon learned that you couldn't learn everything about checkers in a day. The store's proprietor again won all but one game.

"See you Monday, Mr. B," Daniel called out as he headed out the door at four thirty yesterday.

This kid deserved a checkers set of his own. Ernie had saved a youngster from an addiction to video games and replaced Daniel's old yearning with a game that would really exercise his brain.

Daniel's checkerboard would be a twenty-four-inch-square durable folding masterpiece. The checkers would be a set Ernie had as a child; its board had fallen apart thirty years ago. Ernie was determined to have it all ready to give Daniel Wednesday afternoon.

Downtown Barkley looked deserted. It had been a banner day for most of its merchants, but by 4:00 p.m., the customers had migrated to the residential areas to prepare for a night of restaurants and movies.

"Mr. B," Melissa said, "I've got the store as straight and clean as I can, but I can't do much with this front section. We just need more lamps. Have you got any ready in your workroom?"

"No, I sure don't," he said. "I'm caught up on all my orders, but I guess I wasn't prepared for someone like Patty Johnson buying fifteen lamps at once. I'll have to work hard to get a few done Monday and Tuesday."

"I wish there was some way I could help you," she replied.

An idea suddenly hit Ernie. That was obvious by the look in his eyes and, of course, by the pace at which he stroked his moustache.

"I think you could help me very much, actually," Ernie said. "I need some fresh ideas. Do this for me, Melissa: Take a pad and a pen and go back to the storage room where I keep all my supplies. I'll watch the store for you. Write down things you see in there that you think would make a good lamp. Give me an idea of where the bulb should go, what kind of lampshade, anything I need to know to see the lamp you imagine. Give me five or six good ideas."

"Well," she said, "I don't know. I might imagine something impossible to build."

"That's okay," he said. "Just give it a try. If your idea is impossible, I'll tell you. I might be able to make a few changes and still make the lamp."

Ernie thought about change. If he wanted to move things around in the store any time soon, there would be no better time. With all the lamps and juggling supplies sold today, he had space to maneuver.

The building covered twelve hundred square feet, thirty by forty. Some things could not be moved, such as the ten-by-fifteen-foot storage room in the back right corner and the workroom of the same size just to the left of it. The games and juggling supplies needed to stay in the front right, just in front of the cashier station, so that Melissa could keep an eye on the younger customers, more likely to need assistance. The coffee shop needed to stay in the middle of the store, also near the cashier.

What did that leave that could be moved? The books, for one thing. Used books were not a big seller and were low profit. Also the clocks needed to come out of the back left corner to get more exposure. The books could swap with the clock area, putting the time pieces from front to back at the extreme left and the books in the back behind the lamps.

He heard the storage room door close. Melissa held nearly a dozen pieces of notebook paper in her hand.

"Mr. B, promise me you won't laugh," said his temporarily black-haired cashier. "I think you'll either love my ideas or you'll think they're ridiculous."

"I won't laugh," replied Ernie. "I started this, didn't I?"

"Okay," said Melissa. "Here goes. That wooden box would make a great table lamp. College kids would love it! Just put a pole of some kind up through the middle."

"Wait a minute," said Ernie. "That was just holding the other...no, that's a great idea! Go on."

"You've got two or three stuffed animals back there," she said. "Space them a foot apart, hanging from a chain attached to the ceiling. Each animal could hold a light socket."

"Well," the proprietor said, "I've never sold a lamp that had to be attached to the ceiling. But why not? Okay, what else?"

Melissa went to the next page. "You've got a bamboo thingamajig that is just crying for light. If you could wrap a string of Christmas lights around each pole, I think you'd have a masterpiece," she said excitedly. "Add greenery of some kind, maybe ivy, and you could put, like, tropical birds nestled in the middle of it. Here, Mr.

B. I drew you a picture of how it might look. Don't you think it would be great?"

Ernie glanced at Melissa's pencil drawing of the jungle masterpiece. This would certainly be unique. He glanced at Melissa, who almost quivered with enthusiasm, then back at the paper.

"Melissa," he said. "This is incredible. I'll help you start on it when you come in next Wednesday."

"Me?" she asked, eyes big as tablespoons. "I'm going to make a lamp? Wow! Woo-hoo! Woo-hoo! I can't wait!"

If only he'd had a video camera. He had no idea she could do a backflip.

❧

Ernie had a date for church with Cindy Martin tomorrow, Easter Sunday. She left him the responsibility of deciding where they would go—she wanted to see what church was like.

Where should they go? Would a Pentecostal church scare her? Actually, they were known to run a little long. Maybe Baptist, unless they happened on one that pounded the pulpit; that might turn her off.

Ernie thought through several more possibilities. Suddenly his eyes lit up. He knew exactly where he wanted to attend.

He pulled out his billfold and dug out the piece of paper he'd stuffed in there just a few days ago. Grabbing the telephone, he quickly dialed the seven digits.

"Hello, Opal? This is Ernie Bostwick. I want to join you for church tomorrow. What time do we need to be there?"

CHAPTER 11

Cindy Martin oozed with nervous excitement. She wore a sleeveless blue dress covered with yellow butterflies, which seemed to flit about as she fidgeted.

Ernie turned onto State Highway 315 and headed away from Ellerslie. His black Cherokee was freshly washed and waxed and thoroughly vacuumed within.

"I've got an old friend that lives just a few blocks away from you in Midland," Ernie said. He was dressed in a yellow shirt with navy slacks with a necktie sporting yellow daffodils on a blue background. "She suggested this church. In fact, Opal and her niece are going to meet us there. Opal is the liveliest ninety-year-old you'll ever meet."

"How old is her niece?" Cindy asked.

"I'm not really sure. We've never met," he said. "New Life Church should be coming up on the right in about a mile. They're supposed to meet us right outside the front door."

"Before we get there," said Cindy, "tell me something about God. What do I need to know about God before my first time in church?"

The passenger-side tires slipped onto the highway shoulder, and Ernie quickly jerked the car back on the road. What a question!

Ernie quickly thought how to summarize the Bible in a sentence or two.

"Okay, let me see," he said. "Christians believe God made everything that exists. We've messed up God's perfect plan for how the universe ought to work. To make restitution to God would take more than we're able to give, so God made it right by coming to earth as Jesus then giving His life for us by dying on a cross. Since He was God, He came back to life three days later, and that's what we celebrate on Easter."

Cindy sat in stunned silence.

After a half a minute, she whispered, "Wow. I didn't know there was so much to it."

Betty Carollton, Opal, Ernie, and Cindy settled into a row of chairs about two-thirds of the way back in the auditorium of New Life Church. Recorded music played over the sophisticated sound system above the chatter of nearly two hundred attendees. Attire ranged from long dresses and suits to shorts and golf shirts.

"Where are the children?" Cindy whispered to Ernie. He glanced around the auditorium. He could see no one younger than midtwenties.

Opal, on Ernie's other side, pointed to a page inside the worship bulletin. "I think they have a church service of their own," she said.

A trim brunette called from her stage microphone, "Welcome, one and all! It's Easter, so let's stand up and praise the Lord!" Keyboard, guitars, and drums leapt into a high-energy song, and worship took off like a Boeing 747.

ॐ

"If you're new to all this church stuff," said the pastor, Jim Bartholomew, at the end of his sermon, "how about joining our Tuesday night 'Soul Seeker' class? It doesn't matter how little you know about God, or if you've never been inside a church building before. We're real basic on Tuesday nights. There is no such thing as a dumb question. Come be part of a group of like-minded friends. And by the way, this Tuesday, I'm making some of my New York-style cheesecake. Just sign up at the welcome center out in the lobby."

Reverend Bart took a step back and, looking around the auditorium, said, "Hey, it's been great spending Easter morning with you. What a day! We've celebrated the biggest event of all time, Jesus coming back to life after paving our way to heaven. Let me say a prayer, and then we'll go out into the world with ridiculous smiles on our faces, so that folks will have to ask, 'What's up?'"

As Ernie and Cindy walked the Carolltons to their Mazda, Opal reached up and plucked the cotton from her ears.

"I don't think I've ever had so much fun in church," said Opal. "I almost feel guilty about it. Cindy, what did you think?"

Cindy smiled politely. "Miss Opal, there was a lot for me to take in. It was all a little confusing, about dead men walking, and a stone in front of a grave, and the John guy believing without seeing anything. I caught on to the music right away though. That was a terrific band."

Opal replied, "Maybe you could come out Tuesday night, and the group could help you straighten things out. Now, myself, I'll always be a Methodist. I've got a regular church to go to. I may slip back out here once in a while though.

"And, Cindy," Opal added, as she got into her car, "if you can do anything to make Ernie go to church every week, I'd appreciate it. He knows that's where he belongs."

❧

Why did it bother him that French's was open on Easter? They had every right to run their business how they wanted, and Cindy would likely get paid for putting in some very easy hours.

Maybe it bothered Ernie that he and Cindy Martin had to rush through lunch at a fast-food restaurant to make sure she got to work by one o'clock. No, it was more than that. He still held this particular holiday in high esteem in spite of his lack of church attendance. Ernie wished he could explain to Cindy, or somebody, how Easter was the very anchor of his life.

❧

Easter Sunday afternoon could be very quiet for a middle-aged bachelor. Most families were probably hiding eggs about now. Ernie was counting lamps.

About forty lamps made up the store's usual display. One customer Saturday had bought fifteen. That was great, but it also meant he would have to hurry to replace them.

Looking through the remaining inventory, he counted twenty-six lamps total. Four were former candlesticks, twenty-two to thirty-six inches high. Seven floor lamps in the neighborhood of six feet in height, included two former hockey sticks, two completely dissimilar coat trees, a red-handled shovel, a lamp made from the frame of a beach umbrella, and his favorite, the one that had once been a vacuum cleaner hose.

The remaining fifteen lamps were table models, eighteen to twenty-four inches tall. There was the Uncle Sam statue, Winnie the Pooh, three made from stuffed animals, four that had been kitchen pots and pans, the one from a bust of Benjamin Franklin, two from stacks of old books glued together, a wooden nutcracker, a basketball, and finally, the simple lamp made from a plain gallon jug that he'd been trying to sell for two years.

The proprietor refilled his coffee cup with Mocha Cranberry. He rarely made coffee when he was in the store on Sunday afternoon, worried about the caffeine keeping him awake. But this was Easter! Celebrate! Wasn't caffeine known for bringing people back to life? Coffee was an Easter beverage.

❧

After a visit to the storeroom with its various yard sale odds and ends, he looked through the pad with Melissa's lamp ideas. He especially liked her idea of making a wooden box into a table lamp, not because it would be extraordinarily pretty, but because it made him look at things differently. Why not incorporate a light fixture into a bookshelf? Instead of disguising it, light it!

Ernie looked at his stock of odds and ends a second time, trying to see them with a new perspective. Could he attach a pole to the back of a bar stool with a bulb and shade to make it a lighted place to read? An umbrella with a light under it could make a cozy nook in a small room with the proper base. A cheap painting with tiny lights incorporated right into the picture would add pleasant lighting to a small room.

Some of these new ideas would have to wait. The first priority was to get more lamps on the floor quickly.

Unless he was greatly mistaken, Ernie estimated he could convert the dartboard, the three-foot-high artificial sunflower, and the wooden rabbit into lamps during normal working hours tomorrow morning.

As Ernie was getting into his Jeep, it occurred to him that his cell phone was still silenced from this morning's church service. After slipping his key into the ignition, he fished the cell phone from his pocket.

He immediately saw he had missed a call at 1:30 p.m. from Tina Rhodes. *I'll bet she wanted to invite me to watch the kids hunt Easter eggs*, he surmised. *I might as well call while I'm sitting here and explain why my phone was turned off.*

After four rings, Tina's voice came on the line. "Can't wait to talk to you." Before Ernie could say anything, she continued: "Our hands are too full to even pick up the phone right now, but hey, we'll call you back in just a minute. Might be a good idea to leave your name and phone number though, right after the silly beep. Bye."

Ernie hated talking to a machine, but since it was Tina, he said, "Tina, this is Ernie. Sorry I missed you. My phone's been on silent all day. I'll try you again in a little while."

∼

The Dairy Barn wasn't really on the way home, but it had some wonderful meals that wouldn't cause Ernie to have dishes to wash later.

He looked at his watch and decided that quarter after six called for a cookies and cream milk shake. What went with that better than a hamburger steak, whole kernel corn, and mashed potatoes? The obvious answer was, nothing!

All the waiters and waitresses in the Barn wore black jeans, white shirts, and black-and-white checkered aprons. "Can I take your order, sir?" the waiter inquired.

Ernie looked up into the face of his favorite African-American juggler, Teddy Jarvis. "Well, hello, Teddy!" responded Ernie. "I didn't know you had a job at the Dairy Barn. Happy Easter."

"Great to see you, Mr. B," said Teddy. "Guess you've joined the no-cook crowd tonight, huh?"

"I've been down at the store this afternoon, planning my next great lamp building projects," Ernie said, "and I just couldn't stand the idea of messing up my kitchen. How long have you been working here?"

Teddy grinned from ear to ear. "After I discovered your juggling corner in the store, I decided I wanted to buy some real juggling supplies, so I'd better find a job. I came by last Tuesday after school, and they hired me on the spot. This is my third day."

He continued, "Better let me get your order, Mr. B, so the cook can get started on it. I'll stop back later since you're my only customer right now."

After Teddy left with Ernie's decisions, Ernie checked his phone to see if Tina had called again. Nothing yet. Was her phone silenced now? He'd call her after supper.

He thought again about the layout of his store. This really was the time to make changes if he was going to do it any time soon since inventory was low. If he could come up with a plan, he'd call Mike to come in early a couple days to help switch things around.

The left half of the store was lamps, clocks, and books, roughly twenty feet wide by thirty feet deep. Lamps were in the front with clocks behind. The books were on four-foot-high shelves that lined the left wall.

Right now, lamps were his best seller. Should he do something to help clock and book sales, or push lamps while sales were hot? Used books could be profitable if he sold a greater volume since that would allow him to get big orders from the overstock houses. Of course, clocks were already high profit; they needed a new advertising scheme.

"Here's one tremendous hamburger steak meal, Mr. B, ready for consumption," said Teddy, appearing with Ernie's meal. "If you're like me, you'll probably drink half your milk shake first. Let me know if you need anything."

"Well, I did kind of have that in mind." Ernie chuckled. "What would you eat after that?"

"Oh, you really don't want to know," replied the waiter. "But if you did want to know, I'd have to tell you a very deep secret. Whenever Mama makes hamburger steak, I chop it up in little pieces then mix everything on my plate together. But don't tell anybody, Mr. B. They might laugh. Let that be our little secret."

After Teddy slipped away, Ernie started on his cookies and cream milk shake. He glanced at his plate and decided to use his food to figure out his store layout. The corn would be the books, the mashed potatoes would represent the clocks, and the meat would be the lamp section.

Ernie lined the kernels up on the left side of his plate, leaving the mashed potatoes heaped behind the hamburger steak. He sipped a little more on his shake and scratched his head.

Wait! What had Teddy said about mixing things together? The hamburger steak (lamps!) could be mixed in with the whole kernel corn (books!) and the mashed potatoes (clocks!). Genius!

Ernie started cutting his hamburger steak into small squares. After acquiring about thirty lamps, he put a few of the pieces together with a half-dozen kernels of corn and mixed it up with some mashed potatoes. He made two more similar piles and lined them up at the closest edge of the plate. Ernie pondered how his store would look with groupings of lamps and books and clocks together. *Almost like home*, he thought. *I just need a comfortable chair in the grouping.*

Ernie looked up to see a little girl standing by his table, her face spread with a very concerned look. "Mister," she said, "my mama always says people shouldn't play with their food." A young couple was seated nearby, watching their daughter carefully.

"She's probably right," said Ernie. "I was pretending my plate was a store, and every piece of meat was a lamp. The corn was books, and the mashed potatoes were clocks. If I don't stop playing with my food, it will get cold, won't it?"

"That's right," she said, "and besides, the corn should be clocks and the potatoes should be books."

❧

"I'll see you Tuesday, sir," said Teddy Jarvis. "Thanks, Mr. B. I'll be working on my Indian club tosses."

"I'll see you then, Teddy," said Ernie. "Great meal. You're not just a great juggler, you're an excellent waiter."

As Ernie got into his car, he pulled his cell phone out and redialed Jack's wife. *It probably wasn't important*, he mused. *If I don't get Tina this time, I'll just forget it.*

On the first ring, Tina answered. "Ernie, I'm sorry. It's been an awful afternoon."

Ernie was surprised. "Awful? Tina, how can Easter be awful? Did you get tired of hiding Easter eggs? Or did one of the kids get hurt?"

There was silence for a full five seconds on the other end of the line.

Tina's voice cracked as she sobbed. "Ernie, Jack's had a heart attack. We're here at the hospital in intensive care. He's stable. Can you come?"

CHAPTER 12

Peavy Memorial Hospital was only a few blocks from the Dairy Barn. The desk in the main lobby sat unattended. *I'm not surprised*, thought Ernie. *It's seven fifteen on Easter.*

A three-sided sign stood next to the telephone, "Dial 0 for patient information."

He obediently dialed the single digit.

An obviously bored attendant answered, "What name?"

Ernie spoke into the phone, "Could I have the room number for Jack Rhodes, please? He may be in ICU."

The attendant, after a pause of nearly ten seconds, said, "I'm sorry, we have no one listed by that name. Thank you, sir."

"Wait!" Ernie cried out. "I know Jack is in this hospital! I just talked to his wife five minutes ago. Could you check again, please? He's my best friend."

The voice on the other end of the line was obviously perturbed. "I'm sorry, but unless you give me the correct name of a patient, I can't give you any information."

Now Ernie was the one perturbed. No, he was close to being angry.

"I am so sorry, ma'am," he said through clenched teeth. "I meant to ask for the location of *John* Rhodes. Please excuse my blunder."

The voice answered crisply, "ICU bed nine. Visiting ends at seven thirty."

Click.

❧

He tapped lightly on the door of room 9 of the intensive care unit. Tina quietly eased the glass door open and immediately threw her arms around Ernie's neck. He held her firmly as her tears dampened his shoulder.

Jack Rhodes lay sleeping on the narrow ICU bed. An IV connected the back of his hand to a small bag of clear liquid attached to the stainless steel pole at the head of the bed. Another IV provided access for a larger sack of fluid, also on the pole.

Tina eased herself to arms length and said, "He's better now. He'll need a stent put in tomorrow morning. Jack had over a ninety-five percent blockage in the artery going to the top of the heart. Ernie, I didn't think he was going to make it. And all I could do was sit in the waiting room while they worked on him. Every time a doctor came from the back, I thought he was going to tell me they lost him. My nerves were as tight as piano wire."

Tina eased over to the vinyl recliner next to Jack's bed and sat. "Come sit down, Ernie. I've got a lot to tell you."

Ernie moved in the direction of the only chair but said, "I'm afraid they'll be kicking me out in just a couple minutes. Visiting hours are over at seven thirty."

Fire seemed to shoot from Tina Rhodes's eyes. "They'd better not try it! You just got here. I may be small, but I'm a blazing inferno when I'm mad!"

He settled into the chair a few feet in front of Tina. "I put my cell phone on silent when we went into church this morning and forgot to change it back. I just happened to check it when I was leaving the store late this afternoon, and then I guess your phone was not on."

"That's probably when the doctor was talking to Melissa and me," she said. "I turned it on when she left at seven. She's been with me all day."

A male nurse pushed the door open halfway and asked, "Do you need anything, Mrs. Rhodes? Looks like Mr. Rhodes is resting comfortably."

"Thank you, Daniel," she said. "Don't bother my guest here, or I'll be exceedingly upset. I know visiting hours are supposed to be over."

"No problem," he replied. "Your daughter can come back in too, if you'd like. Just as long as we can do our work, that's fine. I'm sorry Jacqueline was rude to you earlier. She tries her best to protect our patients, but sometimes she gets carried away."

Tina said, "Melissa won't be coming back tonight, but I appreciate the offer. Thanks."

The nurse closed the door quietly.

"Tina, give me the whole story from the beginning," said Ernie.

"Ernie, I was going to insist on it," she said. "Then you're going to tell me about going to church. I guess you know I've been praying for that for several months."

Tina stood. "This is a long story. I'd better slip into the restroom first. If a doctor comes in, don't let him leave even if you have to tackle him."

While Tina was gone, Ernie glanced at the monitor above the corner of the bed. Much of it made no sense to him. Lines moved across in regular patterns, probably indicating heartbeat and respiration, among other things. Regular was good, he surmised. None of the numbers at the left of the screen increased his knowledge of Jack's condition. Ernie quickly gave up trying to interpret the monitor.

Jack's eyes opened in slits then closed. Jack whispered, "How's it going, pal?"

Ernie stood up and moved to the side of the bed. He found a place he could grasp a few of Jack's fingers and squeezed them lightly. "I'm glad to be here, Jack. I guess you've had quite an Easter."

Slowly Jack replied, "Yeah. Tina will have to tell you about it." Still whispering, he asked, "Did my wife go home?"

Ernie grinned. "Are you kidding? She's in the bathroom. She's going to be here every minute you are."

Jack smiled, opened his eyes for a few seconds, and nodded.

"I guess all the antacid tablets were trying to tell us something was wrong," said Ernie. "Sorry I was so dull."

"No duller than me," Jack whispered back.

Ernie could hear Tina washing her hands in the room's bathroom. "You better rest," he said. "If Tina tells the story wrong, just smile and let her keep going."

Jack smiled and quickly drifted off to sleep.

❧

"It was just an incredible day before two o'clock," said Tina. "Meagan was home from college for the weekend, Melissa's hair was a relatively ordinary black, and the weather was gorgeous. Sunrise Service was well attended, and the church was absolutely packed at eleven."

Ernie nodded and smiled slightly. He could have commented on his church attendance but thought that might interrupt Tina's story.

"The girls helped me prepare the meal yesterday, so we would only have to heat it up when we got home," she said. "Ham, fruit salad, sweet potatoes, asparagus, cranberry sauce. It looked almost too good to eat. And for some reason, Jack always wants cherry cobbler for dessert on Easter."

Jack smiled slightly at this. Tina didn't notice.

"I'm glad I just had supper," said Ernie, "or your description would be too hard to take."

She continued, "We all headed for the den after the meal. Jack had the Braves on, and the girls and I were swapping sections of the Sunday paper. After awhile, I noticed that Jack was still awake! Ernie, you know he usually falls asleep on Sunday afternoon within minutes of turning the game on."

"I know," he replied. "It doesn't matter if it's baseball, football, basketball, or NASCAR. I make sure I don't try to call him before three on Sunday afternoons."

Tina said, "'Are you all right?' I asked him, just half seriously. Jack started rummaging in his pocket for the

CIRCUS ON THE SQUARE

antacid tablets he's been popping like candy lately. He suddenly grabbed his chest and said, 'Oooh, that hurt!'"

Ernie interjected, "I'll bet that scared you, didn't it?"

"I was shocked and didn't know what to say," Tina answered. "But, Ernie, I want you to know that Melissa started dialing 911 as soon as Jack grabbed his chest. Before I could get my head on straight, the ambulance was there."

"How was Jack at that point?" Ernie asked.

Silence. Tears quickly formed in Tina's eyes. She struggled to speak but just took a few deep breaths instead.

"He was incoherent," she finally said. "Nothing that came out of his mouth made sense. And he couldn't be still, so uncomfortable. I've never seen him sweat so profusely. Ernie, my husband was dying right there in front of us."

"God came through for us again, didn't He, Tina?" said Ernie. "Jack seems stable now, and tomorrow they'll put the stent in. He's going to be all right."

Tina looked deep into Ernie's eyes and nodded then grasped his nearest hand.

"Oh, dear God," she prayed, "how could we ever doubt Your love? When Your son, Jesus, was killed by crucifixion so many years ago, You allowed it as payment for our sins, the only way to bridge the gap between God and mankind. There will never be a greater sign of Your love for us. But today, God, You gave us another great gift, Jack's life. My husband, Ernie's friend, Melissa and Meagan's father will be with us a while longer. Lord, if it's even a month, a year, a few years…he was almost gone. Thank you, thank you, we praise you, from the bottom of our hearts. He lives because you live."

Again there was silence. Tina expected Ernie to pray.

"Oh Lord, king of kings, and our best friend," he began, "I thank You for the fullness of life You allow us to know. Jack is alive, and we praise You, dear Lord. We love the times of great joy You bring us, and there have been a lot lately. But we also appreciate the terrible times like today. You've given us a heart like Yours, and You allow us to know a little of how Your heart breaks when any of Your creation hurts. We thank You for letting us know the heights and depths and lengths and widths of a truly abundant life. All praise to the One who loves us more than we can imagine. In Your holy name we pray, amen."

As he released Tina's hand, Ernie said, "Okay, tell me the rest of Jack's story. What happened when the EMTs came in?"

༺

It was half past eight when Tina finished her story. She sat back in the recliner, tired but relieved that she had gotten the chance to relate it all.

Ernie saw a smile on Jack's face spread all the way from east to west.

Slowly Jack opened his eyes. "There's more you need to hear," Jack said in a whisper. Jack swiveled his head to look at his wife. "Tell him about the angels."

"What angels?" questioned Ernie.

Tina said, "I think he's talking about the people from church, Ernie."

Jack nodded in agreement.

"I really didn't expect anybody to come," she said. "I knew Pastor Olney was at his brother's house in Macon. He and Sandra left right after church. I texted Sandra from the house as they were getting Jack in the ambulance, just asking her to pray. Ernie, within ten minutes after we arrived here, people started coming by to sit with us and pray. They came in couples, singles, families of four. The girls and I were never alone, right up to six thirty tonight. Hilda Brown even brought us some of her ninety-fifth birthday cake, about five o'clock. I didn't realize I was hungry until she brought in the cake. And I thought my girls were going to eat the plate."

Ernie adjusted himself in the chair a little. "I'm sorry you didn't have any peace, Tina. You didn't need to be entertaining folks," he said.

Jack spoke a little louder this time. "Ernie, they were angels. God sent them to support us."

"Jack's right," said Tina. "It might seem like you'd want to be alone. Let me tell you, I needed friends to lean on. And not just anybody. I wanted people around who believed in a powerful and loving God."

She leaned back in the recliner and closed her eyes, finally able to relax. In less than a minute, she was asleep.

෨

The two men were silent for awhile. Ernie decided Jack had dozed off.

He'd better text Gloria. One more person praying for Jack couldn't hurt.

"Sitting with Jack Rhodes in ICU. He had a heart attack today, stable now. Stent tomorrow. Please pray," his message read. Ernie decided that would cover it.

In a minute, his phone beeped, signaling a reply. It read, "Thank the Lord Jack is ok. Playing checkers with my grandson. Will pray now and continue."

☙

The beep from the incoming text message roused Jack. Tina slept on.

Jack whispered, "She was so excited this morning. Tina saw you drive by with a tie on."

Ernie gave Jack a wry smile.

"She knew you were going to church," Jack added.

Ernie let Tina's gentle snoring be the only sound for a full thirty seconds.

"She didn't mention it often, but I know she was praying I'd go to church," Ernie quietly said to Jack. "When did she start praying that?"

"Ever since you've been in town," he said. "Every morning at breakfast."

☙

Ernie looked at his watch and was shocked to see it was nearly ten o'clock. He glanced at his best friend; Jack was sleeping soundly. Tina still had her eyes closed and had not moved the slightest amount in over an hour.

Easing out of the green upholstered chair, Ernie stood erect and carefully stretched his legs. As usual, several joints gave a snap, crackle, or pop.

Tina opened her eyes slightly. "You can't leave," she whispered.

He opened his mouth to protest.

She spoke again. "Not until you've told me about going to church."

Ernie eased back into the chair. He owed her the complete story. "Last Friday, Cindy Martin asked me, just out of the blue, to go to church with her on Easter," he said. "She has no religious background, but she was curious because so many people were talking about Easter. So I agreed to go with her."

"Did she have a certain place picked out?" Tina asked.

"No. She left that to me," he said. "I just reconnected a little while back with an elderly lady that lives in Midland. I used to attend the same church as Opal when I was in college. I called her, and she had a couple of good suggestions."

Tina wanted to ask why Ernie hadn't just gone to church with Jack and her and the family but decided against it.

"Where did you go?" she asked. "Did Miss Opal go with you?"

Ernie said, "We went to a new church a couple miles east of Ellerslie. Cindy and I met Opal and her niece there. I can't think of the name right now, but it had a great band. The pastor wore jeans and a polo shirt."

He reached in his shirt pocket and retrieved the morning worship bulletin. "New Life Church. He had a really good sermon, aimed at seekers or new Christians. I think Cindy liked it, but I know she's got a lot of questions. She should be stopping by for coffee in the morning."

"What about you?" Tina asked.

"What do you mean?" he replied.

Tina said, "Did you like the service? Ernie, I know you're a Christian. I know you have a close relationship with God. You need a church. Is this the one that gets you back where you belong?"

He was quiet for an uncomfortable minute or two. Ernie studied the floor.

She spoke slowly, picking her words carefully. "Today has reinforced my basic beliefs in Christian fellowship. We need each other. Some days one believer is strong, while another is weak. Tomorrow it might be the reverse. You're strong in your faith. That's why I called you today. Ernie, you have denied other Christians your presence for too long. There are days when we all need others. A Christian is part of an army. No one has a right to go

AWOL. You may never need another Christian to carry you. But I really doubt that's true."

Ernie sat a few more seconds then looked at his watch. "Tina, I appreciate your praying for me. I'd better be going."

As he stood to leave, Tina walked over and wrapped her arms around him. "Thank you for coming, Ernie," she said. "You can't possibly know how much Jack and I appreciate your friendship."

As he exited, Ernie called back, "Call me tomorrow and tell me how he's doing."

Tina sat back down, folding her hands in her lap. She leaned her head back and closed her eyes.

Jack said quietly, "You were pretty direct with him, dear."

CHAPTER 13

"Hey, did you know it was us?" she asked. "How's Gloria?"

Nancy Bostwick never was one to beat around the bush. At seventy-nine, she was more direct than ever.

Ernie said, "Mom, I knew that it was second Monday, not the first Monday. You just called last week. But I'm always glad to hear from you."

"I was just curious about your date, son," she said. "I thought we might forget to ask about it if we waited three more weeks."

He decided to fuel the fire a little: "Gloria was doing fine when I texted her last night. I thought it was only fair since I was with Cindy Sunday morning."

"Ooh, texting is the big romantic thing now, is it?" his mother replied.

Bob Bostwick could tell that his son was playing on his wife's curiosity but played along. "Ernie, you're a little old to be burning the candle at both ends. Maybe you should date just one lady at a time."

"Dad, maybe you're right," replied Ernie. "I guess I've been trying to make up for lost time."

Nancy interjected, "Who is Cindy?"

"She's one of my store's regular customers," said Ernie. "Friday night she asked me for a date and, well, she's kind of pretty, and I just couldn't refuse."

Even though all Ernie said so far was basically true, he took the time to fill in all the details for his parents. No need to give them the impression he'd taken a step toward insanity, or made dating a main focus.

"You haven't mentioned church in a long time," his mom said later in the conversation. "This is the first time you've been in years, isn't it?"

"I guess you could say that, Mom," Ernie replied, "but I consider my hour with God every Sunday morning just as good. It gets me recentered for the week."

"I'm glad you do that much, son," Ernie's father said. "You remember the Sabbath and keep it holy. But as a friend, not just your dad, I advise you to get back in church. You don't have to go to church to be a Christian, but you have to be in church to be a *growing* Christian."

That sounded familiar to Ernie, but he couldn't remember where he'd heard it.

Nancy eased away from talking about church. She considered that enough had been said already. "How is the store doing?"

Ernie answered, "Mom, even though my profit stays about the same each month, different areas of the store take turns in leading sales. For instance, it has been a great month for lamps and juggling supplies. Coffee and clocks and newspaper sales have held their own, but books and games have not sold well lately."

"Is there any area that never leads?" asked Dad.

"Hmm, that's a good question," said Ernie. "Now that you mention it, book sales have not had a big month in a long, long time. Maybe I should keep a closer watch on that."

"I'll try to remember to ask you again next month," said Bob Bostwick.

Ernie said, "So, what have you two been doing lately?"

Nancy replied, "Pretty much the usual things. We still walk every morning and go dancing at the Legion on Saturday night. Summer bowling league starts next week."

"Tennis has been a problem," said Dad. "We can't find anybody near our age to play against. Anybody older than fifty can't run worth a flip. We're having to play against couples in their forties now to find any real competition."

Ernie just shook his head.

❧

Teddy and Melissa came through the door at the same time. Her hair was still black, same as the last time Ernie saw her, but it was tipped in brilliant red.

"I'm back, Mr. B," Melissa called out to the proprietor. "Dad is a whole lot better, probably coming home today."

"I've never known you to color your hair in just that style," Ernie added. "Something new you're starting? By the way, you know your hair color has never made a difference to me."

"I promised my dad," Melissa said, "that I'd keep the same color at least two weeks at a time. He said my constant changes weren't giving him enough time to enjoy the 'new me.' But he said coloring the tips would be okay."

"Well, I'm so glad you're here," said Ernie. "Mike was helpful yesterday afternoon, but he can't do everything you can just yet. Teddy, how is your job at the Dairy Barn going?"

Teddy Jarvis smiled from ear to ear. "Sir, it's great. I sure like the pay, but there's a whole lot more to it than that. I had been praying to God for some new place to serve Him, and then I got this job. The more I serve folks, the better they tip, and all I'm trying to do is treat them like I'd like to be treated myself."

Ernie didn't know what to say. People didn't usually say much about religion in casual conversation, but Teddy had done it so naturally.

"Maybe that's like where the Bible says, 'Give, and it will be given to you,'" Melissa said.

"Teddy," said Ernie, "there is no better satisfaction in life than serving other people. And you are both right, God always finds a way to bless His servants. Hey, are you ready to juggle?"

"Yes, sir, Mr. B!" The teen oozed excitement. "I brought a few things, if you don't mind. Some things I need to learn how to handle better."

"Sounds like fun," said Ernie. "Melissa, I'll leave it all to you. We'll be in the storeroom."

Melissa was already making an urn of After Hours, one of the store's two decaf coffees.

❧

"You've got to think catch, not grab," the teacher said to Teddy. "And a football has a way of turning in odd ways no matter how it seems to float on the way up. Your hand has to cradle it as close as possible under its center of gravity as you push it up for another toss."

"Okay, let me try it again, Mr. B," said Teddy. "So you're saying my toss doesn't have to be perfect as long as I can catch the football under its middle."

Teddy Jarvis managed a sequence of eleven tosses of the three footballs before one managed to elude his hand.

"Great! You're getting it now," said Ernie. "Now that you're not so worried about the perfect toss, it's amazing how much more uniform each throw is. Did you bring a fourth football?"

Teddy rummaged through his black duffel bag and produced another one of the pigskins. "I don't know if I'm ready for this," he said.

"It's not what you think," said Ernie. "We can do four footballs together."

For the next several minutes, teacher and student worked on underhand spiral tosses of the footballs back and forth between them. Ernie added a second, then a third, then a fourth football, until they were smoothly relaying the projectiles in a steady rhythm.

Ernie inquired, "Any other strange objects in the bag?"

"Well…maybe," replied Teddy. "Mr. B, I've seen you eat an apple while you juggle." He dug in the bag and produced a bunch of bananas. "What do you think?"

Ernie backed up to the wall and laughed. Teddy frowned. Ernie laughed some more and kept laughing. Teddy was soon infected, producing a high-pitched giggle of his own.

A minute later, Teddy managed, "That was kind of dumb, wasn't it?"

Ernie made himself stop laughing but retained a wide smile. "Actually, Teddy, you could probably figure out how to eat a banana while you juggle. That's what you had in mind, right?"

Teddy nodded his head. "Just juggling bananas is easy, not much different than when I juggle a couple pairs of athletic shoes."

"The hard part, I think," said Ernie, "will be getting the peel started. You'll have to have both hands free for an instant."

"I'll think about it this week," Teddy responded.

Melissa tidied up the coffee area and straightened the magazine rack, never noticing that a ten-dollar bill slipped out of her pocket. She tried to keep her mind off her father, who would be spending another night in the hospital.

"Glen, looks like you're having trouble finding a book," said Ernie in another part of the store. "Can I help you?"

"Just give me another minute," he said. "I thought I knew the author's name, but it slipped out of my mind. It'll be back. You know you're old when it doesn't."

Ernie slipped over to the lamp section, where Melissa was straightening shades. "Mr. B," his helper said, "my mother just called and said Daddy won't be getting out of the hospital. His heart got a little out of rhythm."

"If I'm not mistaken," Ernie said, "that's not unusual for heart patients after they've had a procedure. I'm sure he'll be fine."

Melissa looked for something else to straighten. Finding nothing immediately, she turned off a lamp and turned on the one next to it.

Glen called from the book section, "Okay, I give up. I need help."

Ernie smiled at Melissa and went to wait on his customer.

"So, old man," Ernie said to his Thursday morning Bible study mate, "I guess you couldn't remember the author after all."

Glen gave Ernie a half smile. "I almost thought of it. Seems like it was Bob Kart, something like that. Wrote about a century ago."

"Hmm," said Ernie. "That doesn't ring a bell. Can you remember the name of the book?"

Glen said, "It might have been The Buck that Went to Camp. Does that sound familiar?"

Ernie stroked his moustache for a few seconds. "Sounds like something Mark Twain would write."

"You're close," said Glen. "I think they might have been friends. Maybe the title was something about luck instead of buck. And the guy liked surprise endings."

"Got it," said Ernie.

He quickly walked over to a chair that Henry was occupying and picked up the book off the table next to him. Henry, of course, looked straight ahead and never budged.

When Ernie handed Glen the book, the former math professor's face lit up. "That's it, all right! Ernie, you sure know your stuff."

The book was *The Luck of Roaring Camp* by Bret Harte.

❧

Locking the storeroom, Ernie called out to Melissa, "Register closed out? I'll bet you want to get to the hospital to see your dad."

Melissa was looking on the floor around her primary work areas. "Yes, sir," she called back. "Everything's ready.

Mr. B, I must have dropped a ten-dollar bill out of my pocket. I can't find it anywhere. Mom gave it to me last night to buy some groceries today before I came home. I know I had it an hour ago."

Who had been in the store in the last hour? Melissa could only remember Glen, the deacon from the Pentecostal church. She thought she remembered seeing him bend over one time to pick up something off the floor when he was paying for his book. "That was my ten-dollar bill!" Melissa said to herself.

"I'll keep my eye out for it," Ernie said. "It'll turn up."

She thought, *No, it won't. That hypocrite kept it. I'll never see it again.*

Ernie pulled out his billfold. "Here, take this ten in the meantime. You don't need to spend any more time looking."

Melissa opened her mouth to protest the gift, but her boss shook his head. "It's just a loan. Your money is in here someplace. See you Thursday."

She felt awful about taking Ernie's money. He'd be out ten dollars, and the other guy would be ten dollars richer. But she needed to buy her mom's groceries. Melissa took the money, gave Ernie a quick hug, and went out the door.

❧

Gloria finished chewing her bite of supper and picked up the phone.

"Gloria, it's Ernie," he said. "I hope I didn't interrupt anything."

Why did her heart start to beat faster? *It's only Ernie*, she thought. *Behave yourself.*

"Gloria?"

"Excuse me, Ernie," she spoke up. "I was just finishing my last bite of fish. Don't worry, all the rest is salad. How are you? And what have you heard from Jack?"

"I'm fine," he answered. "Melissa said Jack was going to be coming home today, but his heartbeat got a little irregular. They'll keep him until they get that straightened out."

Gloria said, "I've heard that happens a lot after heart surgery, and it usually responds quickly to treatment. Anything special you called about? Don't forget the grand opening of Mr. Tang's restaurant on May first. He'll want to hear from us how Henry is doing."

"It's on my calendar," said Ernie. "I called to ask if you might like to go bowling tonight."

"Tonight?" she said. Gloria looked at her feet and saw no shoes. She was wearing white gym shorts and a t-shirt with a hole in an inappropriate place. Above all that, she had just removed all her makeup before supper.

"Ooh, Ernie, I'd better not," she finally replied. "I didn't expect to go out of the house tonight, and I've gotten really comfortable. Maybe we could do it another night."

"That's a better idea," he responded. "Well, have a good night. I'll see you soon."

"Good night, Ernie," Gloria said and hung up the phone.

She thought he sounded very disappointed. She wondered if she should have told him she'd go and then run around like a crazy teenager in love trying to get ready.

Ernie, on the other hand, kicked himself for not asking her sooner. He knew better.

A few minutes later, Ernie's phone rang. He grabbed it after one ring. "So you do want to go bowling?" he said.

"No thanks, Ernie. This is Glen," the male voice answered. "Look, I saw a ten-dollar bill on the floor of your store this afternoon, and I thought it was mine. I knew I had carelessly stuffed a ten in my pocket when I got my change from lunch. Ernie, when I got home, I found two tens in my pocket. The ten-dollar bill I picked up off your floor must have been somebody else's. I'll bring it by first thing in the morning."

"No problem, Glen. Thanks," said Ernie. "I know exactly who lost it."

∂

Melissa looked at her cell phone and saw she had a text from Mr. Bostwick. "My friend, Glen, picked up a ten dollar bill at the store. Thought it was his. Found he had a ten too many. Bringing it back in the morning."

Melissa realized she'd been more of a hypocrite than Glen. *To love God with all my heart means to love other people too.*

CHAPTER 14

Well, butter would be okay. Lots of people had butter on their morning bagels. Ernie checked the refrigerator and freezer and found that he was out of butter besides the cream cheese.

That settled it. Ernie had to go to Snead's.

The grocery store parking lot had vehicles in several dozen spaces, in spite of the late hour. Usually he would park at the far end of the parking lot, about a quarter mile from the door, but Ernie wanted to make his purchases and get home to his bed. He'd had more than enough exercise today.

Heading down the dairy aisle, Ernie saw a familiar back, ahead of him by the milk.

"Mike, isn't this your night off?" Ernie said.

Mike Bruce turned and smiled. "I needed some milk for breakfast. Actually, that's not quite true. I had some waffles in the freezer, but I've gotten in the habit of always having cereal when I get up in the morning. I'm either in a groove or a rut."

Ernie had to chuckle at that. "I'm just as bad," he said. "I always have a bagel with cream cheese, and I was out of cream cheese."

"So how was business today?" Mike asked. "You look a little worn."

"Good and bad," said Ernie. "Good meaning a lot of customers, and bad because I'm tired. Our friend Cindy Martin had a paragraph in her newspaper column last Saturday about how good our coffee is, and the past two days we've doubled our coffee sales. And they buy lots of other things too. It seems discovering my store is their big find for the year."

Mike stretched and rotated his shoulders. "Maybe you'll just have to get used to a faster pace," he said. "When I first started working here at Snead's, it almost got the best of me the first couple weeks. But now it's pretty much routine."

"Do you suppose you'd like to try working a couple more mornings a week for me, Mike?" Ernie asked. "I've been wanting to do some extra things, but there's just been no time. Think you could work eight to one on Mondays and Thursdays?"

"Hey, I'd love to try," said Mike. "I might start saving for a new car."

❧

Ernie was a little more excited when he got ready for work Wednesday morning. With Mike working a couple extra mornings each week, he would finally have some time to deal with his stagnating book sales.

He finished spreading cream cheese on two bagels and packed them in a plastic container. Toting the container and a pint carton of orange juice, Ernie got in his Jeep and headed for his shop.

With thirty minutes remaining before opening time, Ernie brewed three urns of coffee but kept the door locked. This was his own time and no one else's. He filled a mug with Cinnamon Blueberry and slowly walked around the area reserved for books, stopping back by the urns now and then to grab a bite of bagel.

What if he discontinued carrying books completely? That would free up maybe two hundred square feet of floor space, or a fifth of the store. Ernie thought about items that might take over that space: candy, luggage, model airplanes, and cars, maybe some type of simple wooden toy. He used to enjoy darts; perhaps he could have weekly darts tournaments.

He caught a glimpse of a car going slowly past the corner of the building. It was probably a local sheriff's deputy, curious as to why Ernie was at his shop so early.

Ernie finished his first bagel then took a long swallow of coffee. None of his ideas for replacing the books excited him. Perhaps he was thinking too big. Reducing his book inventory by half might make more sense. On the other hand, if he were to begin carrying new books instead of used books, what kind would he sell? Maybe Jack Rhodes had a revolving rack of Christian books, or maybe best sellers that would take up less of Ernie's floor space, leaving room for something new and different. Crossword books or find-a-words might be an option.

That car slowly eased by again.

Was there some other handcrafted item he knew how to make? He could think of nothing really unique. Perhaps he could put in a selection of lampshades.

Ernie recognized the vehicle and glanced at his watch. It was past seven fifty. He decided he would let Cindy Martin in. She often was desperate for her first cup of coffee, so why should he cruelly make her wait until eight? Ernie stepped quickly to the door, flung it open, and waved to his customer.

As Cindy got out of her Mustang and headed for the door, Ernie ran to the storeroom and returned with a red welcome mat under his arm.

"Wait!" he called out as she was about to enter. Ernie threw the mat down at her feet.

"It was so kind of you to mention my coffee in your column the other day," he said. "I wanted to honor you by rolling out the red carpet on your arrival, but all I could find was this doormat. Please accept my appreciation!"

She did all she could to stifle her laughter and barely managed.

"Thank you so much, kind sir," she said. "I felt it was my duty to spread the news of such exquisite java." Cindy carefully sniffed the air, and a smile spread across her face. "My favorite! Cinnamon Blueberry!"

The journalist was used to being Ernie's first customer on Mondays, Wednesdays, and Fridays, and dutifully weaved through the lamp section, turning on half of the appliances. She then filled a blue mug that had the words "This is the day that the Lord has made" printed in yellow on both sides with her favorite coffee.

Ernie had settled into the green recliner and was sipping from a white mug. "So where has your editor sent you today?" the store's proprietor asked.

"Word has it," she replied, "that Senator Pride will be in town to cut the ribbon at the new golf cart factory. I must be there amidst the smiling manufacturing chiefs to cover the news but also to discretely ask questions about our senator's frequent fact-finding trips to Hawaii. My editor says I've got the charm to pull it off."

"I'll pray for you," said Ernie, "and I promise that will work."

"Really?" she asked.

The bell over the front door announced the arrival of the second customer of the day. Gloria carried a basket covered with a yellow cloth. "The door was unlocked, Ernie. Are you open?"

Cindy jumped up from her seat. "So that's who makes those amazing blueberry muffins!" Cindy said. "What an aroma!" She carefully folded back the cloth atop Gloria's basket to reveal more than a dozen plump muffins. She reached for a small paper plate and snared one of Gloria's creations. "They're still warm! You have just made me very happy."

Gloria directed, "Ernie keeps some butter in the little refrigerator under the coffee. Try a little, spread on half of your muffin."

Cindy found a small container of butter on the middle shelf of the little refrigerator and proceeded to follow Gloria's advice.

"Ooh, delicious! What a great idea!" she cried.

Ernie and Gloria watched Cindy Martin get into her Mustang and drive off.

"She's kind of cute, isn't she?" said Gloria.

Ernie responded after a little thought, "Yes, she really is. And wacky and high-strung. Unpredictable. But you know, I think God is getting her attention. You and I need to do all we can to encourage her journey."

Gloria was surprised at the direction her question had sent Ernie's thinking. What she was hoping to uncover was, if he had any romantic interest in Cindy Martin. His remarks didn't touch on that at all.

"Gloria, let me ask you something," said Ernie.

Gloria looked Ernie straight in the eye, eager to hear his next remark.

"You have a grandson that recently learned to play checkers," he said. "I wonder if that is the same boy that has come in and played checkers with me recently."

"Do you know his name?" she said. "My grandson's name is Daniel. I do remember picking him up here last Wednesday."

"That's him," said Ernie. "Blonde. Maybe ten years old."

"Actually, you're a little off," she said. "Daniel is only nine. His birthday is coming up. And by the way, could you make me a clock for his birthday? You had one in here that you made from a baseball bat some time back. I think he would love that."

Ernie asked, "When is Daniel's birthday?" The checkerboard he was making for the boy was done, so Ernie could present it as a birthday gift.

"His birthday is Monday," she said. "Can I pick up the clock on Monday afternoon?"

"No problem at all," said Ernie. He leaned close to Gloria and whispered, "It's hanging above the cash register. It was one of my all-time favorites to make. I'll mark it 'Sold.'"

&

Wednesday afternoon when Mike came into work, Ernie said, "Mike, call me if you get busy. I just want to run to the hospital for a few minutes to see Jack Rhodes."

"No problem," said Mike. "I'll hold down the fort."

After asking at the desk for the room number for John Rhodes, Ernie made his way to room 312. "Millions of places in the world," Ernie grumbled to the empty elevator, "and I'm in the only one where Jack Rhodes is known as John!"

Jack was sitting in a chair with his feet propped on his hospital bed, reading a magazine. "Hey, Ernie! How are you? Glad you came by," said Jack.

"Looks like I was lucky to catch you," said Ernie. "You look healthy enough to be sitting at home. When are they letting you out of prison, er, I mean, the hospital?"

Jack smiled and pointed to wires running out of his pajama shirt pocket. "I've got to wear this heart monitor for twenty-four hours, ending at ten tonight. If it shows a normal series of readings, they'll let me go. I'm going to miss this food though. Ernie, did you realize that there are over thirty different colors of Jell-O?"

"That's amazing," said Ernie. "Say, Jack, before I forget it, let me pray for you. I don't know if I've got the special prayer God is looking for in your case, but I need practice being a little more bold in my faith. Okay?"

"Thanks so much, friend," said Jack. "I've seen God answer a lot of your prayers over the years. I'd be honored."

Ernie Bostwick bowed his head then decided to get on his knees on the floor. "God, my great friend and guide and the best healer ever, take a look at my friend, Jack, here. You made his heart, and you know it's got a lot more years left in it. Shore it up, Lord, heal it completely. Make Jack's heart better than it's been in years. You've touched a lot of lives through him. We need him back on the job, inspiring us all to a greater witness. Please, Father, let him be whole again. Thank you, Lord! You are incredible, awesome, and abounding in steadfast love. Lead us, Lord, even when we're slow to follow. In Jesus's name, amen."

As soon as the amen was voiced and he stood up, Ernie's cell phone rang.

"Am I speaking to Ernie Bostwick?" the elderly man's voice on the other end questioned.

Ernie knew the voice but couldn't quite match it with a name.

"Yes, it is," Ernie replied. "Who might I be speaking to? You certainly sound familiar."

"I'm the one who expected great things from you, and in all the years you worked for me," the voice said, "you never let me down."

Ernie cupped his hand over the phone and said to Jack, "Excuse me a few minutes. I've got to take this call." Jack nodded, and Ernie quickly stepped outside the room.

Ernie spoke into the phone, "Mr. Best! How are you, sir? It's great to hear your voice!"

"How is retirement going, young man?" asked Jack Best. "You certainly earned it, but I sure hated to let you go after just thirty years."

"Thank you, Jack," Ernie replied. "I'm running a little store here in Barkley, so I'm still busy in my retirement. I don't make a lot of money, but I'm really happy at what I'm doing."

"Good, good," said Jack Best. "What kind of things do you sell? Are you going to run me out of business?"

"Not anytime soon, I don't imagine," said Ernie. "You've got about a three thousand store head start on me. I sell lamps and clocks that I make, old-time games, used books, juggling supplies, and fresh brewed coffee. And I get plenty of time to chat and make friends."

"Sounds great, Ernie," said the Best-Mart founder. "Look, the reason I called was to ask a favor of you. I need to borrow some of your people skills. You always were a great judge of people, and you know how to get the most out of employees."

Ernie said, "Thank you, sir." His right foot and left eye started to twitch.

Jack Best continued, "I need someone to go into my Perry store and see what's going on. You'd be kind of a secret shopper. Chat casually with several of the workers. See if they're happy, what they think of the manager. Get some opinions from the customers. Ernie, I rarely fire a manager, but I really think that store is grossly underperforming. Maybe there are factors that don't show up in the balance sheet."

"Jack, you were always good to me," said Ernie, "and I'd love to help you, but the employees know me down there. Probably a lot of customers would remember me, too."

Mr. Best quickly answered, "You'd be surprised to know that only Kate in photography and Freddy Owens, two employees that followed you from West Point, are still there from when you were the manager. But you're right about the customers. Hmm."

Silence covered the next ten seconds.

Ernie spoke up, "You know. I think I'll do it, Jack. I'll disguise myself a little, and I think it'll work out. I've got a young friend who knows a lot about dying hair. I'll get her to add a little color to my mop of hair. This could be fun."

"Fabulous. I knew I could count on you," said Mr. Best. "Call me back and let me know next week what you found out."

Ernie answered, "Sure will. I suspect I'll go next Tuesday or Wednesday."

After a short pause, Jack Best spoke again.

"Did you say juggling supplies?"

❧

When Ernie returned to his store, Mike was sitting in a folding chair, sipping a cup of coffee.

"Have you been busy?" Ernie asked.

"I guess you'd call it that," he replied. "Besides selling a few papers, I've spent most of my time helping one customer. There's a guy down the street that's opening an antique shop. I think it's one of Gloria's buildings. He was looking for used books to add the proper atmosphere to his store. He wasn't as worried about authors as he was age. The older the book, the better."

Mike got up and walked over to the register. "Let's see. He spent a little over two hundred dollars. I'm glad you had some extra boxes around."

Ernie glanced over at the book section of the store. Some of the shelves were completely empty, while others had a half-dozen or fewer books.

Mike said, "The best part was when he noticed the book in Henry's lap. He really wanted it. He finally asked Henry, really politely, if he could see it. You know Henry. He didn't say a word. The guy's face turned three shades of red when he realized he was talking to a mannequin."

CHAPTER 15

"Last time we talked about Jesus praying in the Garden of Gethsemane," said Gloria. "We'll go on in Matthew 26 to Jesus's betrayal by Judas and arrest."

In Sam Myers's absence, Ernie had the green recliner today. Mandy sat in the plush blue recliner and stretched her long legs in front of her. Marietta claimed the red-cushioned rocker ("It matches my hair," she said). Mack, Glen, and Gloria occupied the matching blue upholstered chairs.

After Gloria read verses 47 through 56, she remarked, "What a contrast in friends! Judas betrays Jesus with a kiss, and another disciple defends Jesus with a sword."

"I suspect the ten other guys just stood there," said Mack.

Glen said, "They were probably shocked at what was going on. It's not always easy to know what to do."

"Still, they should have done *something*," said Mandy. "Their friend needed them."

Gloria said, "How many of us have failed to help when a friend needed it? I suspect we all have. Maybe we've said something weak, like, 'If there is anything I can do to help, just call me.' That's a good intention. When a friend is under stress, they don't have the strength to organize a help squad."

"Yeah, but it wouldn't have helped Jesus if everybody got arrested," said Mack.

"Do you all remember our conversation last week about friends that would stick with you through thick and thin?" asked Marietta. "Many of you told me that you can find friends like that in a church. Well, I finally did. I went to a church this past Sunday that surrounded me with love, instantly. Three of the single ladies and I went out for lunch together one day this week, and it's like we've known each other for years. They just love me like I am, red hair and all. I believe they'd walk over hot coals with me."

Ernie said, "That's great, Marietta. But I've had friends like that in churches that would stick with me until the coals were lit, then they backed off."

After a few seconds of silence, Mack cleared his throat. "That's the kind Jesus had in the scripture Gloria read. Friendship takes a lot of strength."

Gloria added, "That's so very true, Mack. In fact, it takes more strength than is humanly possible without Jesus."

Ernie couldn't help but wonder where Marietta had gone to church. Even on Easter Sunday, people had time to reach out to her with a friendship she was looking for.

Mandy said, "Gloria, why do you think Judas betrayed Jesus?"

"I'm not sure," she replied. "I don't think he was trying to get Jesus to start the new kingdom like some have said. If that were the case, I think he would have tried to get the Romans to arrest him, not the religious establishment. Mandy, you've been a little quiet today. What do you think?"

The tall blonde took time to formulate an answer. "Judas never had a lot to say. I don't think he ever was convinced that Jesus was the Messiah. He probably was trying something drastic, to see if Jesus could convince him with the way he reacted."

"That would be pretty drastic, all right," responded Glen. "Friends don't put friends in a life-threatening situation. No matter what Judas believed, Jesus had done more than enough to win his friendship."

"I agree," said Marietta. "Friends trust what you say and do until you do something to kill that trust. They don't push you to prove yourself. They take you for who you are."

&

After the rest of the Bible study group had gone, Ernie poured himself another cup of Seattle Sunrise. Gloria had moved to the rocker.

"I happen to know where Marietta went to church last Sunday," Gloria said. "She was sitting on the right side with several of the younger ladies from the Happily Singles class."

"She was at your church?" Ernie asked, obviously surprised.

"I'll have you know," she replied, "that my church is full of friendly people. I just didn't want to suggest it to her before. I don't want our Bible study to be a sneaky way to make Northside members."

Ernie and Gloria sipped their coffee. Mike walked around in the games section, showing a young mother possible presents for her daughter.

"Did you go bowling the other night without me?" Gloria questioned.

Ernie shook his head. "No, I didn't think I'd enjoy going by myself. Who would believe me if I bowled a perfect game?"

She said, "Surely someone would notice that you were jumping up and down and yelling. That's not normal for you."

He couldn't help but chuckle at the thought. No, it took a lot to excite him.

She added, "Do you want to go bowling with me tonight?" Gloria could feel her face flushing just a little. She was a little surprised at her boldness.

Ernie didn't take much time to decide. This was payback for when he had asked her to go bowling on short notice two nights before.

"That's a great idea," he answered. "Pick you up at seven?"

∾

Melissa still had black hair today, but the red tips had migrated a few inches further up the strands of her hair.

"Mr. B, the lamp section is looking better," she said. "Mike must have been a lot of help to you today."

"He certainly was," Ernie replied. "He still can't hold a candle to you, but he's improving."

"Aw, thank you," Melissa said. "My dad got home today. Thanks for going to see him yesterday. He really appreciated it."

"He's a great friend," said Ernie. "I'm glad he's better."

Teddy Jarvis burst in, making the bell over the door dance with all its might. Throwing his right arm skyward, he announced, "It's showtime!"

All the response he got were two pairs of surprised eyes.

"Mr. B, my church is having a talent show Sunday night. Can you come?" Teddy asked.

Ernie replied, "I take it you signed up to do your juggling act. You'll be great."

"Thank you, sir," Teddy replied. "You're a great teacher!"

Melissa ventured, "Are you the only one juggling?"

"Well…" Teddy said slowly, "mostly." Teddy paced back and forth a few steps.

Melissa went on, "I don't suppose you signed up a partner for part of the act, did you? Maybe someone to do some doubles juggling with you?"

Teddy bit his lip, evidently having a hard time with his answer.

Ernie smiled wide and said, "Why, thank you, Teddy, I'd be glad to juggle with you!"

Huge lights seemed to go on in Teddy's eyes. "You would? Really? Oh, thank you, Mr. B! I knew you'd do it!"

"What time should I be there?" asked Ernie.

Teddy Jarvis replied, "It starts at six, but I guess it would be good if you got there by quarter 'til. It's Greater Mount Zion Missionary Baptist Church over on Hightower Road. It's only two blocks from the Dairy Barn."

"I'll be there," said Ernie. "Teddy, I'm looking forward to it."

☙

A fifteen-year-old Chevy Lumina pulled into a space across from Ernie's. Melissa watched as an elderly lady got out and quickly headed for the store. She wore jeans and a bright yellow knit top and looked to be about five foot four.

As she entered, Melissa walked toward her and said, "Welcome to Ernie's."

Ernie Bostwick was just exiting his workroom. When he saw his new customer, he called out, "Miss Opal! You found me! What a pleasure to see you!"

"Wow! I smell some great coffee in here," replied Opal Carollton. "Anything decaf?"

"Yes, ma'am," said Melissa. "We have one called After Hours, and also Evening Delight."

"I sell more After Hours to the young crowd," said Ernie.

"I'll have that then," said Opal. "Young lady, what is your name?"

"I'm Melissa Rhodes, Miss Opal," she replied.

"Melissa, I just love your hair! If my hair wasn't so thin," said Opal, "I'd try some new colors myself. At my age, I'd be dyeing my head more than my hair. Just set my coffee next to the red recliner. I want to take a look around the place."

As Ernie began walking around the store with Opal, he asked, "Where's the new Mazda you had at church Sunday? Was that your niece's car?"

"Heavens, no," she shot back. "I'm in Betty's old rattletrap today. She doesn't drive it enough to keep it running smooth. I had to get it out on a straight stretch, to blow the soot out of it. It sputtered a little at sixty and seventy, but after that it was fine."

Ernie stopped and stared at Opal for a moment, but she kept on walking.

"Where in the world do you get these lamps?" asked Opal. "She sure has some imagination, whoever she is. And a lot of skill."

"Why, thank you, Miss Opal," Ernie answered. "She is me. I made all of these."

As they continued through the clocks and used books, Opal said, "I'll bet you have a blast in here. This is quite a place. Let's sit down and have some coffee before it gets cold."

Ernie said, "Opal, let me treat you to a molasses cookie to go with your coffee. Melissa, if you don't mind, please bring us a couple cookies."

As she took a few sips of coffee, Opal replied, "Why, thank you. My, this coffee is certainly good. You must sell a lot of it."

"It does do quite well, but regular coffee always sells better than decaf," said Ernie. "There are a lot of people that can drink caffeine any time of day. Not me."

Opal stood up when she had finished the cookie and set her coffee mug down. "Time to see the rest of your store."

Ernie followed her to the rows of shelves with classic games. Every step or so, Opal would pick up one of the games and smile and say something like, "Ah, I remember playing this," or, "We used to play this quite often," or, "I'm surprised you can still find this one."

Opal stared at the array of juggling supplies. After a few moments, she turned to Ernie and asked, "Can you juggle, Ernie?"

"Oh, yes, ma'am," he said.

She stepped back a couple steps and said, "Well?"

Ernie gave her a questioning look. Opal raised one eyebrow.

"Oh," said the store proprietor and reached over to grab four rubber balls.

Melissa turned to the customer she had just finished waiting on and whispered quietly. They made their way over to where Opal and Ernie stood.

Ernie cleared his throat. "Umm, I began juggling when I was about seven, I think. Dad always had worn-out tennis balls around the house, and I had run across an article on juggling in the old red encyclopedias we had."

Ernie deftly juggled three rubber balls without any trouble.

Opal picked up the fourth tennis ball. "I used to watch my cousin juggle. He was really good. Sometimes I'd throw an extra ball in to surprise him."

The elderly lady tossed the ball into the midst of Ernie's other three juggled balls. He incorporated it into the scheme without any trouble.

Opal picked up a fifth ball. "You are amazing. Care for another?" Opal tossed the new ball to Ernie. With obvious effort, it also became part of the show.

"Five balls is difficult," said Ernie. "I usually don't try it unless I'm juggling double. With that, he tossed the last ball back to Opal without stopping his juggling of the other four.

Opal tossed it right back. Another came out of Ernie's rotation, and she deftly tossed it back.

"Oh my gosh!" exclaimed Melissa. "I can't believe this! Miss Opal, you're amazing!"

Ernie and Opal finished touring the store and returned to their coffee.

Opal looked back at the book section of the store. "Looks like there is extra space in that part of the store. Does it usually have more books, or are you making some changes?"

"That's very perceptive, Opal," said Ernie. "We did just sell a hundred or so books to one person. But I have been thinking of making a change in that part of the store. Books have usually been a very slow seller, at least in the last six months. I've been pondering what might be a better use of the space."

She pondered the information for a couple minutes then said, "I know one thing you could certainly use."

"Why, thank you," said Ernie. "What is it?"

Opal turned in her chair to look Ernie directly in the face. She said, "Nothing in this store says you're a Christian. There's no indication. That's hiding some very important information."

Ernie showed obvious surprise. Could Opal be right? Everything in the store was wholesome and family-friendly. He shied away from books that were the least bit scandalous. There was a Thursday morning Bible study, but everybody brought his or her own Bible. Yet he could think of nothing that showed obvious Christian leanings, except a mug that declared, "This is the day that the Lord has made."

"I'll work on it," said Ernie. "I promise, I will."

As Melissa clicked off lamps before heading for home, Ernie called out, "If you've got a minute, I need to talk to you about my hair."

She finished turning off lamps as her wonder grew at what he'd just said. "Mr. B, you'd probably get more help from my dad. But I like the way you comb it all the time."

"No," Ernie said, "I need it to look different just for one day. I've got to spy on a Best-Mart store as a favor to my old boss, and I don't want anybody to recognize me. Can you tell me how to color it a dark brown? If possible, I need it to wash out after a day." With a smile, he added, "I can't think of anybody who knows more about changing the color of their hair."

CHAPTER 16

Ernie's 180 average eclipsed Gloria's average by six pins, but both were thrilled at their improvement.

"We need to do this again soon," said Gloria. "How about next Thursday?" She was stunned when she realized she was asking him for a date for the second time in a week.

Ernie smiled. "Let's do that. Bowling felt a little more natural tonight," he said, "and I think four more people noticed my checkered ball. Didn't we see somebody take a picture?"

"I'm not sure they were photographing you," she said. "It might be they noticed the man in the next lane bowling a perfect game."

Ernie shrugged, and said, "Which would sell more papers, a checkered bowling ball, or a game with no mistakes?"

She decided to not answer that question. Instead, Gloria asked, "Dairy Barn?"

❧

Melissa pulled up just as Ernie got out of his Jeep. It always impressed him how carefully she drove. His high school employee exited her 1997 Honda Civic and called out, "Good morning, Mr. B."

"Good morning, Melissa," he replied. He waited for her, then they crossed to the store together.

"Is your dad about back to full strength now?" Ernie asked as he pulled his key from his left front pocket and reached toward the doorknob. A few pieces of broken glass crunched beneath his shoe.

Melissa suddenly grabbed Ernie's arm and shouted, "Wait!"

She stared at the front door. "Oh my God."

Ernie followed her gaze and saw that a plate-sized section of glass was missing next to the doorknob.

Ernie managed to barely beat Melissa in dialing 911.

❧

The deputy walked up to the door, reached his gloved hand through the hole in the glass, and turned the knob to open the door. Melissa and Ernie cautiously followed Officer Paulk into the store.

"You two stand right here for a minute," Officer Paulk said. "I doubt the suspect is still here, but let's be sure." He slowly worked his way around the store, checking behind bookshelves, inside the other rooms, and eventually the checkout station.

"Okay," the deputy said. "All clear. Mr. Bostwick, you know your store better than I do, but it looks to me like the suspect only wanted money. I think you'll find that nothing else is missing. It's kind of a mess back here by the cash register though."

Ernie and Melissa joined Officer Paulk at the cash register. The old machine had taken quite a beating. If the burglar had just pushed the little open drawer button, the cash drawer would have been easily accessible.

"Mr. Bostwick, how much money would you guess was in the cash register?" the deputy asked.

"Not a dime," Melissa spoke up, still looking a little dazed. "We always take it all out. And I always leave the drawer open. I don't understand why he gave the machine such a torture."

"That's my fault, I'm afraid," said Ernie. "I accidentally pushed the drawer shut when I reached for a piece of paper on the floor, just before I left, and didn't bother to open it back up. Who would have thought that it would matter that one time?"

The officer reached down to pick something up. "Ernie, I don't remember your carrying any sporting goods. Was this in the store?"

In the officer's hand was a significant remnant of a baseball bat. A piece of paper dangled from it, proclaiming, "Sold."

Daniel's birthday present was ruined.

☙

"Somebody run a lamp through the door?"

Mike Bruce stepped around the glass repairman working on the front door. The service man finished glazing and stepped back to look at his work. Satisfied, he began cleaning up the area.

Melissa continued making a fresh urn of Mocha Cranberry. "We had a break-in sometime overnight," she said. "Nothing was missing, but they destroyed the empty cash register." The disabled machine had been set to the side. A smaller, more modern model sat in its place.

Ernie stepped out of his workroom. "Good morning, Mike," he said. "Surprise, surprise."

"I hope they catch him," Mike said. "It's probably some drug addict that hasn't worked a day in his life. He should have known there wasn't much in here he could sell. 'Psst. Hey, buddy, wanna buy a Monopoly game?'"

"I hadn't thought about it like that, Mike. I make a decent living off our sales," Ernie said, "but my most valuable commodities are lamps and clocks, and they are easily recognizable. They'd be hard to pawn."

"I think it might have just been somebody down on his luck," interjected Melissa.

Mike said, "Whoever it was, he needs to be prosecuted. Replacing the register and the glass in the front door cost Ernie a bundle."

Ernie returned to his work on a clock added to the front of an electric fan. The clock mechanism clung to the inside of the wire mesh guard that protected fingers from the fan's blades. The stem poked through the middle of the guard, then the clock hour and minute hands were fixed to the stem on the outside of the guard, bent to match the curvature of the fan exterior. To protect the clock hands, Ernie now hot glued on a plastic piece that had formerly been the bottom of a small refrigerator container.

Every time he thought about the burglary, Ernie could feel his blood pressure rising. He thought, *Why this store? Did people think I'm rich?*

The loss of the old cash register didn't bother him that much. He probably should have already replaced it. The bigger loss was the baseball bat clock that was to be Daniel's birthday present next Monday.

Setting the finished fan clock on a smaller table, Ernie strode to the storeroom. Moving stools and candlesticks, pans and coat trees, he worked his way to the furthest corner of the room. Leaning against the wall was a Louisville Slugger baseball bat with Dave Cash's signature inscribed near the trademark. Ernie carried it to his workroom.

He thought through the steps it had taken to make the former baseball bat clock, now ruined. The work would be a little tedious, but he could put in an hour or so on Sunday afternoon. He thought through how he had embedded the little square box that housed the clock workings.

He stood stone-still. "Mr. President, we have a problem," he said to himself. This particular project called for a clock mechanism with a longer stem, and he didn't have any in stock. The earliest he could get one would be next Tuesday, a day too late. Ernie slipped out for a coffee break, wondering if there could be a solution.

Melissa stayed busy selling newspapers and coffee, also finding time to explain the strategy of classic board games to young parents, and how to begin learning to juggle to patrons of various ages. Mike spent his morning showing off Ernie's unique lamps and clocks.

Ernie sipped Mocha Cranberry from a mug that proclaimed Proud to Be Humble. He always found solutions to knotty problems as he viewed life from the green recliner.

He wondered if there might be a way to make another baseball bat clock using only a standard stem. If he could manage that, he had all the equipment he needed. *No*, he mused. *A short stem would only allow a thin veneer of wood over the square workings. It would crack too easily.*

Melissa made a new urn of Java Jamaica. "Mr. B," she said, "I love this old clock you made out of a barrel. You're so good at seeing a clock where nobody else would imagine it. How long have you had it?"

Ernie replied, "That's actually one my mom made around forty years ago. She taught me everything I know about making clocks. She made me use all that space inside as a clothes hamper. She finally bought me a laundry bag, so she could just carry it to the laundry room, instead of having to nearly invert herself to empty my barrel."

Mike followed a customer to the cash register, carrying three lamps and a stack of used books. It reminded Ernie that he still needed to solve the problem of rearranging or eliminating the used book section.

An idea flashed through his mind. Used books. Rearrange. Used clocks? Maybe there was a clock in the store that Ernie could borrow a long-stemmed mechanism from. He got up and walked through the array of clocks. They all had standard stems. He looked carefully a second time. They definitely all had standard stems.

Ernie sat back down and sipped a little more coffee. His eyes wandered around the store, finally stopping on…

The barrel!

No. He would not desecrate that treasured heirloom. "Lord," Ernie prayed, "if You've got a long-stemmed clock workings lying under the corner of Your throne, could you kick it on down to me?"

"Ernie, it's a shame how kids are brought up these days," said Mike. "There are a lot of kids that have no father around, and the mother has to raise the kids on government assistance. They never see anybody in the family actually go out and earn a living, so they don't know what to do as an adult when the money runs out."

Mike couldn't help but straighten up a few things before he left for the day. It was getting harder to make the dwindling inventory of books look like much, but he decided a few here and there looked better than all the books on one shelf and none on several others.

He continued, "When I knew my money wasn't going to last until Social Security kicked in, I didn't take out a loan or break into a store. I went out and found a job. Some folks would have considered it beneath them to stock shelves in a grocery store, but it's honest work. I don't mind a few sore muscles."

Ernie smiled, but he could not quite hide his resentment. "I'd be happy to know that whoever broke in here, he at least has sore muscles from swinging the baseball bat."

Ernie handed Mike his pay envelope. "I appreciate you, Mike. So do you think you'd like to keep on working Monday and Thursday mornings? It was a lot of help to me this week, but I know you have other things to do besides work."

"Sure," responded Mike. "My life is actually pretty simple. No wife, no kids, no pets. I think those two extra days will not be a problem. I'll see you Monday." He stuffed the white envelope into his pocket and slipped out the door.

&

Gloria Smith entered the store, toting a large paper sack.

"Is it that time again?" called out Ernie. He remembered that the last time Gloria brought a bag in, she'd brought new clothes for Henry, the mannequin. "I kind of like Henry's present outfit."

She glanced around to see if there were any customers. Seeing none, she said in a quiet voice, "I've got to get rid of this. I hate it. It was a gift from a relative. I thought perhaps you could rob it for parts."

With that, Gloria removed a birdhouse from the bag. It was obviously made from recycled wood, most likely from an old barn. It was painted an odd shade of orange. The piece epitomized the term *sturdy*, and Ernie wondered if there were an uglier gift in the whole town.

"Well, I don't know," said Ernie. "At first glance, I don't really see anything I'd want to save. I don't need another doorstop."

"Oh, excuse me," said Gloria. "Let me show you the other side." She turned the birdhouse around, and Ernie could see that the monstrosity was more than a birdhouse. It was a clock.

"I thought perhaps you could take the clock parts out and just throw away the rest," she said.

Ernie examined the birdhouse clock more closely. The clock mechanism seemed loose and probably could be removed easily. The numbers glued to the outside would probably not come off cleanly.

It occurred to him that whoever had made this clock was a beginner. The workings did not fit the birdhouse well; the stem stuck out too far.

He suddenly said, "Thank you, thank you, thank you, Lord! And thank you, my friend. This is exactly what I need to finish a very special clock. Hallelujah!"

❧

Sleep? How could he sleep?

Ernie glanced at his bedside clock, its red figures glowing in the dark. It was quarter after twelve, and he'd turned the lights out at ten.

The break-in had been more inconvenience than tragedy. The glass man repaired the window in the door quickly, and of course, no money or merchandise had been stolen. The ruined cash register should have already been replaced, so perhaps that was a blessing in disguise.

What bothered him most was the destruction of the baseball bat clock, intended for Gloria's grandson. If nothing extraordinary happened on Sunday, he could still have the birthday gift ready by Monday.

Why, he wondered, would someone break into his store? He had loved his customers, every one, since he'd opened in Barkley. He treated everyone with respect.

The Bible said, "All have sinned and fall short of the glory of God." He could certainly vouch for that. He was a sinner and so was everybody else. The person that ruined his cash register and broke the baseball bat clock was a sinner. All people disappoint God every day. Yet this was personal. *Why did he have to get me involved?* Ernie pondered.

This would not be a Sunday to visit any church. He didn't want to encourage anybody else, or change any sinners, or smile at people he didn't know. At this point, Ernie was too disappointed with the human race.

CHAPTER 17

S unday never allowed bagels. Eggs waited patiently throughout the workweek to get their chance to be the main ingredient in an omelet. Their best friend had been sliced jalapenos for several weeks.

Today the eggs had no other friends.

The grated sweet potatoes fried noisily as Ernie washed the yellow apple.

By the time the jalapeno omelet was ready, the counters were cleared and washed. He slid the sweet potato hash browns onto his plate and filled the remaining space with omelet.

Today the Sunday comics were destined to be funny. Ernie had noticed, over the last two years, that every third week he laughed more at the comics than on the previous two Sundays.

He spread the paper out next to his breakfast plate and paused for prayer. "Dear God, my Father, Lord, and best friend, I thank you. You've given me friends, a business I love, and food for my table. Lord, bless Gloria and all my friends at their worship services this morning. I am especially grateful for Jack's healing. Lord, help me walk in Your ways. In the strong name of Jesus, my Savior, amen."

Breakfast was delicious. He guessed wrong on the comics. None of the paper, in fact, measured up to its normal standard. He would have done better to eat another breakfast rather than read the paper.

Eleven o'clock. Church began, the church of one.

Hadn't Ernie sung these same songs every Sunday for months now? No, one song he'd only sung a few weeks. He wished he could remember more of the words from last week's praise songs at New Life Church. Maybe he should get out some of his old cassettes during the coming week and remind himself of some old favorites.

Praise seemed right, no matter what the song. Ernie sang with enthusiasm for nearly twenty minutes. God blessed Ernie every day, there was no doubting that. It had been something of a gamble, leaving the store manager position with Best-Mart after thirty years. Retiring at age fifty-two meant he would have to be a little mindful of his cash flow until Social Security kicked in.

But it had been a decision steeped in hundreds of hours of prayer. The ongoing conversation with God led him to an empty building in downtown Barkley. Gloria Smith, the owner, had offered him bargain-basement rent on the building with one condition: let her start a weekly Bible study that would meet in the store during regular store hours.

Ernie bid good-bye to Best-Mart and the pressures of working for a large corporation. His hobbies now became his vocation. His smile returned.

Today in the tenth chapter of the Gospel of Luke, Ernie read the scripture passage known as "the parable of the Good Samaritan." He knew the story well. In years past, he would feel guilt when the priest and then the Levite walked past the mugging victim, thinking he might have done the same. Scripture has a way of changing Christians though, and Ernie knew he would now stop to help someone in distress. That was just who he had become. Many faces came to mind as Ernie read, people he had helped.

Unbidden, Tina's words came to mind. *Ernie, you have denied other Christians your presence for too long.*

Ernie grinned a wry smile. "Lord, that's a strange twist," he said aloud. "Instead of the church person walking by the man, You're telling me that I'm a man that would walk past a needy church."

A familiar *synchronized* feeling let Ernie know that he had indeed understood God's message to him. There were needy persons in the church that he alone could reach. He had a unique background and way of looking at things. Ernie's theology might not be conventional, but it had a perspective that was just what some struggling Christian needed. He was 'hiding his light under a basket,' as the Sermon on the Mount said.

This might be the last meeting of his one-man church.

The birthday clock was finished. Ernie had allowed two hours for the project instead of just one, and it had taken every minute. The clock workings from the old birdhouse had been an unusual size, slightly smaller than what he usually used. The stem projected further, of course, but it was also slightly fatter. Little adjustments have a way of eating away the minutes.

Ernie wished he'd hidden the first bat clock. The signature on the bat was a current player, and maybe Daniel would have recognized the name. Dave Cash had been a great player decades ago, but the name would mean nothing to a kid today.

He put the clock inside a cabinet and locked the cabinet door. As he cleaned up his workbench, Ernie looked at his watch. He'd better hurry. Teddy needed him to be at the church just an hour from now.

As often as Ernie had been to the Dairy Barn, he'd never noticed the blue sign on the corner, advertising "Greater Mt. Zion MBC, 2 blocks." After making the indicated left turn, he saw sidewalks full of all kinds of people, including ballerinas and dancers of all kinds, kids in karate attire, men in tuxedos, pirates with parrots. He decided he'd better park the Jeep in the first available spot. This talent show was going to be big.

He retrieved his big blue duffel bag from the Jeep's backseat and started walking. The tall brick church's parking lot was completely full as far as Ernie could tell. Cars ranged from new luxury models to nearly antique pickups and decade-old SUVs.

The stream of walkers headed for the double doors of a building labeled Family Life Center. Teddy stood near the left door, looking at each face, and waved energetically when he spotted Ernie.

"Mr. B," he said, "I've got my stuff in one of the Sunday school classrooms. Let's practice in there. Man, I'm nervous!"

"You just need a little warm-up," said Ernie. "You've performed in front of people before. Piece of cake."

Teddy blurted out, "There must be three hundred people in there! I'm number twenty, out of twenty-five acts!"

"Just remember to have fun," Ernie said, "and let yourself enjoy being with the audience. There's not a million-dollar prize, is there?"

"I think it's twenty-five dollars for first place," answered Teddy, "then ten for second and five for third."

Ernie reached for his billfold. "Tell you what. I know that you're really good, so let me take the pressure off. If you win less than twenty-five dollars, I'll make up the difference, and I'll also give you twenty-five for your church's offering. So like the Bible says, do your juggling 'as unto the Lord.' Okay, let's practice."

Teddy went through his five-minute solo act, including some banter he would use with the audience.

He then pretended to introduce Ernie and spent a few minutes in doubles juggling. Teddy seemed relaxed and confident.

"I've been working on a big finale," he said, "but only if I feel sure of myself."

Ernie inquired, "The banana?"

"You guessed it," Teddy replied. "I've done it right just a couple times, but if I'm doing good, I think the audience would be okay with a decent attempt."

"Go for it," said Ernie. "You'll be sorry if you don't try."

☙

The audience exhibited many shades of skin color, especially shades of brown. Ernie realized that there had once been a time when he would have felt almost embarrassed to be such a minority in a large gathering, but he felt genuinely at ease tonight.

A tiny ballerina, surely no older than five, twirled on her toes and leapt across the stage, only stumbling twice. The audience applauded wildly. Two young boys told a series of *knock-knock* jokes, and those in attendance laughed as if they were hearing professional comedians. Acts ranged from instrumental to vocal to acrobatic, and everyone received a warm response.

After an hour and a half of entertainment, Teddy eased from his seat. "I'd better go backstage. There's only one more act before mine," he said. "Do you want me to just call you up from the audience?"

Ernie stood up. "No," he answered, "I'd rather come in from offstage. Looks like you're going to be one of the best acts of the night."

"Thanks," said his young juggling student.

"And now," said the master of ceremonies, "our own Teddy Jarvis will display his phenomenal juggling skills." Teddy strode on stage amid energetic applause, put down two equipment bags, and pulled out three tennis balls. He immediately began to juggle.

"Great, huh?" he asked the audience. They responded with mild applause. Teddy pulled another ball from his pocket without missing a toss and added it to the trio of floating spheres. Spontaneous applause erupted, increasing markedly when he pulled a fifth ball from his other pocket and added it to the mix. He continued with all five balls for about thirty seconds without dropping the first ball.

Teddy looked intently at a lady in the third row and said, "I couldn't always afford five tennis balls, so I learned to juggle just about anything. My favorite has always been footwear. Ma'am, excuse my asking, but could I borrow one of those beautiful red high heels you're wearing?"

The forty-something woman smiled shyly then reached down to remove her shoe. Teddy scurried down to retrieve it. "Could I get another volunteer? How about you, sir?" A tall teen boy quickly removed his basketball shoe for Teddy.

"Whoa! I've never juggled a size nineteen before. And one more," Teddy continued. "Friend, do you suppose I could borrow your baby's little shoe? Yes? That's perfect?"

Teddy Jarvis immediately started juggling the three very different shoes. He jogged back up the steps to the stage as he juggled then began a smooth back-and-forth kind of dance. The audience responded with warm applause. He added a few under-the-leg tosses, then a couple from behind his back. Finally catching the shoes one by one, he asked a young girl in the front row to return the foot apparel to their owners.

"How many of you," he asked, "have ever seen two persons juggling together?" Only four or five hands were raised of the three hundred people in the audience.

Teddy said, "Please let me introduce you to my young partner, Mr. Ernie Bostwick!" Ernie strode on stage from behind a side curtain amid warm applause.

Someone in the back called out, "Hi, Mr. B!" causing a lot of chuckling. Ernie was sure the voice was Melissa's.

"Hey," said Teddy, "where's the stuff?"

"What stuff?" asked Ernie.

"The stuff we're supposed to juggle," said Teddy.

"What did it look like?" Ernie wondered.

"It was in a canvas bag," his partner said.

Ernie said, "Was it a big bag?" He held his hands about three feet apart. Teddy held his own hands two feet apart. Ernie brought his hands in to two and a half feet apart. Teddy Jarvis then expanded his hands to about two and a half feet apart then walked over and compared his expanse to Ernie's.

"Yeah," said Teddy.

Ernie said, "Oh, it's right here." He reached behind the curtain and produced the blue canvas bag. The audience erupted with laughter.

Ernie reached into the bag and threw Teddy an Indian club, which was much like a bowling pin, only thinner and sporting a red knob on top.

"Another one," called Teddy as he tossed the club from hand to hand with a complete revolution in between. Ernie quickly tossed him a second club.

"Another," said Teddy. The boy quickly had all three clubs flipping easily in a hypnotic pattern.

Ernie stood up now with two more Indian clubs in his hands. Ernie tossed Teddy a fourth club. "Take it back," Teddy urged, but Ernie shook his head.

Instead, Ernie tossed a fifth club to his partner.

"No, no!" Teddy said with alarm. He tossed one of the pins back to Ernie, who promptly tossed it back. Every time Teddy tossed a club out, his partner tossed it back, at a faster and faster pace. Before the audience knew what was happening, the two were smoothly juggling five clubs between them. Wild clapping sprang up, accompanied by whistles and cheers.

The two jugglers caught the clubs and bowed to their admirers.

"What a great audience!" said Teddy. "You make me feel like I'm really special. I'd like to try something new, especially for you."

Ernie turned and gave Teddy a thumbs-up gesture then departed to the left of the stage.

Teddy stated the obvious, "This is really hard work. And I guess some of you know that teenagers like me eat a lot just to keep our strength up."

Someone in the middle of the crowd yelled, "You can say that again."

"So," Teddy continued, "somewhere in this bag, I brought a piece of fruit, just in case I got desperately hungry."

A voice that sounded very much like Melissa Rhodes called out, "I'll bet you're going to eat an apple while you juggle!" Many people seemed to murmur agreement.

"Actually, I'm not all that fond of apples," the juggler said to no one in particular. He rummaged in the canvas bag for several seconds, finally finding what he was looking for.

Several people in the audience spontaneously blurted out, "A banana!"

Teddy Jarvis now had everyone's attention. He began to juggle two tennis balls and the banana in high, slow arcs. Gradually the rhythm changed so that the balls followed each other in rapid succession then the banana after a slight pause.

Suddenly, Teddy snapped open the banana with both hands then, on successive tosses, yanked the peel back a few inches on each side. For a few rounds, the balls and banana went in steady rhythm. The juggler carefully tossed the banana in a vertical position so that the peel hung down out of the way of the fruit.

Finally, Teddy grabbed a bite of banana. A collective gasp went up from the crowd. On his second bite, "Wow!" echoed throughout the arena. Teddy flashed a wide grin.

On his third bite, he missed his catch of both tennis balls. They bounced away in two different directions, leaving him holding only a half banana. All the light went out of his countenance.

Everyone in the audience stood, applauding vigorously. Many called out, "Bravo! Bravo!"

Ernie could not have been more proud if Teddy were his own son.

Ernie Bostwick took the long way home. The lonely country road gave him a chance to reflect on the night at Greater Mount Zion Church.

Teddy was certainly the star of the night. It wasn't just his skill at juggling though. His home church loved this teenager. Even before the talent show, several came up to hug Teddy and offer best wishes.

That was a church at its best, thought Ernie. *It was like a big, loving family.* He knew that if Teddy had fumbled everything in his juggling act, he would still have received loving applause.

Was this a unique church? No, from what Gloria had said after Thursday's Bible study, her church had that same quality.

Or so she said.

The Jeep began to slow down even though Ernie still had his foot on the gas pedal. Why would it do that? He pushed a little harder on the pedal, but it seemed to make no difference. Then he glanced at the gauges on the dashboard.

The fuel gauge registered significantly below E. He pulled to the side of the road as the car slowed to a stop.

It was nearly midnight. He was a mile from town and out of gas.

CHAPTER 18

A black Jeep Cherokee on the side of a country road doesn't show up very well in the middle of the night. Also it soon became obvious that few people are out at midnight on Sunday night.

Another car went by without stopping. He couldn't blame them. He never stopped for a car on the side of the road, reasoning that he really didn't know anything about automobile engines. Now if he saw that it was a lady who had a flat tire, he'd stop to help. He could change a tire.

Ernie would give it a few minutes more, then he'd start walking to town. It was probably less than two miles home and would take less than thirty minutes on a good day. He'd have to walk a little more carefully tonight, making sure he stayed on the road.

He wandered around to the back of the car and opened the trunk. He was sure that he didn't carry a gas can in the trunk, but it wouldn't hurt to check. He was not surprised to see no container there.

Should he call a friend for help? He looked at his watch. He certainly wouldn't get any but the closest friend out at a quarter past midnight. The only friend dear enough was Jack, and he was still recovering from his hospital stay. Ernie would never ask Gloria to come out by herself at this time of night.

An old white Chevy drove by, slowing slightly but not stopping.

Well, maybe it was time he started walking. He could leave the Jeep here for the rest of the night; when Mike came to work Monday morning, they'd bring a can of gas out here and bring the Jeep back to town.

Car lights appeared from the other direction now. The vehicle slowed then pulled over next to Ernie's Cherokee. It was the old white Chevy. The driver rolled down his window and said, "Friend, looks like you could use some help. Car giving you trouble?"

"I guess there's nothing really wrong with the car," said Ernie. "I just let it run out of gas. I didn't think about the extra miles I've driven lately. Makes me feel kind of foolish."

"Oh, that's no big thing," the elderly African-American man said. "You probably just had a few extra things on your mind this week. These kids talk about multitasking, but I think you've got to be able to focus to keep anything at the front of your mind."

Ernie shuffled his feet a little then asked, "Do you suppose you could give me a ride home? It's only a mile or two." He realized this was a total stranger, but maybe he would have mercy on his situation.

The other car pulled to the side of the road, and the driver came across the road. "I'll do you one better than that. I've got an empty gas can in my trunk, been doing some lawn mowing, and we'll go get you some gas at the station next to the Dairy Barn. Now, if you'd rather stay here with your car, I can be back in a few minutes. My name's Earl Barber."

"Let's go," said Ernie. "I'm Ernie Bostwick. Thanks so much!"

"Hey," said Earl, "you're my little buddy Teddy's helper, aren't you? That boy sure has talent. There was no competition when it came down to awarding first prize tonight."

The two men got in Earl's car and headed for the gas station. Earl said, "Now where do you suppose Teddy learned to juggle like that?"

"He loves to practice," said Ernie. "And he's not afraid of trying new things. I've been teaching him what

I know about one afternoon a week, but that banana stunt was all his. I've never seen anybody else try that."

They rode in silence for the rest of the trip to the station. Earl jumped out and retrieved the gas can from his trunk. Before Ernie realized what he was doing, Earl had swiped his debit card at the pump to pay for the gas.

"You didn't have to do that," protested Ernie. "You've done enough already."

Earl replied, "No, no, when I do something to serve the Lord, I always want to be generous about it. One day I may be the one by the side of the road, and I want God to send somebody like you to help."

On the ride back to the Jeep, Ernie found out that Earl was a bachelor too. He had lived in Barkley his whole life and had been a member of Greater Mount Zion about two years. "I was a heathen before then," he told Ernie. "I spent my time trying to make money. I was the center of the universe. But now God has changed all that. I'm doing all I can to live my life for other people. And let me tell you, brother, that's living. There's nothing like it."

After Earl Barber emptied the five gallons of gasoline into the Jeep, Ernie got in to make sure the engine started. He turned the key, pumped the gas pedal a few times, and the engine roared to life.

"Now, don't try to pay me, Ernie," said Earl. "A lot of times that's the first reaction people have. Comes down to it, I did this for God, and I owe him more than I can ever repay. You just look for a way to help somebody else."

"That's a deal," said Ernie. "I'm glad God sent you my way. You were there before I even had a chance to pray."

Earl pulled out his wallet and handed Ernie a business card. "If you ever need a hand, just let me know."

"Thanks again," replied Ernie.

❧

Ernie parked the Jeep in the garage and entered his house. He continued his conversation with God that started just after he left Earl Barber.

"I think I'm starting to get your point, God," Ernie said aloud. "People need each other, and Christians need other Christians. There is some church that needs me as much as I need them, and I've been keeping Your blessings all to myself."

It was late. He crossed to the bedroom and changed into pajamas, but Ernie could tell that God wasn't going to let him sleep right away.

He went through his usual routine of brushing his teeth and cleaning his glasses. He laid out his clothes for Monday. His mind was still engaged with God, so Ernie grabbed a pen and legal pad from his home office and settled into a chair in the living room. He propped his feet on the foot stool and closed his eyes.

Why did Earl Barber stop to help? Nobody else tonight had even slowed down. It was because he was a Christian, the kind Ernie had always wanted to be, the kind he had once been, and the kind he was determined to be again. He wanted everybody else to live out their faith; it was time he did the same.

"Lord," Ernie Bostwick prayed, "I'm ready to listen. I've kept a part of my heart closed to you for years, but it's time for me to open up. I decided a long while back that churches were so full of undedicated and hypocritical people that I'd do better just worshiping at home every Sunday. I guess that was purely my decision, not yours."

He adjusted his position in the chair a little. His mind wandered to the last church he had attended regularly, a little storefront church in Perry.

The River had great musicians, and a young preacher that loved the Lord and everyone who came through the door. The never-churched, the outcasts, the seekers, the Bible nerds all found a loving home at the River. Reverend Hatcliff formed the motley bunch into a force for good works in the city like none had seen before. He knew that serving others was something everyone in the church could agree on. Once engaged with the River, the system of small group studies carried the congregation to greater knowledge of the Bible and God's love.

The church grew and changed rented locations three times in two years to accommodate the swelling numbers. When Ernie first attended, talk had begun of building a permanent location.

There was something about land and buildings that started to erode the fellowship at the River. At first, disagreement was congenial, but over the course of a few months, two sides developed, the "build it and they will come" opinion and the "we should keep renting" group.

Reverend Hatcliff wanted to build, but an important and influential member could not be persuaded to agree. After three years, the pastor resigned, and the River became a contentious group with no direction. It could be said as of the church in Ephesus, "You've left your first love."

The experience soured Ernie on the institutional church. How could people, once so much in love, turn on each other? How could bricks and mortar be stronger than the bonds of fellowship? If a church put ownership and acreage above God, he would do better to worship by himself.

Ernie left the church. Kate, one of his workers at Best-Mart, tried several times to get him to come back to the River but to no avail.

"You're so good with people, Ernie. You could be a healing influence," Kate pleaded. "We need people like you now more than ever."

He persistently refused to attend. Instead, Ernie started "the church of one," replicating the River's order of worship each Sunday at his own home.

Now years later, God was persistently urging him to return to corporate worship.

"Dear God," Ernie prayed, "I'm listening to You now. I give You permission to tell me why I need to be in a church. It's not that I've forgotten the Sabbath. I love You with my whole heart."

Ernie sat quietly, waiting for a word from God. God did not have to answer him, he knew, any more than He had to answer Job. But Ernie felt sure God was going to.

A quiet thought slipped into Ernie's mind just a few minutes later. It was a familiar voice, the voice of his friend Jack's wife, Tina. Ernie heard a replay of something she had said at the hospital a few days before: *Some days one believer is strong, while another is weak. Tomorrow it might be the reverse. You're strong in your faith, that's why*

I called you today. Ernie, you have denied other Christians your presence for too long. There are days when we all need others. A Christian is part of an army. No one has a right to go AWOL.

Ernie got up from the chair. He paced around the living room for five, then ten minutes.

Looking out the living room window into the darkness, he spoke directly to God. "Ernie Bostwick, recently AWOL, reporting for duty, Lord. Put me where You will. Forgive me, Lord. I thought I had a better idea, but somehow I temporarily forgot my rank."

The night was short, but the sleep was outstanding.

Monday morning in the interval between bagel half number one and bagel half number two, Ernie decided he knew where God wanted him the following Sunday morning. Still he decided to make a list of what he hoped to find in a church now that he was definitely returning to regular attendance.

Music was important. Contemporary music really stirred his heart. Then again, he had heard the old hymns sung with such fervor and conviction that they brought tears to his eyes. He wanted to be part of a church that sang to God.

He wanted Bible preaching. It was okay for a pastor to read only a few verses, but let them be the foundation of the sermon. He knew that there were good ideas that were well-accepted in present culture on how to live a good life, but a sermon was not the place for them. He wanted to know what the Bible said. Explain and expound the Word of God to him. Whether or not the Bible sounded pleasant or not, the centuries had proven that there was no better guidance for life.

And Ernie wanted a church that got people involved. The church was God's army, and no one should be allowed to just watch while others served. He needed to serve. He had been out of the action for too long.

But no matter what Ernie wanted in a church, he knew he would go wherever God led him.

As he was leaving for work, Ernie noticed the business card that Earl had handed him in the dark last night, lying on his dresser. It said, "Earl Barber, president, Avery Oil Distributors. Serving thirteen southeastern states."

Earl obviously didn't have to drive an old white Chevy. It was a testimony to his new focus on other people instead of himself.

The man's words came clearly to mind: *I spent my time trying to make money. I was the center of the universe. But now God has changed all that. I'm doing all I can to live my life for other people. And let me tell you, brother, that's living. There's nothing like it.*

CHAPTER 19

What's this world coming to? thought Ernie. For weeks, the only coffee Cindy would drink was Cinnamon Blueberry.

"I'd like to try something special this morning," she said. "Maybe something exotic, something different." Cindy looked at the other two urns next to her forsaken favorite. "Ooh, maybe this Java Jamaica is what I'm looking for."

She filled the orange Unguarded coffee mug and took a sip. Her eyes squinted as her mouth formed a frown.

"A little strong for your taste?" asked the store's proprietor.

She quickly took another sip. "Excellent, I would say. It just surprised me a little."

"I like to have your favorite coffee ready when you come in. What should I make for Wednesday?"

"Surprise me. Maybe something else I've never tried before."

Ernie settled into the green recliner with a mug of Seattle Sunrise. "I think you like to keep people guessing. I've been reading your column lately. One time it's a review of a business, another time we get a play-by-play of a disagreement you had with your fifth-grade teacher, and still another time you author a beautiful poem."

"I think I have a fear of a comfortable routine becoming a rut. I don't want to miss anything by living on autopilot for too long."

"I know exactly what you mean. I've decided that my life needs a charge. I've decided to find a church to be a part of. My life took all kinds of crazy twists and turns back when I was a churchgoer."

Cindy quietly stared at Ernie a little while, sipping her coffee.

She challenged, "I'll bet you don't know where I'm going tomorrow night."

He stroked his moustache a few times then held his chin between his right thumb and forefinger. "Is Senator Pride coming to town? You really gave him a rough interrogation last time about his Hawaii trips."

She smirked. "He deserved it. But, no, that's not it."

"Taking ballroom dance lessons?"

Her laugh was her negative response.

Ernie thought carefully. Suddenly his eyes widened with a look of disbelief. "Don't tell me you're going to New Life Church!"

"You have hit the nail on the head. The preacher makes a killer cheesecake."

"So I guess that means you went last Tuesday too. I don't remember your signing up while we were there on Easter."

Cindy responded, "No, I just dropped in. I decided that I'd let it be a test. If they had a problem with me just showing up, maybe they weren't as friendly as they claimed to be."

"And?"

"Not a problem at all. I didn't really learn anything new. That little summary you gave me just before we got to church said everything that Reverend Bart covered last Tuesday. You really know this Christianity stuff, don't you?"

The bell over the door announced Gloria Smith's arrival. Ernie called out, "Gloria, grab a cup of coffee and come join us."

"On the house?" she asked.

Ernie wasn't sure how he should respond.

Gloria said, "Just kidding! Boy, the look on your face was priceless." She found a mug that proclaimed "You're

#1" and filled it with Aloha Dark. She chose one of the red straight-back chairs, a good complement for her orange-and-red paisley blouse.

"Gloria," started Cindy, "I went to church on Easter to see what it was like. I'm still trying to figure out why people go to church. I mean, the music is okay, and the talk is entertaining, but some people just never seem to miss."

"What did Ernie say?" asked Gloria.

"I was just about to ask him when you came in the door."

"Then I guess I'll let him go first. Ernie, why do people go to church?"

He decided he would refill his coffee mug before he answered. Sitting back down, Ernie smoothed his moustache a couple times. "Let me go at the question from a different direction. I haven't gone to church for years, except for Easter with you, Cindy. I believe that God wants a relationship with every person. Once you accept that relationship on God's terms, other people can help you grow closer to God. Unfortunately, sometimes other people can have the opposite effect. That's why I chose to quit church."

Cindy asked, "So church is for mutual encouragement?"

Ernie was about to answer, but Gloria spoke first. "That's right. It can be a real growth experience, but it's a matter of give and take. Each person gives to the group and receives from the group. We can learn about God by reading the Bible, but it's hard to put it altogether by ourselves. One person might understand one concept very well, but be confused by something else. The songs and the preaching are helpful too as they present another person's understanding of a human's relationship with God."

"It takes awhile to put it all together," said Ernie. "It really takes a lifetime. Do you understand how to start a relationship with God?"

"I'm beginning to." Cindy glanced at her watch. "Hey, I'd better get to work. I've got to be in downtown Columbus in forty-five minutes. Bye!" She left two dollar bills on the counter by the cash register and made her way to her black Mustang.

"That was dumb."

Ernie was surprised but decided not to respond. He was fairly certain he knew what Gloria meant, but he thought it best to let her complete her thought without his interrupting.

Gloria sipped her coffee, waiting for Ernie to ask for her clarification, but he just calmly looked at her. She shrugged her shoulders and gave him a half smile, which still did not elicit a response.

Neither wanted to give in. They were both determined to make the other one speak first.

He finally smiled and said, "You're right."

"Right about what?"

"It was dumb."

"It was?"

"I think so."

They both quietly sipped their coffee for a minute, then Ernie began to chuckle. Gradually his chuckle became a laugh then a stream of laughter and then a geyser. Gloria joined in, knowing full well how difficult it would be to stop.

Jack Rhodes arrived amidst the hilarity and joined in the contagious laughter. "Er...errrrn...hee-hee-hee." Jack doubled over then stood up and tried again.

"Ernie...hee-hee, hoo-hoo-hoo. What's so, what's so, so...funny, hee-hee-hee." It was the best he could do.

Gloria made a successful, heroic effort to get control of herself. She paced back and forth, never letting herself look at Ernie. She patted her face a few times then stopped dead still. "Jack, a friend asked us why people go to church, and we never mentioned anything about worshiping God. It's not funny, really. It was dumb."

☙

Jack was about to slip out the door right behind Gloria, when Ernie called his name and motioned him back.

"Jack, what day will you next be going to the Best-Mart in Perry?" asked Ernie.

"Day after tomorrow. Why, need something they sell?"

Ernie stroked his moustache a few times before he spoke. "I'm going to be there that day. I promised Jack Best that I'd go in and check it out for him as a secret shopper. He said there seems to be a morale problem, and he needs to know more about it. If you see me, act like you don't know me."

"Aren't there people working in that store that remember you?"

"Only two. He told me who they are, so that I can avoid them. Your daughter is going to help me dye my hair brown, and I'm hoping that will be enough to fool any customers who knew me."

"How about a hat? You'd look great in a fedora."

Ernie laughed. "Jack, I'd better let as much brown hair as possible show. I'm going to wear jeans too, and nobody there has ever seen me that relaxed."

"Wow, this is so cool! I've always wanted to meet a spy. 'Ernie Bostwick, 007. Retail spy.' Is he paying you?"

"We never discussed money. Jack, this is just a favor for an old friend. I'm going to have a lot of fun with this."

"Okay, but remember, the General is tough. He might not react well if he knew you were digging up information on him."

❧

Ernie decided that Henry had finally finished the book he gave him to read. It was time to move the mannequin out of the used book section to another part of the store.

The coffee shop wouldn't do. None of Ernie's regular customers would be surprised by Henry's presence, and lately he just could not spare a chair for someone who never bought any coffee or added to the conversation.

The chairs at the checkerboard needed to be available for when Daniel came in to challenge grownups to a game or two. That was really entertaining. The kid could really embarrass old checkers experts who didn't realize how well Daniel could play.

Ernie carried the well-dressed mannequin to a spot next to the cash register. He faced Henry slightly toward the door, looking a little over the head of anyone who might be paying for their purchase. Henry's right hand rested on the counter, giving him an extra measure of steadiness.

Ernie stood back a few feet to admire the mannequin's pose. He stepped in to raise Henry's left hand to waist height and placed an empty foam cup in it. A new customer might think Henry was deep in thought as he held a cup of coffee.

❧

"Welcome, Patty! So good to see you again," said Ernie. "You said you'd come back one day when you had time to look at my selection of clocks. Is this that day?"

"After I get a cup of coffee," said Patty Johnson. "I so enjoyed it when I was in here with Gloria awhile back. Cindy Martin's mention of it in the newspaper reminded me that I needed to get some more coffee soon."

"I just brewed some Mocha Cranberry. Care to try some? I believe you had Gloria's favorite last time, Aloha Dark."

"I think you're right, I did. How did you remember?"

Ernie smiled. "A good merchant remembers his customers' likes and dislikes. It shows how much their business is appreciated. By the way, Patty, have you met Henry?" Ernie extended his hand toward his advertising associate.

"Why, Henry, it is so nice to finally meet you. Gloria has told me so much about you." She winked at Ernie. "She told me how she helped you rescue him from a fate worse than death. I'm sorry I spoiled your fun, Ernie. I'll bet you get a lot of laughs from people who assume he's real."

The bell over the door announced the arrival of two customers. The middle-aged couple immediately let their eyes roam around the store, obviously a new experience for them.

"Welcome to Ernie's," called out the proprietor. "Can I interest you in some coffee?"

Eddie and Sarah Smith both smiled. "We recently read about your store in Cindy Martin's newspaper column and decided this would be a good day to visit," Eddie said.

"Yes, we certainly want to try some of your coffee," said Sarah. "Cindy raved about it."

Ernie moved over to the coffee urns. "How about a cup of my favorite, Seattle Sunrise? It's stronger than most American coffees but not an espresso."

"That's good for me," said Sarah. "Eddie would prefer something a little stronger, I think." Her husband nodded his head.

"All right. That's Seattle Sunrise for her, and Aloha Dark for him. Why don't you have a seat? We'll join you. I'm Ernie Bostwick, the proprietor, and this is Patty Johnson."

The Smiths chose two of the straight-back chairs.

"Good morning, Ernie," Gloria called out as she danced through the door.

Patty turned abruptly and greeted her new best friend. As she turned, she bumped Henry's elbow, sending him twirling away from the counter. She was able to catch him before he fell, but the acrobatics caused Henry's left hand to clunk to the floor.

Gloria saw an opportunity.

"Oh no! Patty, what have you done? Oh, horrors! Have you no respect? Don't Henry's years in the service to our country mean anything to you? How dare you!"

By this time, Eddie's and Sarah's eyes were huge.

Patty cried out woefully, "I'm so sorry, Henry! Please forgive me. Are you all right?"

Henry didn't say a word. He leaned unsteadily against the counter.

Ernie picked up Henry's hand from the floor. "How can I help you, old friend? Do we need to rush you to the VA hospital, or do we just jam your hand back on your nub?"

At that, Sarah Smith gave a little shriek. Her husband did his best to comfort her.

Ernie said, "Maybe we'd better just sit you down in one of these chairs, Henry. You must be in shock. You haven't said a word." Ernie carefully eased Henry into the green recliner.

The visiting couple stared at Henry, now seated next to them, unblinking eyes staring off into space.

Eddie suddenly understood and started to laugh. His wife slapped him on the shoulder, but he laughed even harder.

"It's a mannequin, dear," said Eddie.

Sarah burst into laughter, which ignited Patty and Gloria, then Ernie. Soon they were all out of control, tears streaming down all their faces. Gradually, order was restored, and Gloria produced a tissue for Sarah to dab away her tears.

"Whew!" exclaimed Eddie. "All that after just one sip of coffee. Best java I ever had!"

Patty brought a fifth clock to be checked out. "You are really creative, Ernie Bostwick. Your clocks make the ones I have at home look so ordinary. One or two more ought to be enough."

"Are these all for one house?" Ernie asked.

"Every clock in my home has a cord. The last time the power went off, I decided that it was time I went to all battery-operated clocks. Besides, the cords were never long enough to quite reach the outlets unless I settled for putting them a little left or right of where I really wanted them."

"Now all you'll have to worry about is keeping a few AA batteries handy."

Patty's eyes suddenly brightened. "Have you ever tried converting an electric clock to batteries?"

He stroked his moustache a few times then took off his glasses and stroked his chin. He looked at the clocks Patty had brought up for purchase then glanced at the ones still on display.

After a little while, he said, "That might be fun to try sometime."

"I'll tell you what. I'll bring you one of my old wall clocks to experiment with. If you can convert it, I'll buy it back for five dollars."

"That's a deal."

CHAPTER 20

Every time he came out of his workroom for a cup of coffee, he could tell that Melissa was not quite looking him in the eye. She seemed to be focusing just above him. Ernie tried to put it out of his mind. He had to finish the silver bell pole lamp today for the lady from Midland, if at all possible. Tomorrow would be Ernie's spying expedition as Jack put it.

The trick with this particular lamp was balance. Most pole lamps could not handle a heavy shade like this silver bell. After a few months, they were no longer vertical and leaned more and more as the years went by. Ernie had attached a cable directly opposite the heavy shade from which hung an antique lead weight. All that remained to complete the project was to shine the metal parts with silver polish.

When he finished, Ernie attached a tag with the price and the customer's name and carried the lamp out to a spot near the cash register.

"Melissa, thank you for being willing to work on Wednesday this week," said Ernie. "I'm sure that by the time you get here from school, Mike will be ready for some help. It'll be his first time working all day by himself."

"I'm glad to help, Mr. B." She was still looking a little above him.

"Melissa, are your eyes bothering you today?"

"No, sir, they're fine. Why do you ask?"

"Because you haven't looked me in the eye since you got here. It's like you're looking just above my head."

She giggled. "I'm sorry, Mr. B. I guess I've been staring at your hair. You haven't forgotten that I'm going to dye it for you tonight, have you? I've never done anybody else's hair, and I'm just thinking through the process."

"Still willing?"

"Oh, yes, sir. I'll try to not think about it until after supper."

Teddy Jarvis arrived with a bright orange duffel bag.

"Whew!" said Melissa. "Teddy, turn out the lights on that thing, you're blinding me."

"I don't suppose," inquired Ernie, "you bought that bag with the prize money from last Sunday night's talent contest?"

"Yes, sir, Mr. B. From now on, my juggling gear will travel in style."

"Any bananas in there?" asked Melissa.

"That really was a tremendous trick," said Ernie. "I don't know why no one has done that trick before. I've just never heard of it."

Teddy replied, "I know why you haven't heard of it. That was a mess. Once I got the skin peeled back, it was sticky and slippery. I think I'll stick with apples from now on."

"I want you to know I worked hard to get the spot right after your juggling act," added Melissa. "I thought my song was so appropriate."

"It did seem like more than a coincidence," said Teddy. "I didn't know there was a song named, 'I Go Bananas for You.'"

☙

Ernie watched his pupil's tosses carefully. The rhythm was good, but Teddy often had to reach for the catch with his left hand.

"The toss from your right hand, from behind your back, needs to land a little more to the left of center, Teddy. We need to allow the left hand to catch and toss in a smooth arc."

Teddy made the adjustment. Each ball rose from his left hand was snatched at its highest point with a downward catch by the right hand and was tossed back into the air from behind his back to land again in the left hand. The beginning two tosses looked a little awkward, but by the time the third ball was in the air, the pattern they produced was extraordinary.

"Am I ready to try it with Indian clubs, Mr. B?"

Ernie shook his head. "No, you'll need a little more practice at home. Flipping those clubs will be quite a bit more complicated. Let's try replacing one of the tennis balls with a softball."

The extra size and weight of the softball threw Teddy off for a full ten minutes. The toss from behind the back hit the back of the teen's head more than a few times. By the time his forty-five minute lesson was over, his rhythm had returned.

"Thanks, Mr. B. See you next week. I'll be practicing." Teddy headed for the door.

"Wait a minute, Teddy," said Ernie. "I want to ask you something. Last Sunday night as I was headed home, I ran out of gas. A gentleman from your church, Earl Barber, was nice enough to help me out. I was really impressed that he would stop when nobody else would."

"Oh, he's like that, Mr. B. Church has really changed him. Five years ago, none of us kids even wanted to walk by his yard because he'd always yell, 'Get out of here, hoodlums!' He owns Avery Oil."

"I saw that on the business card he gave me. Why does he drive that old Chevy?"

Teddy chuckled. "I told him one day that he ought to buy a new car. He said he didn't need it. That would just give him less money to help other people."

"So what does Earl get out of helping other people?"

"Looks to me like it's made him the happiest man in town."

❧

As she exited, Melissa reminded Ernie, "Mom said supper is at six, chicken pie. Wear old clothes in case I mess up more than your hair."

Ernie smiled and nodded, locking the door behind her. He took a slow stroll around the store, making a mental note of items he needed to order and checking to see that all was ready for Mike to run the store by himself the next day.

Ernie planned to leave from his store around nine. He would get to Perry before eleven, shop for a few things in the Best-Mart while noticing all he could, then eat lunch at a fast-food restaurant. He decided he would spend lunch, writing down all he could remember about his morning shopping visit, then go back to check on anything he might have missed. His best information would come from casual conversations with customers and employees.

A few more books had sold today. He really had to do something with the left end of the store. If he continued to let the inventory of used books dwindle, he would soon have a space about ten feet square to do something new with.

It would be great if he could make space for Teddy to do an occasional juggling demonstration. The kid was getting really good! Of course, he couldn't expect him to put on a show more than a couple times a month. What would he do with the space the rest of the time?

Forty or fifty years ago, coffee shops would have poetry readings or folk singers on the weekends. Nobody did that anymore. Cindy sometimes wrote poetry.

Some furniture stores had artwork for sale on consignment. Maybe that was a possibility. How do you find an artist?

He decided to pray about the extra space. His own ideas were getting him nowhere. *What could it hurt?*

Ernie prayed aloud as he walked. "Dear, precious God, help me. Some space is developing in my store, and I don't know what I should do with it. I don't know whether to sell a new line of books, or maybe baskets or sports equipment. Nothing comes to mind. I've got an idea that you were somehow behind this new space. If that's the case, you already know my best use of every square foot of it. Lord, I am just going to leave it up to you. I'll be patient. I'm not going to rush ahead. I thank you and praise you. I want everything in my life to honor you. In Jesus's name, amen."

Ernie continued to walk. He glanced at his watch and decided that he'd better head on home to change clothes. He didn't want to be late for Tina's chicken pie.

Use it for ministry.

Ernie abruptly stopped walking. There was no sound, but he knew that voice.

God had spoken to him. Ernie Bostwick. God answered his prayer. In less than a minute.

Ernie had forgotten to contribute to the conversation at the Rhodes's dinner table. Few could blame him. Tina's chicken pie was incredibly distracting. All he could think about was the wonderful time his taste buds were having.

"Tina," he finally offered, "this chicken pie makes the one I produce taste like a kindergartner made it. I don't know what you do that's different. My crust is like yours. I use carrots and peas and corn, and surely we both use cream of chicken soup. What's different?"

Melissa's mom smiled coyly. "It's a secret. I can't tell you."

Jack said, "You see, Ernie, if you don't know how she does it, you'll always be eager to come to our house when Tina's serving this chicken pie. We've got to keep some leverage."

"It's the thyme," blurted out Melissa.

"Shhhh!" Tina gave her daughter a stern look.

"You cook it longer?" asked Ernie.

Tina smiled and slid her thumb and forefinger across her mouth to simulate zipping her lips closed. Ernie looked at Melissa and then Jack and got the same sign.

"Hmm," the store proprietor said. "Well, since you won't tell me the secret, you'll have to invite me back every month. I think I'll need some of this chicken pie for as long as I live."

Melissa said, "Let Mom tell you about the time she took her chicken pie to the Cave. It's the stuff legends are made of."

"The cave?"

"The Cave is what the youth room is called at our church," said Tina. "The huge room in the basement has been given over to our teens and their youth minister. Parents and other church members take turns, providing supper for the youth group on Sunday nights. A couple years ago, when it was my turn, I decided to feed them chicken pie. I asked Melissa how many kids usually come, and she estimated ten. 'But one time we had twenty,' she said.

"Well, I didn't want to run short, so I cooked four nine-by-thirteen pans for them. Unfortunately, midyear exams started the next day, and the only ones that showed up were the youth minister and two other boys, plus Melissa."

Ernie started to chuckle. "I'll bet this house ate chicken pie for a week!"

At that, Jack and Melissa burst into laughter. "Are you kidding me?" said Jack. "We didn't bring a single bite home. Tina thought they were even going to eat the dishes!"

Tina slipped into the kitchen with their empty plates, returning in just a few minutes with dishes of vanilla ice cream.

Ernie ventured, "Do churches still treat their youth groups like a separate congregation? That always seemed problematic to me. Once a kid graduates from the youth group, he or she is expected to immediately worship like all the adults."

"That's about the time they head off to college," said Jack. "A lot of them get into a college ministry with a worship service geared just for them."

"And when they come home," said Ernie, "they find that their old church has nothing like that for them. Each church needs somebody to teach the young adults."

"Some of them try to hang out with the youth group," added Melissa. "They figure out before long that they just don't fit there anymore."

Tina said, "I wish we could do a better job with young adults. They usually end up just dropping out. The ones that get married and have children pretty soon seem to be the ones that find a place in their old church."

"They just need somebody to show they care," said Melissa. "It almost seems like the adults want the ones in their twenties to flounder."

Tina interrupted, "Ernie, we'd better let Melissa get started on your hair. She's got a test to study for."

Turning to Melissa, she added, "Please don't use that blue on him. I saw you had some on the counter."

Melissa poked out her lips. "Momma, you know I'm saving that for myself!"

❧

Ernie looked at his reflection. *Who* is *that man?*

"You can look more in just a minute, Mr. B," said Melissa. "Let me use a brush to work a little more color into your moustache."

The teen carefully applied more hair color with the tiny stiff-bristled brush. After a couple minutes, she stopped and examined her work. She put down the brush. "Now you can look."

He stared for a full minute before saying a word. Surely no one would recognize him in Perry. In fact, even those who knew him in his childhood had never seen his brown hair with this hint of red.

"Great job, Melissa! This is perfect. Can you take a picture?"

Melissa retrieved her camera and took two shots, one from the front and one from the side.

Ernie said, "I'll bet you don't know what I'm going to do with them."

Jack piped up, "Pin them to that bulletin board in the post office?" He laughed at his own joke. "The FBI is always looking for some spy."

"No, I'm going to send them to my parents. I'll tell them that I ran across my twin, only he was twenty years younger."

Turning to Melissa, he asked, "How much do I owe you?"

"Well, the hair color only cost seven dollars."

"That's a bargain. How much would I have had to pay in a beauty salon?"

"About thirty, I think."

Ernie quickly pulled out two twenty-dollar bills and handed them to her. "Tip included."

He glanced at his watch. "Jack, Tina, I'd better go. I've got a few more things to plan before I do my secret shopper trip tomorrow."

Tina handed Ernie a small container as he headed for the door.

"What's this?" he asked.

"Chicken pie. You take the rest. There's just enough left for one person. If we keep it, we'll just fight over it. Hope everything goes well tomorrow."

CHAPTER 21

"Good morning and welcome," Mike called out.

Cindy headed straight for the coffee, as usual. She grabbed the pink mug that proclaimed "Coffee is a girl's best friend," and filled it with Seattle Sunrise. She took a few steps toward the comfortable seating nearby but was surprised to see Ernie was not in the green recliner this time of day.

The newspaper reporter wandered around the store for a few minutes, occasionally stopping to sip coffee. Heading back toward the cash register, she called out, "Mike, where's Ernie today?"

"He went to his house for a minute. He'll be gone most of the day, but he'll stop back in for a minute before he leaves town."

"Ernie? Leaving town? Where's he going?"

"Uh…I'd better not say." Mike immediately busied himself with checking how full each of the three coffee urns was.

Cindy's mind started to race. Ernie must be going to a doctor. Maybe he's going to one of the big hospitals in Columbus. Or if he's going to Macon, it must be something to do with his heart.

"Is Ernie all right, Mike?"

"Oh, he's fine. He's just got some business out of town."

She decided Ernie must be going someplace with a woman, that's why Mike wouldn't tell her. He probably thought it would bother her. It must be Ernie's landlady.

The bell over the door announced the entrance of another customer.

"Hi, Cindy," Gloria Smith said. "So good to see you today. You're usually heading out the door by the time I finally get here. You must be working nearby today."

"Actually, I'm not. I've got a big interview in Perry later this morning."

Mike's head suddenly turned in their direction.

Gloria said, "I guess I've decided this is housecleaning day, so it's Barkley for me all day. Where's Ernie, Mike?"

Mike Bruce parroted out the same answer he gave Cindy earlier, about Ernie going home for a few minutes, then he'd be gone all day.

"How is the store fixed for muffins and cookies?" said Gloria. "I can bring some this afternoon, if need be."

"Tomorrow morning will be soon enough," he replied. "I know your Thursday morning Bible study tends to go through a lot of muffins though."

"Okay. Just tell Ernie I'll bring some of everything first thing in the morning."

❧

At 8:50 a.m., Ernie stopped into his store just to check if Mike needed anything before Ernie left for Perry. He was hoping not to see any regular customers. He didn't want to spend the time explaining his appearance.

"Everything going okay, Mike?"

"So far, so good," he replied. "I'm already on the third urn of Seattle Sunrise, and Aloha Dark is running a close second. Most of the newspaper crowd has been here. Ernie, there's one thing you need to know."

"What's that?"

"I heard Cindy Martin say she'll be in Perry today. Wouldn't it be wonderful if she happened to turn up at Best-Mart? Better keep a lookout."

❧

The miles eased by. Ernie needed this travel time to ponder his message from God that his spare space in the store was to be used for ministry.

What exactly did that mean? Jack Rhodes sold revolving racks of Christian novels and self-help books. Could he make a special collection of lamps and clocks with Christian symbols? He still liked the idea of Teddy performing some juggling a couple times a month, but that's probably not what God meant by "use it for ministry."

The time Opal visited, she said he needed something in the store that "said Christian," something that made it plain where Ernie's highest priority was. It wouldn't be difficult to learn to make tee shirts with Christian symbols or sayings on them. Then again, carrying a line of clothing could get complicated. He'd soon be carrying caps then handbags.

Better keep a little more focus on driving. That deer almost decided to make a mad dash across the highway.

❧

Ernie waved to the twentysomething man gathering up carts outside Best-Mart.

"Great day, isn't it?" There was no reply. *Oh well. Probably had a rough night last night.*

Ernie tried again. "Been working here long?"

The young man replied, "Too long. But it's a job."

"Can I have one of those shopping carts? I sure would like one that rolls quietly, instead of the bumpity-bumping kind I usually get."

The Best-Mart employee pushed one cart, then another, finally finding that the fourth he tried rolled smoothly. "It's your lucky day, sir. You can sneak up on people with this one."

Ernie stuck out his hand. "Thank you." Reading his name badge, he added, "Thank you, Tom. I appreciate you."

Just inside the door, Ernie heard someone call out a cheery "Good morning. Welcome to Best-Mart."

The lady was tall and slim and probably seventy-five years old.

"Good morning, ma'am. I'll bet you'd rather be out in the sunshine, riding down the highway in your red convertible with your hair blowing in the breeze. It's a great day out there."

She gave Ernie a big smile. "Oh, I'm satisfied to be here, greeting fine people like you. Anyway, I never did figure out how to get the top down on my old pickup truck."

"Does Freddy Owens still work here?"

"Funny you should ask. He'll be relieving me as greeter here at this door at noon. Do you know him?"

"Haven't seen him in years, but I used to enjoy his company. Which way is the deli, ma'am?"

She turned and pointed. "Go straight ahead until you get past these pizzas and take a left. I'd walk over there with you, but if I get any farther from the door, my boss will get upset. You have a good day now."

The two ladies behind the deli case didn't notice Ernie standing there right away. He decided he'd get a few slices of cheese to nibble on as he shopped.

The plump African-American woman said to her coworker, "He did his best to not let me leave to see about Jessie's broken leg. One more minute, and I would have bit his head off! The ambulance picked her up at school, sirens blaring. She was scared to death. When I got to the emergency room, Jessie just burst into tears. Doesn't that man know that a little girl needs her mama at a time like that?"

The slim red head shook her head. "I know he's got a heart. He's got to. But he doesn't show enough evidence for anybody to prove it."

"Is your daughter better now?"

The first woman jerked her head around in surprise. "Is your daughter doing all right now?" Ernie said again.

Looking flustered, Lola Jackson said, "I'm so sorry, sir. I didn't see you come up. Can I get you something?

And yes, my daughter is fine now. Thanks for asking. That was eight weeks ago, but I guess I'm still upset about some of the things that happened."

"Give me about four thick slices of Swiss cheese, please. I've got to have some energy to get my shopping done."

Lola quickly filled Ernie's order. He handed her a ten-dollar bill, and she gave him his change and receipt.

He motioned for the red-haired worker to join them at the deli case.

"Dear God, our heavenly father, thank you for healing Jessie. Now, Lord, help us all to leave past hurts behind and live for today, for today is a great day. In Jesus's name. Amen."

Both ladies looked stunned but happy as Ernie waved and headed down the next aisle.

Lola called out, "Be sure to keep your receipt!"

There were actually a few things Ernie wanted to buy today. He could always use more bagels, and he knew he was getting low on sliced jalapeno peppers. One of the lamps in his living room blew its bulb last night, so he needed a package of 100-watt lightbulbs. Teddy was on his mind too; Ernie hoped to see something of unusual shape that Teddy had never juggled before.

Ernie spent two hours in the Best-Mart, putting very little in his shopping cart but engaging dozens of customers and employees in conversation.

He looked at his watch and decided it was time for lunch. He'd find some quiet fast-food restaurant where he could write some notes on what he had experienced in the Perry Best-Mart today.

Only four checkout lanes out of twenty were in operation. At least four customers waited in each lane. Ernie was relieved to see a self-checkout lane.

He passed the bagels over the scanner. *Ping*. He placed them in a shopping bag then scanned the jar of jalapenos. *Ping*.

After scanning and bagging everything but the five juggling objects, Ernie put the first bag back in his cart. He decided the toy dinosaurs would provide a real challenge for Teddy, having long tails and an off-center center of gravity. The first green dinosaur scanned well as did the next three. The last one, however, just did not ping. Ernie tried scanning it backward to no avail. He scanned it left, right, upside down, still nothing.

He looked around for help. The nearest cashier looked at him and shook her head. The man over at the service desk just shrugged his shoulders.

A customer walking by said, "Their boss won't let them help anybody at self-help. That's why nobody uses it."

Ernie stared at the machine and stroked his moustache. *There's got to be a way to do this.* There wasn't any need to get the dinosaurs if he could only get four; Teddy needed five to be really challenged.

A little blonde girl came over to talk to Ernie. Her mother stood a few feet away, looking over a long shopping list.

"Watcha doin'?"

"I'm trying to buy five dinosaurs, but only four make the machine ping."

"Did you try it backward?"

"Yes, and every other way I could think of."

"Why don't you just put it in your bag and do one of the other dinosaurs again?"

Ernie started to say why that would not work but stopped himself. He looked down at the little girl, and she stared back at him, as if waiting for him to do what she said. He dutifully put the fifth dinosaur in the bag and got out one of the first four. He ran it by the scanner. *Ping.*

As the little girl turned to walk away, Ernie said, "Thank you, friend."

"No problem."

❧

The Best-Mart in Perry had problems for sure. The biggest of which was employee morale.

Employees couldn't work efficiently if they were always looking over their shoulder to see if the boss was nearby. He obviously worried about adherence to the letter of each company rule.

There seemed to be agreement among customers and employees alike that the General had no heart. There was no evidence that he cared for the employees as people. Though he always treated the customers exceptionally well, his unfair treatment of the workers made customers suspicious that he loved them just for their buying power.

Employees did not help each other, afraid that their boss would accuse them of laxity in their own responsibilities. Workers were unsure of how to earn a promotion since extra effort was not uniformly rewarded.

It all boiled down to the Bible principle popularly known as the Golden Rule, to treat others as you'd want them to treat you.

Golden Rule? All the gold at the Perry Best-Mart had turned to lead.

~

Jeff Marsdale made the best burgers in Perry. Thankfully, not everyone knew it. Ernie had been able to write out a good summary of what he'd seen at Best-Mart without running into any old acquaintances. Then again, no one would have recognized him. Melissa had done a wonderful job with his hair.

"Was everything all right, sir?" asked the owner and cook. As many times as Ernie had eaten here, a few years back, Jeff had no idea that he knew him. Ernie just mumbled and smiled and nodded his head without looking away from his pen and yellow pad. That evidently satisfied Jeff, and he went on to another table.

"Oops!" A lady dropped her pen on the floor as she was passing Ernie. He quickly retrieved it and handed it to its owner as she stooped to pick it up.

Cindy!

She stared at him intently. "That's a wonderful disguise," she said quietly. "Are you in trouble?"

Ernie chuckled softly and motioned for her to sit down across from him.

❧

As they emerged from the burger joint, Cindy said, "I'm done for the day. I've just got to write up my interview when I get home tonight."

"There are just a couple of things I want to check on in Best-Mart before I leave town," said Ernie. "I need to check on the service desk somehow, and I need to walk by the meat department to see how fresh the items look."

"So, are you going to return something you bought earlier?"

"I wish I had thought about that. I didn't buy anything I want to take back. I guess I could take something back then go buy another just like it."

Cindy said, "I'll help you. The restrooms are right next to the service desk, aren't they? We'll go in the store together like we're husband and wife. While I'm using the facilities, you hang around outside like husbands do. That will give you a chance to listen and observe customers and employees at the service desk."

"That would work. But then you'd have to stay with me while I finish my observations at the meat department. You don't mind?"

"It'll be fun. If anyone thinks they might recognize you, they certainly aren't used to seeing you with a wife. They'll know they're mistaken."

Ernie wasn't entirely comfortable with the plan, but it would work, and he could get back to Barkley.

"Let's go in my car," she said. "We can come back here to pick up your Cherokee."

❧

Wandering near the restrooms while he waited for Cindy, Ernie heard bits of an animated conversation at the service desk.

"It looks fine to me. Are you sure you want to return it?"

The customer nodded sheepishly.

"Let me check with my manager."

Ernie was careful not to look in that direction. The Best-Mart chain famously asked no questions about returns. What was going on here?

He heard the desk phone click down. "The manager will allow your return. Try to shop a little more carefully next time."

Ernie thought, *An embarrassed customer usually becomes a former customer.*

"Ready to look at some steaks?" asked Cindy.

❧

As Cindy drove him back to his car, Ernie wrote himself a note to emphasize to Jack Best what a great meat department he'd found in the Perry store. In fact, the store had many fine attributes. However, none of them would be able to overcome the poor employee morale. Ernie knew from personal experience that poor morale was always linked to poor customer service, and both were a reflection on the ideals of the store manager.

CHAPTER 22

S omehow rainy days didn't affect Ernie's profits. People still stopped by for their daily paper. The coffee customers lingered for a second or third cup. Even though fewer people came in the door, they stayed longer and talked themselves into buying a little more.

"Man, you sure have changed," said Glen. "You were okay in the Bible study group yesterday, but when I stopped by in the afternoon, you were a man on fire. You were in your workroom. Then up here, taking a sip of coffee. Then back to the workroom. Then bringing a couple lamps to the front. That day in Perry was like a fountain of youth for you. Thank God you've settled back down today."

"I just realized how great life is without the pressures of managing a Best-Mart," said Ernie. "Here, I can set my own pace. If I want to rush around one day then take it easy on a day like today, nobody is stopping me. Did I ever tell you that I used to take blood pressure medicine?

Within a year after I opened this store, I was back in the normal range."

"Ah, you're the kind that doesn't need stress to get things done. You must make, what, a couple dozen lamps a week? And yet you still have time to sit with people like me and have a cup of coffee just about every morning. Ernie, you're a man who appreciates his friends."

Ernie smiled broadly at Glen's last remark. He took a long drink of coffee.

Gloria collapsed her umbrella as she came in, shook it, and leaned it against the wall just outside the door.

Ernie said, "Glen, I've always tried to do as the Bible says, 'Love your neighbor as yourself.' You never know when you're going to need other people."

"Have I had Hazelnut Supreme before?" Gloria asked Ernie. "It certainly smells good."

"Maybe not. I realized this morning that I don't make it very often. I'll have to be more careful."

Glen began putting the sections of his *Wall Street Journal* back together. "Guess I'd better be going. They depend on me down at the sub shop to handle the cash register when the lunch crowd comes in."

Ernie glanced at a nearby clock and saw that it was half past ten. "I think you just enjoy seeing the money come in. Hey, can you send me a ham and cheese sub in a couple hours?"

"Sure, Ernie. Same stuff on it as usual?"

"Extra jalapenos. Maybe I can liven up this rainy day."

Gloria settled into the chair across from Ernie with her Hazelnut Supreme as Glen exited. "I never did hear where you were Wednesday. Mike was really close-lipped about it. I decided it must be a doctor's appointment."

"No, I was just doing a favor for an old friend. Jack Best wanted me to do a 'secret shopper' survey of his store in Perry. He said sales were lagging, and he needed to understand why."

"Were you able to give him any clues?"

Ernie got up to refill his coffee. "It's definitely an employee morale problem. If the manager would just enforce one simple rule, he'd see a dramatic change."

"One rule would change everything? I can't imagine any solution that simple."

"Gloria," Ernie said, "if the manager would tell his staff, 'From this day forward, we are going to obey the Golden Rule, treating others as you would want to be treated,' it would make an incredible improvement. If enforced, it would mean that employees would treat each other fairly, they would show genuine concern for the customers, and the whole store would be a happier place."

"You really think that would work?"

"When I became the manager of the Best-Mart at West Point, we had this same kind of morale problem. I suffered with it for a couple months, but then I laid down the law. That law, the Golden Rule. Everything changed for the better in just a few weeks."

Gloria and Ernie were silent for a few minutes, quietly sipping coffee and staring into space.

"I've seen that same problem in the church," said Gloria. "I'd like to say that my church is immune to that, but it's not. We all get self-centered at times. We forget to help the needy. We correct people in a less-than-loving way. I've even seen people drop out altogether, when loving other church members gets too difficult."

"I guess that's why it's called the Golden Rule. It's as valuable as gold." He added, "And, by the way, that's not why I dropped out of church."

"No? Ernie, I believe you said people in your church couldn't agree on whether to build or to keep renting. You left, but you could have used your people skills to help heal the divisions. Isn't that the Golden Rule? Wouldn't you want folks to work on settling their differences instead of walking out?"

Neither of them spoke for a full minute.

Finally, Gloria stood up. "I apologize, Ernie. Sometimes I'm too outspoken. Please forgive me."

Ernie shrugged his shoulders. "You are forgiven. I'm glad you consider me a dear enough friend to speak frankly to."

"Thank you. I appreciate that. I'll see you a little later with a refill on your muffins and cookies."

ॐ

After Gloria left, Ernie started working on a clock he set into a multiple-picture wooden frame. Most of the spaces he left for photographs, but in one of the five-by-seven-inch spaces he put a clock face, made from adhesive shelf paper on a thin sheet of wood veneer with stick-on numerals.

Before he got very far, the weather showed dramatic improvement as did the traffic. Ernie had to set aside his project to wait on customers. Even the sandwich Glen delivered at one o'clock sat idle for an hour. Ernie couldn't complain. By midafternoon, he had sold seven clocks, two sets of Indian clubs, four lamps, and more coffee than usually sold by day's end.

Melissa would arrive in just a few minutes. Ernie sat down with a cup of coffee while an elderly couple pondered which board game to purchase for their great-nephew.

Gloria had said some things that might have sounded harsh a few days earlier. God was already pushing Ernie to get back in church, so her words were more encouragement than insult. He did need to find a church and stick with it, thick or thin, no matter what might arise. According to the Golden Rule, that's what he would want others to do for him. God needed people who could be a congregation's glue.

But that didn't mean he would stick with the first church he visited. He would do his best to discern where God thought he fit in.

❧

Ernie had to laugh. "What did your dad say?"

"He took it pretty well. He knew I needed a change, and he appreciated the sacrifice I had made for him."

Melissa was no longer black-headed. Her hair was a neon shade of green. The world had finally regained its balance.

"Mr. B, the coffee is pretty low. I guess you must not have made as much since it was a rainy day. I'll put on some After Hours."

He smiled and said, "Good idea. Actually, I sold more than usual. I'm so glad you're here."

Ernie spent the next half hour bringing new clock and lamp creations from his workroom. Thursday's "getting ahead" on lamps and clocks had suddenly become "just keeping up with demand."

"Melissa, I want you to help me make a special lamp tomorrow. You had some great ideas on how I could use that bamboo thingamajig, so I'm going to let you help me bring your scheme to life."

"Really? Mr. B, I don't know a thing about making a lamp. Thank you! Wow, I can't wait."

"I think you'll do well. You've seen a lot of my work, so you know a little about how I put things together."

❧

Cindy made a show of easing in the door. Ernie had never seen her this relaxed and unhurried.

"I've been looking forward all day to a cup of your fine decaffeinated coffee. Do you have any After Hours made, Melissa?" Cindy collapsed into an upholstered chair.

"Yes, ma'am. I just brewed it a few minutes ago. Can I bring you a mug full?"

"Please."

Ernie gave Cindy a curious look. "Shouldn't you be in a bit of a rush? You always fly through here on Fridays, desperate for coffee as you hurry to French's. Don't let us make you late."

Cindy's face shown like the sun. "Thanks to the raise I got this week, I am now only working at French's on Saturday. My Friday nights have been restored. I can finally really enjoy my four thirty Friday cup of coffee. Oh, I have so looked forward to this."

Melissa handed Cindy her coffee in a green mug that read "Celebrate!"

Ernie asked, "Any particular reason for the raise?" Then he answered his own question. "Maybe your boss appreciated the hundreds of extra papers sold when you exposed our eminent senator's lavish lifestyle at taxpayers' expense."

"Bingo. Along with all the other fine reporting I do."

Melissa had made her way to the far end of the store. She made it a habit to carefully straighten anything out of place at the end of each day.

"So, I suppose you'll take it easy tonight," said Ernie. "Maybe cook a frozen pizza, kick your feet up, and watch a little bit of television?"

"What I really want to do is talk you into trying out a little restaurant in Midland with me. Ever been to Kathy's Soup and Sandwich?"

"Now, Cindy, do you expect me to drop everything I had planned to be your escort to a sandwich shop? It's pretty short notice."

"What did you have planned?"

"Actually, I was going to cook a frozen pizza, kick my feet up, and watch a little bit of television."

"Shall we go to Midland right after you close then?"

"Hi, I'm Clint. What can I get y'all to drink?" The waiter wore jeans and a lime-green knit shirt with the name of the restaurant embroidered on the pocket.

"Hello, Clint," said Cindy. "Goodness, will I get bulging muscles like you if I eat here regularly?"

The waiter laughed. Ernie just smiled and shook his head. "You'll have to excuse my friend, Clint. Newspaper reporters are always very direct. I'll have a medium root beer. And you, Barbara Walters?"

"We're celebrating tonight, Clint. What's the most expensive drink you have?"

Clint gave Cindy a wry smile. "I'm afraid our fresh-squeezed lemonade is only a dime more than the rest. Good enough?"

"Sure. I can afford it."

"I'll be right back with your drinks."

Ernie took a long look around Kathy's. It obviously had been a residence originally. The kitchen was separated from the room in which they sat by a three-foot-wide counter with cabinets above it. The cook smiled back at the customers as she worked. Perhaps she was Kathy. There were three other dining areas, including a screened porch, plus three private dining rooms (former bedrooms?). It was almost like eating a meal at your neighbor's house.

"Do you cook, Ernie?" Cindy asked.

"Nothing elaborate, but, yes, I cook breakfast and supper every day. I carry my lunch to work most days. I guess I've gotten a lunch sandwich delivered most Thursdays lately."

"I rarely cook. It's just too lonely, eating at home by myself. I grew up, thinking of meal time as a social event. But I'm usually a cheapskate at restaurants."

"Most people who don't do their own cooking are overweight. I would have never guessed that you live on restaurant, cooking. You've got such a slim figure."

"Why, thank you, Ernie," Cindy said. "I'm pleased that you noticed."

Clint returned with their drinks. "Have you looked at the menu? I can come back for your order if you need a few minutes."

"I'll have a sub on whole wheat," said Cindy. "So I can have two meats and then as many other toppings as I like?"

"That's right," said Clint. "Go for it."

"All right. Start with turkey and ham, with lettuce and tomato. Let's see. Mushrooms, alfalfa sprouts, and green olives. And I guess I'd like honey mustard."

"That sounds good. And you, sir?"

Ernie considered ordering something very simple, but he couldn't resist the urge to compete with his tablemate. "I'd like a sub on whole wheat too, Clint. Let me have salami and bologna with spinach, tomato, jalapeno peppers, ripe olives, guacamole, and American cheese, with Dijon mustard."

"Great. What kind of chips do y'all want with that?"

Cindy and Ernie simultaneously said, "Plain."

The waiter laughed. "Are you kidding? Plain? After all that? Plain it is."

❧

Cindy finished the first half of her sandwich and took a long drink of lemonade. "What do you think?"

Ernie looked at her quizzically. "About what?"

"About the restaurant. Is this a place you'd recommend?"

"Certainly. My sandwich is great, and even the root beer tastes special. How about you?"

"I like my sandwich too. Ernie, you've got to try my lemonade. Take a sip." She pushed her glass in his direction.

He picked it up and sipped carefully, looking toward the ceiling as if hoping to explain the taste by some words written high in the room.

"Mmm. That's really good. Say, are you reviewing this business in your column next week?"

"Bingo. But that doesn't mean I'm not mixing business with pleasure."

"Oh, I'm sure," Ernie said with a smile.

"So how is the meal, folks?" said their waiter, Clint.

"God has blessed us with good company and food," answered Ernie.

"I agree," said Cindy.

Clint seemed to suddenly get an idea. "Hey, y'all go to church, don't you?"

Cindy said, "Sure." Ernie nodded.

"I've been writing a song," said Clint. "Can I play it for you? Just tell me if you think it's good enough for church. Let me grab my guitar." He walked briskly away.

"Cindy, you've only been to church one Sunday."

She countered, "You've only been once lately yourself. He didn't ask us if we were regulars."

Clint returned with his well-worn acoustic guitar. "Okay, let's see."

It's been too long, too long, since I've been inside these doors.

It's been too hard, too hard, living out here in the cold.

I don't know why I always pass by, but today I walked right in.

It's not like I thought, I don't feel condemned.

It just feels like coming home.

Lord, I feel your love, and your arms embracing me.

This time I'm going to stay. The wanderer is home.

"That's as far as I've gotten so far. I got started on the second verse, but it's not quite done. What do you think?"

"It's going to be great," said Ernie.

"Boy, I wish there was someplace like the old-time coffeehouses," said Cindy, "where people could read poems and play songs they're working on."

"Yeah, and short stories and that kind of thing," said Clint.

Ernie felt a tap on his shoulder. He swiveled in his chair, but there was no one there.

"Maybe there could be, like, a Christian open-mike night at some shop. Too bad this place doesn't have any big room for something like that."

Ernie again felt a tap on his shoulder. Again, there was no one there.

"Ernie, are you okay?" said Cindy.

❧

After saying goodnight to Cindy, Ernie started toward home. All during the drive, he couldn't get his mind off the taps on his shoulder.

Was it just a muscle twitch? Maybe. He had had a lot of coffee to drink today. Maybe he'd had too much caffeine lately. Then again, those two were the only twitches he had felt tonight.

Maybe it was a nervous reaction to part of the conversation. Let's see. They were talking about songs and poetry and short stories. Nothing in that to be edgy about.

Perhaps it was the need for a coffeehouse that gave Christian artists a chance to share their talents. He had never given that much thought. You couldn't really call his store a coffeehouse, at least not entirely.

But then, he had been trying to rearrange his store a little, and God had told him to use the extra space for ministry.

Was that God tapping on his shoulder?

CHAPTER 23

There it was, in the middle of the floor, whatever it was. Before the day was over, these bamboo poles of various lengths, anchored in concrete, would become a lamp.

"Melissa, we can't work on your project until Mike comes in at ten. I thought perhaps we could toss some ideas back and forth about it until then."

"Wow, I can't believe I'm actually going to make a lamp," said Melissa. "You'll have to do most of the work, Mr. B. I'll just supply some ideas."

"That's exactly the way I want it."

Melissa continued to get the store ready for opening but regularly glanced at the bamboo arrangement.

"Mr. B, would someone want this lamp to read by? I originally pictured it as providing some soft general lighting. Not bright illumination."

"I think you're right. It certainly calls for multiple bulbs, so you would want them low wattage."

Ernie sipped on some Seattle Sunrise and glanced at the morning headlines. He already had plenty of ideas on how this finished lamp should look, but he was reluctant to put down any original concepts Melissa might come up with.

❧

Glen, newspaper under his arm, was about to leave when he saw the bamboo poles in the concrete pot. He stopped in his tracks and stared for a few seconds. He noticed Ernie smiling at him.

"I know you, Ernie. You're waiting for me to ask what this thing is. I've done it a million times, and you always give me one of two answers. You're going to say either, 'It's a lamp,' or 'It's a clock.'"

Ernie just continued to smile. Glen was just naturally inquisitive.

"I'm going to throw you a curve this time, buddy. I will just stifle my curiosity. Just tell me this: what was this thing originally?"

Melissa chimed in before Ernie could answer, "It was an art project at college for some guy, but his mother couldn't remember anymore about what it was supposed to represent. She just remembered that he got an A for the project."

Glen turned to look at Melissa. "An A?" He looked back at the odd sculpture and shook his head. Glen headed for the door. He had his hand on the door handle but stopped. He slowly turned to look at Ernie.

"All right. You win. It'll worry me all morning if I don't ask. Ernie, what is that?"

The proprietor laughed out loud.

"It's a lamp."

&

"Mr. B., it looks like it would be just right for a college dorm room. It's too different to really fit in a house."

Ernie replied, "I can see it sitting in the lobby of a small office. Melissa, are you still planning on going to Columbus State next fall?"

"Yes, sir. So many of my friends want to go far away to college to get away from their parents. Not me. I love my parents. They are a gift from God, and I know they still have a lot to teach me. I'll just commute every day."

"Nobody could have better parents than Jack and Tina Rhodes. But aren't you afraid of missing 'the college experience'?"

"I think a lot of that is just kids with raging hormones who don't know how to be responsible yet. I want college to prepare me for life, not mess it up. And I need to stay anchored in my church. Most college kids set God aside for a few years just when they need Him most."

Ernie walked around the lamp-to-be, pausing every few steps to consider possibilities.

Melissa said, "I think it needs extra bulbs besides one on the end of each stick. Maybe one about halfway up each one?"

"And colored bulbs, maybe blue or purple, right?"

☙

Suddenly customers were everywhere. Mike quickly and courteously rang up purchases. Melissa was kept busy, making new batches of coffee, refilling sugar and creamers, and serving cookies and muffins. Ernie explained to customers how he made various clocks and lamps, took orders for made-to-order lamps, and generally directed traffic.

The young lady was ordinary yet stood out from the crowd. Short black hair surrounded a blemish-free, tanned face. A turquoise T-shirt coordinated well with slightly faded jeans. It was the tattoo of a thin red snake on her right forearm that really attracted attention.

"Good morning. Can I help you find something? I'm Ernie," said the proprietor, extending his hand.

She smiled quickly but declined to shake his hand. "One of my friends said you carried a few books. I need Walt Whitman's *Leaves of Grass* for a class. Do you have anything that old?"

"I try to carry classics like that, and some of the best new books. I think I've got it."

She followed Ernie to one of the wall bookshelves where he quickly retrieved the book.

"Do you read much poetry?" Ernie asked. "That is a lovely tattoo, by the way."

"The two subjects are related, actually. I had a streak of lousy boyfriends a few years ago. After an especially hurtful breakup, I started writing poetry. It was good therapy. And that's when I got this tattoo. To remind me that all men are snakes."

He laughed. "I hope some decent men eventually come into your life. Trust me, there are good ones out there. You read poetry to write better, I suppose."

"Yes, that's why I'm taking the class."

Only a handful of customers remained in the store now. Melissa showed juggling supplies to a ponytailed man in his forties. Mike straightened clocks and lamps.

"Come try some of our coffee," said Ernie. "Free for you today."

"Thank you, I think I will. Although a lot of my worst memories have started with a man saying 'Can I buy you a drink?'"

"By the way, I'm the proprietor. I started this store about three years ago."

"Pleased to meet you, sir. My name is Callie." She picked out a gray mug with green letters that proclaimed "Lord, help!" and followed Ernie to the coffee urns.

"My favorite is Seattle Sunrise. The Hazelnut Supreme sells best. And the Pomegranate we rarely make. It seems to appeal to a different kind of customer, I guess."

Ernie refilled his Seattle Sunrise and headed for his favorite chair. Callie wasted no time in selecting Pomegranate.

"I've always been curious about tattoos," said Ernie. "Do they hurt?"

"Some people don't mind it. I could barely stand it when I got this red snake. I've never felt such pain in all my life. But it was a price I had to pay. I never wanted to be used by a guy again. I needed a strong reminder. One pain stood for the other, you know?"

Ernie had to look away for a minute before he spoke. When he looked back, he looked directly in Callie's eyes.

"My heart was ripped out of my chest many years ago. I thought I wouldn't be able to go on. I'd done all the right things, I thought. I got a good education, a good job, and I was sure I'd found someone I could spend the rest of my life with. When she saw things differently, well…"

Ernie noticed that Gloria had come in and stood at a distance. She seemed to have something she needed to see Ernie about, but this was no time to interrupt the conversation with Callie.

"How did you get through it?" Callie asked. She smiled broadly. "Did you think about a tattoo?"

Ernie had to laugh. "No, that never occurred to me. I just threw myself into my assistant manager job at Best-Mart and prayed a lot. I can honestly say that God was the way to new life for me."

"Funny you should say that. Just after that first tattoo, I started going to church. I don't know why. That was a few months ago. I've been a Christian now for about a month."

Ernie looked at her quizzically. "First tattoo? You've got other tattoos? I thought you said it was painful."

Callie turned her left wrist up for Ernie to see a small, multicolored heart. "This will be my second and last skin art. This is my Jesus tattoo and stands for His everlasting love."

Ernie smiled and leaned back in his chair. "I'm glad you found a love that won't let you down."

"This is really great coffee, by the way. Can I try another flavor?"

"Sure. Maybe you'll get hooked, and you'll be a regular customer."

He noticed Gloria going out the door. She seemed in a hurry.

ॐ

Ernie wound the string of Christmas lights around each pole of the bamboo structure, thirty large bulbs in all. He knew he'd have to secure them into place a little better, but he first wanted to see what Melissa thought.

His original intent was to use ten or twelve 40-watt incandescent bulbs. It would have required a lot of wiring, and more time than he would usually spend on a lamp project. Melissa decided that Christmas lights would have a similar effect but doubted any could be found in April.

She had no idea of the variety of objects in Ernie's workroom.

He slipped the plug into the nearest electrical outlet and turned off the overhead lights in his workroom.

"Melissa, I'll watch the register for a minute. Come take a look at how our lamp is coming along." Ernie closed the door and came to the front of the store as Melissa headed for the workroom.

"Wow! That's great! Have you still got some of that tan tape you said you used on Cindy's lamp to secure the wires to the bamboo poles?"

"Maybe we should use green tape since the cord on the string of lights is green."

"Oh, that's right, Mr. B. Then wind some artificial ivy up the poles too to make it look more natural."

"Good idea. Do you know what Gloria Smith wanted? She didn't stay very long."

"She just said she wanted to ask you something." Melissa looked around to see if any customers were nearby. Satisfied that no one was within earshot, she said, "Do you think Gloria was going to ask you for a date? Maybe you should call her."

"Since this is Saturday, she was probably going to invite me to church again. Won't she be surprised when I walk through the door tomorrow?"

"Mr. B, I'm impressed. That's two Sunday mornings in one month. Are you going to start going to church every week?"

"Definitely. Like your mother said, it's not about what I can get out of a church, but what I can give. God has been very patient with me. I'm back in the fold."

"I'll tell my mom that our prayers have been answered. Why that particular church?"

"I...guess I don't know. God just said to visit there first. But I'll still be meeting your family for lunch, so save me a place."

~

He watched Melissa's car pull out as he locked the deadbolt from the inside. Ernie liked to spend a few minutes walking around the store at the close of one week to get a sense of what needed to be done to start the next week.

Many empty spaces called out for clocks, and nearly as many pleaded for lamps. The ponytailed man had bought juggling supplies as if there would be a shortage in the next few weeks. Coffee had also had a good week.

Surprisingly, used books sales had rebounded. The new best sellers had very little sales this week. God seemed to be leading Ernie in a new direction in this part of the store, but he needed to spend more time in prayer to sort out the heavenly message. It did not seem prudent anymore to completely discontinue books, but

Ernie remembered Opal saying that nothing in the store really witnessed to his Christian faith.

Use it for ministry. Ernie clearly heard God speak to him four days ago. He was determined to follow God's directive. As he considered that message, the image of the lamp he and Melissa had created today popped into his mind. He knew it must be part of the solution.

CHAPTER 24

Ernie wondered if he'd heard God right. Is this really the church he was supposed to be in today?

Important ingredients were missing. Nobody met him in the parking lot, so Ernie had to find his way to the right building and the right door. An usher smiled and handed him a worship bulletin when Ernie found the sanctuary, but the young man may not have recognized that he was a visitor, or perhaps this church didn't treat visitors as treasured guests.

Once he decided on where to sit, no one paid any attention to him except a very senior woman. She smilingly informed him that she usually sat in the exact pew he was in but to never mind as she could sit somewhere else. He apologized and sat elsewhere.

At about ten minutes before eleven o'clock, the sanctuary suddenly began to fill with people. Evidently Sunday school had just ended. Several sizeable groups of people entered together, chatting amiably.

Where was Gloria? He was sure she never missed a Sunday. He wanted to see the surprise on her face when she spotted him here after the many invitations she had issued him. Of course, it would be helpful to have a friend to guide him through any unfamiliar parts of this church's order of worship.

The choir entered the choir loft, wearing dark blue robes with white stoles. Gloria was the fifth singer to enter, but sat in the second row, blocked from his view by a tall, blonde soprano.

Suddenly someone tapped Ernie's shoulder. "Wow! You're here! Can we sit with you?"

He saw the red snake before he saw her face. "Callie, it's so good to see you. I was hoping I'd see somebody I knew. Please do sit with me!"

"Let me introduce you all to Ernie. He has a great coffee shop in the village along with a lot of other incredible things. Ernie, I don't know your last name. This is Mandy, Kate, Frank, Liz, and Arnie. We are the young adult class, also known as the future of the church.'"

"Ernie Bostwick. Callie and I are already on a first-name basis. By the way, you never told me your name either."

"Johnson."

The piano started playing louder, and the choir stood. The congregation quieted immediately. "Call to worship," Callie whispered to Ernie.

Gradually, he grew more comfortable with the worship service. It resembled the way things were done in the church he attended at the end of college. He would have preferred a less formal service like at the River.

During the offering, Callie whispered, "See the lady at the end of the second pew?"

Ernie nodded slightly. The tiny, white-haired lady reminded him of Opal Carrollton, looking at least eighty, but obviously full of energy.

"She's our Sunday school teacher. You've got to meet her. She's the craziest, most loving person ever."

When the pastor stood to deliver the morning sermon, Ernie recognized that he was an every-morning customer. He whispered to Callie, "I didn't know Dan was a preacher. He comes in my store every day."

"I like him. He calls me California. His wife is a sweetheart."

Ernie had never asked Dan what he did for a living. He didn't want to measure people by their occupation. Dan never lingered at the store. He just bought the *Columbus* paper and a coffee to go. Ernie usually did a better job of getting to know his customers.

It was an amazing sermon. The pastor seemed to have no manuscript or notes, allowing him to keep eye contact with the congregation. He used the full width of the stage but didn't wander from his focus on the subject, "win them with patience." He concluded with a call to prayerfully and patiently win friends to Christ.

As the service ended, some rushed out the door, some eased toward the narthex, while others stood, seemingly without a care for what they had to do next.

"We'll be here same time next week," said Frank. "Plan on sitting in the same seat."

"You're one of us," said Kate. "We claim you. Any friend of Callie's is our friend too."

Ernie smiled. "But I'm not a young adult."

"You are now," said Liz.

"Come on, we've got to introduce our friend to Jana," said Callie.

Gloria was coming out of the choir loft, heading for the narthex. She couldn't help but notice the group of young adults gathered around Jana Huffton at the front of the church. It still amazed her that an eighty-four-year old could bond so completely with the young adult Sunday school students.

She stopped, midstride. Ernie Bostwick was in the gang! Ernie had come to church. She could see that it would be useless to try to fight through the crowd to welcome him. "I'll stop by the store in the morning," she told herself.

‍

"So how was it?" said Tina. "We've been waiting here ten minutes already. You either had a great time, or the preacher didn't know when to quit."

"Mama, God didn't make a rule that church has to get out by noon. Maybe the pastor was especially inspired today and had a lot to say." Melissa looked at Ernie expectantly.

He saw the waitress coming to get their drink order, so Ernie just smiled instead of answering questions about his attendance at church.

"I'll have unsweetened tea instead of coffee, Brenda," he said. "How has your day been so far?"

"Pretty busy, Ernie," the young mother replied. "I think there's been some kind of convention over at the motel this weekend, and they're all stopping here to eat before they head home."

"How is Johnny doing with his juggling?"

"He practices all the time. That was really thoughtful of you to remember his birthday with that little starter set. He's starting to juggle four balls now. And you know, I think it's helping his self-confidence."

"That's great," said Ernie. "It wouldn't be the first time a kid conquered his shyness by juggling."

Brenda turned to the others. "The usual drinks for the rest of you? Melissa a root beer, Tina unsweetened tea, and coffee for you, Jack?" Tina and Melissa nodded.

"Remember, I switched to decaf," said Jack.

Brenda nodded. "Help yourselves to the buffet. Don't miss the garlic mashed potatoes. The cook is especially proud of them."

Ernie popped up and headed for the buffet, leaving Tina's questions about church unanswered.

"The church service didn't have any big surprises," said Ernie. "The music was good although my taste runs a little more contemporary. But they did it well. The sermon was great. Now, they could have put a little more effort into their hospitality. I guess no one has ever trained them how to handle visitors."

"They may not be used to having visitors," said Melissa.

"You're right, dear," said Tina. "Hospitality is just a matter of treating others like you would want to be treated. Somehow people don't naturally do that in church."

Jack asked, "Are you going back? You said God told you to go there this Sunday, but was there anything that would make you want to return without a second command from God?"

Ernie smiled warmly. "Yes, I'll certainly go back. I've been adopted into a herd of young adults. Melissa, remember the girl with the red snake tattoo?"

She nodded. "Callie was there?"

"Yes, and she and her young friends all sat next to me and really made me feel at home. They declared that I should sit next to them from now on. I was late getting here today because they had to introduce me to their Sunday school teacher."

"So I guess you're saying," interpreted Jack, "that it only takes a few thoughtful people to make a visitor want to return to a church."

"I think that's right. If only one person had welcomed me well, I might or might not go back. It made a difference that it was a group."

Melissa said, "Was Gloria there? She's been inviting you to her church for awhile."

"I saw her when the choir entered, but then somebody taller sat in front of her. I doubt she knew I was there."

"Ernie," said Tina, "I'm convinced God wants you planted in a church to help others as much as to help you. Did God give you any ideas how He might want you to serve in that church?"

"Hmmm." Ernie worked on cutting up a piece of ham as he pondered the question. The others at the table likewise took the opportunity to bite and chew.

Brenda came by to refill their drinks. "Certainly is quiet. Somebody pass out insults?"

Ernie chuckled. "Looks like it, doesn't it? No, they just asked me how I was going to serve in my new church. It's only my first Sunday there! What would you say, Brenda? If you were new in a church, how would you offer to help?"

"Well, people think, since I work here on Sunday, that I don't go to church. Actually, I go to Trinity Baptist every Sunday night. To answer your question, I could see on my very first Sunday night there that somebody ought to have a class for the kids during church. They were just fidgeting and writing on bulletins and napping. So I volunteered to be their teacher while the adults had church. I really love it, and the parents are very grateful."

"Brenda, I could tell you were a Christian by how you treat other people. I guess I never really thought about when you might worship," said Ernie. "Thanks for the good idea. The pastor is one of my regular customers. I think I'll talk to him about what the church needs."

❧

Ernie stared at the television with his eyes struggling to stay open. What was that ringing in the middle of the baseball game? Was it a fire alarm? Did it mean that somebody just hit a home run? Maybe the manager was calling the bullpen.

He finally realized his telephone had interrupted his nap. Quickly standing and traversing the distance to the wall phone, Ernie forced himself to shake off the vestiges of a splendid Sunday afternoon nap.

"Ernie, this is Jack Best. Bet I woke you from a nap."

"Yes, sir. How did you know?" said Ernie.

"Just going with the percentages. Most churchgoing men in America take a nap on Sunday afternoon. Ernie, I want to thank you for your good work at the Perry store. I'm going to move the manager there to be an assistant at a larger store and find somebody else for Perry. I think that if I keep the General's pay the same but put him where he has a great manager to observe, I can turn him around. Now I just need to find the right man for Perry."

"That's great, Jack, and very generous. I agree with you that the Perry store can thrive again with the right manager. It's a great location, and a great town."

"I'm sending you a check, Ernie. I know you didn't ask for any pay to be a secret shopper for me. Just consider it a 'consultant fee.' Take a friend out to eat or buy something for your store."

"Thanks, Jack. I'm glad I could help. So, what kind of manager are you looking for?"

Jack Best paused for just a few seconds. "Ernie, the Perry store really did well while you were there. I need to find someone with some of your same qualities. I need a servant leader. I guess it would help if they were a Christian because they understand about treating other people like they would want to be treated. You can't really do that for very long if you're not a Christian because people will take advantage of you and hurt you. It takes God providing extra strength."

Ernie thought of past experiences, working as a Best-Mart manager. Jack was right. There were always employees that would take advantage of the manager's kindness. They didn't last long though. Self-centered behavior had a way of catching up with a person. "What else, Jack?"

"And I need somebody who is naturally outgoing, not out of training, but because they really care. Employees can tell if the boss really has compassion, or if he is just trying to say the right thing." Jack continued, after a pause for breath. Ernie remembered that Jack Best had a respiratory problem that limited his physical stamina. "Ernie, you were a great judge of abilities. I need more managers like that who can get the right employees in the right jobs."

"Jack, that's a product of the caring you talked about earlier. If the manager sees each employee as a real person, he'll do all he can to get to know them. As he learns their struggles and celebrations, he will know what they like to do and what they have the ability to do."

"There you've got it," said Jack. "I'm looking for a servant leader who lives by the Golden Rule, someone who authentically cares about the persons under him and wants to see them succeed. Ernie, if I could only persuade you to come out of retirement, I'd have just the manager I need."

"I'd be tempted to take you up on it," said Ernie. "I really loved those folks."

"Double what you were making when you retired. How about it? You could quit after six months. That's all it would take you to get that store back on track. Then you could retire again and have another great story to tell your friends and relatives."

Ernie was silent. He prayed silently, though he doubted this was the Lord's plan for him.

His mind brought up a picture of his store, and he thought about the half-empty book section. *Use it for ministry*, God had said.

"Ernie, are you still on the line?"

"Jack, thank you for the offer. I know I could turn that store around, and it probably would not even take six months. I live by the Golden Rule, and it doesn't take long to convince other people that it works."

"Then we have a deal?"

Again Ernie was silent. Twenty seconds slowly passed.

"No, Jack, I need to stay right where I am. God is doing something here, and I can't walk away from it. It's really going to be great, probably the biggest service to God that I've ever done. I will pray for you though, that you'll recognize the right person for the job. Jack, I know you believe in God, so depend on Him to supply your needs. And let me know if I can be a spy for you again. I kind of enjoyed it."

"God bless you, Ernie. You're a good man."

CHAPTER 25

The four days since Jack Boot called now seemed like weeks. Ernie Bostwick produced over thirty lamps in that span with a somewhat different, fresh look. Melissa's idea of using multiple bulbs on a lamp inspired him to try three, four, or even seven bulbs on various lighting fixtures. The result was phenomenal. The new lamps were selling quickly.

Other parts of the store were changing too. Two new coffee varieties were due to arrive any day. Yesterday a new type of juggling rings made its appearance in the store.

Now Ernie stood, pondering the used book section. How, Lord, could he use it for ministry? As Opal had said, nothing in the store revealed that Ernie was a Christ follower. Now was his chance to amend that.

Just looking Christian is not the same as doing ministry though. If God said to use space in the store for ministry, surely that should include action. How could Ernie reach out with floor space?

๛

Would Gloria be here for her Bible study today? Ernie hoped so. She never missed, but Gloria had not been in the store since Saturday. That was when she left in a hurry while he was talking with Callie Johnson.

Perhaps he should have paused long enough to speak to Gloria. Surely Callie would have understood, but Ernie had not wanted to interrupt the deeper-than-expected conversation.

She would be here. This Bible study was an important way she served the Lord. He would apologize as soon as she came in the door.

He also needed to remind her of an upcoming event that had significant implications for Gloria, himself, and Henry.

๛

"Ernie, I'm Dan Miller, pastor at Northside Church. I saw you in worship last Sunday. Glad you came!"

"Thank you, Dan. I recognized you as one of my regular customers, but I've never been inquisitive enough to ask your profession. Have you just been at Northside a few months, or is that just when you discovered our coffee?"

"I've been here about a year. Gloria Smith heard that I love coffee and insisted that I try the coffee here. It didn't take me long to become a regular customer."

Ernie said, "If I'm not mistaken, you usually get Seattle Sunrise. That's my best seller."

"That's pretty accurate. I have Cinnamon Blueberry about once a week. So how did you like our worship service?"

"I was impressed with the sermon. Your message was direct and biblically sound. I've got to admit that my first preference in music is contemporary rather than traditional."

"We would love to mix in some contemporary music, but right now, we just don't have the musicians. Ernie, where did you last attend?"

Should he mention his three years of Sunday worship at home?

"Dan, I attended a church in Perry when I lived there called the River. At one point, we had a lot of conflict in the church, and I stopped attending. I really missed teaching Sunday school, but the disagreements were too distracting for heartfelt worship."

"I understand. I've been through enough church fights for a lifetime. I hope you'll sense enough love in

Northside to come regularly. I'm sure God wants you to put your knowledge to work in encouraging others."

"Thank you. I've promised some friends that I'd be back next Sunday."

"Good, good. We'll see you then."

❧

Jack, Melissa's father, pointed at the short and squat coffee urn next to the usual three. "What's this?"

"That's brand new today. I've got a few special customers that prefer decaf coffee even in the morning."

Jack first looked astonished then produced a wide smile. "I thank you, friend, and so does my cardiologist." He gave Ernie his biggest salesman's handshake.

"Come sit down, when you get your coffee, Jack. I may have some business for you." Ernie settled into his favorite green recliner.

"Okay, but I don't know of anything in this store I carry."

Ernie took a big swallow of Seattle Sunrise. "I have an elderly friend that came in here a few weeks ago for the first time. Do you remember me mentioning Opal Carrollton? She lives in Midland with her niece."

"Sure do. You and Cindy went to church with them on Easter."

— CIRCUS ON THE SQUARE —

"Opal looked over the place thoroughly then said something that has been bothering me ever since. She said that nothing about Ernie's revealed my Christianity."

Jack sat quietly for a minute, looking slowly around the store.

"She's right, Ernie. But what did she expect? Your faith is revealed in how you treat people. You don't just hang a sign out."

"Do you have any Christian products, Jack? What kind of display do you put in stores that is obviously Christian? I don't want to leave people wondering if I'm just a nice guy or if there's something that gives me strength to live a better life. I want people to know about God."

☙

At about fifteen minutes before ten, Gloria walked slowly and carefully through Ernie's front door. She made her way to the coffee urns, carrying her Bible and a notebook in a canvas bag.

"Hello, Ernie."

He humbly began, "Gloria, I apologize for not taking the time to speak to you last Saturday. It was very rude of me. I could see that you had something important you needed to say to me."

— 323 —

"Oh, that's no big deal. I could see you were in a deep conversation with a customer."

"Then you forgive me?" Ernie said. "When you didn't come in the store for several days, I knew I'd offended you."

"Ernie, friends don't get offended that easily. I turned my ankle Monday morning, and the doctor said to stay off it. I so wanted to tell you I saw you in church, but I was stuck at home. I'm much better today."

"I'm so glad," said Ernie. He paused a few seconds then continued, "Tomorrow night is the grand opening of the restaurant where you and I found Henry. Gloria, would you be my date to Dan-O's Chinese Restaurant?"

Her face lit up like sunshine. "I most certainly will. That's exactly what I wanted to propose when I was in here last Saturday. In fact, I wouldn't be surprised if Dan-O Tang were looking for us to make an appearance. I wouldn't want to disappoint him."

❧

"If we are the body of Christ, like I just read in 1 Corinthians 12, then we should each look like Christ in some way," said Gloria.

Only Glen was missing from Bible study this week. Still, it meant that six upholstered chairs didn't have to be supplemented by a metal folding chair.

"A church is not complete then if it doesn't have some of all kinds of people," said Mack. "I think my church has a lot of people who are Christ's hands and feet, but we lack his good judgment."

"The Bible says that if you lack wisdom, pray. God will provide." Mandy had grown a lot in her Bible knowledge since she joined the group in January.

Gloria asked Mack, "Do you suppose God wants every church to be alike? I wonder if we are meant to be a little lacking."

"So that new people have a place to fit in," said Marietta. "God leads seekers to the right church so that He can meet the needs of the person and the church."

Ernie was doing his best to be more listener than talker today. God was telling him something about why He wanted him at Northside. Was he meeting a need of both the church and himself?

Marietta had found just what she was looking for at Gloria's church. Although Ernie had not found all that he expected this past Sunday, he had the similar experience of a small group of people taking him in immediately.

"If we are all part of the body of Christ," said Sam, "I think I'm a forearm. I have a gift for connecting people in the church. The ones that do the work like the elbow and the wrist. I may not look like I'm doing much, but I think I'm pretty necessary."

"We've got a lady at my church," said Mack, "that has a gift for calming down folks that get agitated or get their feelings hurt. You know how excited we Pentecostals can get sometimes. She's never head of a committee, but she may be the most important person in the church."

Ernie turned to the slim blonde next to him and asked, "Mandy, I know you haven't been going to church but a few months. What have you found to be the most important part of the body of Christ?"

"For me, it's the encouragers. They make it a habit to tell others that they are doing a good job, or that tough times don't last forever, or that they like your smile or your handshake. They treat you like it's important to them that you showed up today."

"That's the lubricant for all the joints in the body," said Sam. "They make everything work more smoothly."

"Okay, let's look back at something else," said Gloria. "The eye or some other part, it said, can't tell another part that it's not needed. Yet I've seen members of churches who seem to be roadblocks. If they would just move out of town, it looks like the church could serve God better. What am I missing when I think that way?"

"Maybe we're not seeing a deeper problem that they're struggling with," ventured Marietta.

"I've found," said Mack, "that sometimes roadblocks make you look to find a better route. Like when the city tore up Main Street a couple years ago. I started going on Elm and discovered some of the most beautiful flower beds in town. It got me to work in a better mood."

Sam added, "Maybe Paul was talking about those roadblock people when he said he had a thorn in the flesh that God didn't want to take away. It made him lean on God a little more."

Ernie had to speak. "God brings new people into a church to renew it. Yet too often the members want to make the new person just like them. They miss a great opportunity. If the visitors aren't allowed to be who God made them, they take their gifts to another church."

"It's important to remember," said Gloria, "that God fits the church together. From our human standpoint, we decide that some people will never be able to belong to the same church. But for God, nothing is impossible. He has a plan how everything should work. The pieces will always fit if we let God use people as He wants to."

"Doesn't it also mean," said Mandy, "that there is a right church for each of us? No two churches are alike. They all have a different combination of people. God meant it that way."

"And there's no reason for anybody to not be in church on Sunday. There's enough difference in churches that everybody can fit some..." Sam stopped midsentence. "Oops. Sorry, Ernie. I wasn't talking about you."

Ernie laughed. "No offense taken, Sam. My stay-at-home Sundays are behind me now."

It hit him like an errant basketball. What a great idea!

"Melissa, I know you just got here but would you mind if I ran down to the thrift store for a few minutes?"

His green-haired helper answered, "I think I've got it. There aren't any customers in here right now. Need something for a lamp?"

"No, I need to find some good used clothes for a friend. I'll be right back."

After reaching the First Baptist Thrift Store in the next block, Ernie headed for the corner with men's clothing. He didn't see any medium dress shirts and stopped to look around.

"Can I help you, Ernie?"

Carol Young, the volunteer on duty, stepped up to his left. "If you're looking for something dressier, we've got a special section in the side room."

"You read my mind, dear friend. I need a dress shirt and black slacks for a man a little slimmer than me and a couple inches taller."

She led Ernie to the side room. "How about a long-sleeved white shirt in a medium?" she asked as she handed him a shirt.

"Great. I think he needs pants with about a thirty-two-inch waist and about the same inseam."

"About?"

"Anything close will probably do."

Carol stared at him for just a moment then held up a pair of black pants. "Here's a thirty-two by thirty. Okay?"

"Great! And give me that black hat with the blue hat band."

Ernie was in and out of the store in less than five minutes.

"Want to go to church with me Sunday?" said Cindy. "Now that I only work at French's on Saturday, I think I'd like to make church a part of my life."

"That's a pretty big step. Let's see, you've been on Easter, then a couple of Tuesday nights, right?"

"Well, actually just one Tuesday. I didn't quite make it that second time. I've been thinking about it, and it all sounds good."

Ernie took a couple sips of coffee. As usual for the half hour before closing, business was winding down.

"What part sounds good?"

Cindy said, "Just the church kind of life in general. I know there must be a God. It seems obvious to me. Everything about the way things in the world are put together seems orderly and planned out. My life needs a lot more order. When I look at you and Gloria and Melissa, I can see that you have something I don't."

"Well, I haven't really been to church much lately, except two Sundays."

"Yes, but I know you believe in God. There's some kind of extra strength behind you. Me, I've been trying to do life on my own strength."

"Cindy, you're right. Without a relationship with God, there are a lot of things in the past few years that I couldn't have handled. Jesus Christ is the answer to the most important questions in life."

"Tell me more."

Melissa walked up. "Mr. B, I'm sorry to interrupt. Could you tell this lady how to play cribbage? She wants to buy a game for her son's birthday, but isn't sure which one."

"Sure, Melissa. I'll be right there."

Ernie stood up from his chair. "You'll have to excuse me, Cindy. Work calls. I promised some people I'd attend Northside Church this Sunday. I'd be glad to meet you there. I'll be the older guy with a group of twentysomethings."

"Wow, that sounds interesting. I'll see you Sunday."

CHAPTER 26

What does a person wear to a restaurant grand opening? Gloria had been to movie opening nights, theater opening nights, even to the grand opening of a playground. There probably was no reason to treat it like a prom.

But this was Ernie, and somehow that made it different. She wanted him to feel comfortable being with her.

Gloria sat down in the chair in the corner of her bedroom. This was the chair she studied her Bible in, and did deep thinking in, and prayed in. Now seemed to be a good time for deep thought.

What did Ernest Bostwick really mean to her? First, he was a renter. He had been a joy in that regard. His monthly rent on his store always arrived in her mail a couple days before it was due. He didn't make demands for building improvements, just routine repairs. Ernie had been glad to let Gloria lead a Bible study in his store every Thursday morning. Then again, her incentive had been to lower his rent by two hundred dollars a month, so it was not terribly surprising that he consented to the Bible study. On the other hand, he chose to participate as much as he could and gave every attendee free coffee.

Ernie had become more than just a renter. He was a customer, buying muffins and cookies she made, for sale in the store.

He was also a dear friend. Ernie Bostwick had, at times, been a shoulder to cry on and, at other times, been eager to help her celebrate her joys. He was a caring listener and kept in confidence any deep secrets she shared.

How much of a friend was he? Would people consider Ernie her boyfriend? Heavens, no! This would only be the fourth time they'd been out together, and she knew he had been out with Cindy Martin a little too.

The most important thing, she had to admit, was that Ernie was a person who had isolated himself from other Christians. God was using her as one means to bring him back into a church. It didn't have to be her church although it looked like that might be the will of God. Ernie Bostwick, when back on the front lines of God's army, could be incredibly important in leading others to

Christ and in encouraging other Christians. He just had amazing relational skills. God wanted to use him.

Gloria loved being with Ernie and would like to see their relationship blossom. It hurt her to realize that her first priority was not to bring Ernie closer to Gloria, but to God.

❧

The black Jeep Cherokee pulled into Gloria's driveway a scant minute before six o'clock. Ernie never wanted to be late, but he knew enough about women that he knew they would be getting ready for a date right up to the last minute, so he really didn't want to be early either.

He was only halfway to the door when Gloria came out. "I'm all ready," she said. Her gray and pink pantsuit complemented his dark gray slacks and pink shirt incredibly well. "This will be quite an adventure. I haven't had anything more Chinese than an egg roll in ten years."

"I've been hungry for a couple hours. I hope you don't mind if I don't use chopsticks. I think I'd starve."

"I don't mind at all. I could use them, but every time I do, I get food on my clothes. If they don't have any real silverware, I've got two plastic forks in my purse."

Ernie chuckled as he opened the Jeep door for her. "That's what I call being prepared."

But she wasn't prepared for what she saw when she started to get in the car. Another man was riding in the backseat, staring straight ahead through sunglasses.

"Oh!"

"You don't mind, do you?" Ernie asked.

Gloria reached out her hand to the man, saying, "So glad you could join us. I'm Gloria."

Ernie had covered his mouth with his hand, evidently holding back some kind of emotion.

The man in the back did not respond to Gloria. She slowly retracted her hand. Ernie still stood by her door.

"I'm sorry, Gloria. I was sure you had met Henry."

"Pleased to meet you, Henry. *Henry?* You dummy, what are *you* doing here?!" Gloria stepped back out of the car and swatted a laughing Ernie Bostwick. She couldn't help but join in the hilarity, her knees growing weak as she exploded in laughter. Ernie caught her in his arms, and they stood laughing for another minute before he loosened his hug.

Ernie helped Gloria into the car a second time then came around to the driver's side and got in. "I thought Dan-O might enjoy seeing his old pal again. How does he look?"

Gloria turned in her seat and looked over the mannequin. Henry wore black pants, a white shirt with a blue print tie, and a black hat with a blue hatband. "I think you did a great job. How much did you have to spend on his outfit?"

"Let's just say it was north of five dollars and south of ten."

"How are we going to get him in the restaurant?"

"I asked Henry if he was hungry. He didn't say anything, so we'll just let him sit in the car."

"Welcome, good friends! Kim, this is Ernie Boston and Gloria Smith. We met one night when I was cleaning out things from the clothing store. Ernie and Gloria, this is my wife, Kim." Dan-O Tang beamed from ear to ear. The restaurant was very nearly full of customers.

Ernie reached out to shake Kim Tang's hand. "Pleased to meet you. I'm Ernie Bostwick. Dan-O did a good job of remembering our names."

Gloria shook hands with Kim and Dan-O then said, "Dan-O, we are so happy we could be here to celebrate your grand opening. We brought another friend to see you, but he didn't want to get out of the car. Can you come out to say a word to Henry?"

Dan-O looked puzzled but kept the wide smile on his face. "Certainly!"

Kim said, "I'd better stay inside and watch over the workers. You go ahead."

Gloria, Ernie, and Dan-O stepped outside to Ernie's Jeep Cherokee.

Ernie said, "Henry, here's Dan-O to see you." Ernie opened the back driver's side door, and Dan-O stepped up to Henry's side.

Dan-O called out, "So good to see you, Henry." Henry didn't make any move to acknowledge Dan-O's presence. "I'm glad you could come, sir."

Ernie eased up to Dan-O's side. "He never speaks. You remember the night we met that I saw Henry upside down in a box by the dumpster?"

Dan-O put his forefinger to his chin, deep in thought. Suddenly he burst out in great guffaws, putting his hands on his knees to keep from falling over. Tears began to roll down his cheeks, inciting laughter in Ernie and Gloria.

"You got me that time! Oh, that's a good one. He looks so real the way you have him dressed up. Gloria and Ernie, I am so glad you came! You made my day even bigger than it already was. I thank you! Now, come eat."

❧

Empty soup bowls sat next to their plates. Ernie dipped another piece of pork into the red sauce in another small bowl.

"I'm sure your sesame chicken can't possibly be as good as my sweet and sour pork, Gloria. This is incredible."

"Your sweet and sour pork may be incredible, but this sesame chicken is the best thing I've ever eaten. If every item on the menu is this good, the Tangs will make a fortune here. Are you going to have dessert?"

Ernie finished his mouthful and replied, "That depends. Do you have to go straight home?"

"Well, I didn't really dress for bowling."

"I was thinking along the lines of miniature golf. Do you putt-putt?"

Gloria shook her head. "Ernie, I had to give it up. I'm too good. I just embarrass anyone I'm with."

He grinned. "Let's do it then. I'm not easily embarrassed. Maybe we can get a shake at the Dairy Barn afterward."

"That sounds wonderful. But don't say I didn't warn you."

After they finished eating and declined the waiter's invitation to order dessert, Gloria and Ernie headed for the door. "I want to speak to Dan-O and Kim before we leave," said Ernie.

Kim Tang walked up after they had only taken a few steps. "How was your meal?"

Gloria spoke first. "Excellent. Please thank the cook for us. We look forward to coming back soon. Right, Ernie?"

"We'll certainly try. It really was good."

Dan-O came up just then. "I told Kim that she must see Henry before you leave. The last time she saw him, he was dressed in less than rags."

❧

As they drove to the miniature golf course, Gloria ventured, "That was a pretty sizeable tip, wasn't it? Something like twenty-five percent."

"I guess people consider me a pretty generous tipper, though there are only a few dollars difference, usually, between an average tipper and a big tipper. I can afford a little extra every now and then if it helps someone feel appreciated. I like to invest in people."

"You really care about people, don't you? It shows in all you do."

"I do, because I enjoy it. Gloria, when I first became a Christian, I cared because I wanted to be like Jesus. He is my example and my leader, my lord. But it was almost like a duty. I was doing it to please him."

She looked a little puzzled. "That all sounds right."

Ernie was visibly excited about this subject. "But I found out why Jesus wants me to care. It's fun! It has made my life so much better. God wants me to have the most blessed life possible. I really enjoy doing good for others. I enjoy the way they love me back. And when they don't, I still enjoy their reaction. I know I'm making the world better by making *my* world better."

Gloria reached over and touched his arm. "You're a good man, Ernie Bostwick."

ॐ

She tried one putter and then another. The fifth candidate seemed just right. "It's not just the length. The balance feels just right on this one."

Ernie smiled and grabbed a putter. "This one will do. I'll use a bright yellow ball. Pink golf ball for you?"

"That's right. How did you know?"

"It matches your outfit."

They waited at the first hole for a teen couple to finish. The course had two windmills, jungle animals, bridges, and palm trees. There were about a dozen people scattered over the eighteen-hole course.

When the boy and girl ahead of them finished the first hole, Ernie said, "Ladies first?"

"I'd be glad to. Thank you." Gloria placed her ball on the eight-inch-square green starting pad. The cup was twelve feet away, straight ahead and slightly uphill. She lined up the putt, studied it for about four seconds, and then tapped the ball firmly. It went straight for the hole and rattled in. She smiled with satisfaction.

"Good, but I'd better be careful not to hit it too hard."

Ernie just said, "Hmm."

He stroked his moustache a few times then stepped back. He looked at the metal side rails about four feet apart. Stepping up, he placed his yellow ball on the green pad. He lined up his putt then stared at a spot on the right rail, halfway to the cup. With a smooth, firm stroke, Ernie caromed the ball off the rail and into the hole.

"Good shot," said Gloria. "Why didn't you hit it straight in?"

"It worked, didn't it?"

The next hole had a right angle to the left at the eight-foot mark. The cup was then twelve feet farther away, partially guarded by two upright pipes, twelve inches apart.

Gloria hit her pink ball straight into the angled rail at the first corner. It gently rolled toward the hole and stopped within three feet. She stepped up to the ball and hit it straight into the middle of the cup.

"Good work," said Ernie. "I'm glad you went first."

He addressed his ball and hit it in the same direction as Gloria, but a little harder. It just missed the hole, bouncing off the end rail. It stopped two feet away from the hole, but one of the three-inch pipes was between the ball and the hole.

"Ooh, that's a shame. That was a good shot, Ernie."

He studied the situation from several angles then stepped up and banked the yellow ball into the cup. "Was that okay?" he asked Gloria.

She smirked and headed to the next hole.

After nine holes, Gloria was five under par, three strokes ahead of Ernie.

I can see why you're so good at this," said Ernie. "You always hit the ball straight."

"And you're always looking for an angle."

"Correction: I'm always looking for a way to have more fun."

On the second half of the course, Gloria continued to do well. The exceptions were the two windmill holes. The blades of the windmill came down to a fraction of an inch from the putting surface, sweeping in front of a tunnel that was the only route between the starting pad and the cup. Gloria had trouble timing her stroke to miss the blades of the windmill and got a four on both windmill holes. Ernie avoided trouble there.

At the end of the course, he trailed Gloria by two strokes. "Should I be embarrassed?" he asked.

"Only slightly," said Gloria.

இ

Ernie and Gloria settled into a red vinyl booth near the front of the Dairy Barn. "I'm glad we stopped here," she said. "Supper seems so long ago."

"Chinese food has a reputation of not lasting."

The waiter arrived for their order. "Don't I know you?" said Gloria.

"You certainly do," said Teddy Jarvis. "I'm Ernie's number one juggling student. I've seen you at his store several times."

"Still like this job, Teddy?" said Ernie.

"Yes, sir. I really enjoy serving people and seeing the looks on their faces when I bring their food."

"You and Ernie have a lot in common," said Gloria. "You get your joy in bringing joy to others."

"Yes, ma'am. Now what joy would you like to order tonight?"

"I'd like a medium vanilla shake, please."

"And you, Mr. B?"

Ernie stroked his moustache a couple times. "Let me try something adventurous, Teddy. If I order a vanilla shake, what could I add to it?"

"Lots of things. There's banana, peppermint, chocolate candy, caramel—"

Ernie interrupted, "That sounds great! Make it a medium."

❧

"I'm just curious," said Gloria as she finished her milk shake. "You said in Bible study yesterday that your days of staying home from church are over. Does that mean you'll be at Northside every Sunday now?"

"I'm not really sure. I know that God wanted me to start there. I'm coming back this week because the young folks I sat with last week invited me back. I get the feeling God will show me a place I'm really needed."

Lord, let it be at our church, she prayed silently.

CHAPTER 27

I s this the same church?

Young men and women were greeting everybody that walked up to Northside Church today even before they got to the door. Their sincere smiles and enthusiasm were contagious.

As Ernie left his Cherokee, a tanned black-haired man stepped toward him. "Hey, you're back! Good to see you again, Ernie." Arnie extended his hand in greeting.

"I knew you had a place for me," said Ernie. "It's the only place in town where I'm called a young adult."

"There's a place at Northside for you, I promise. We'll be sitting in our usual spot once the service starts."

"It's great to see you again, Arnie."

Ernie continued on toward the sanctuary door. A short red-haired lady met him and said, "Welcome. It's a great day. I'm Sandra."

"Good morning, Sandra. I'm Ernie Bostwick. Are you part of the young adult Sunday school class?"

"Yes, I am. We volunteer as greeters every Sunday." With a twinkle in her eye, she said, "Consider yourself greeted." Sandra threw her arms around Ernie and gave him a quick hug.

"Last Sunday was my first visit here. How did I miss the greeters last week?"

Sandra's face grew more serious. "That was my fault. I had a messy breakup with my boyfriend, and my classmates spent the time between Sunday school and church praying for me."

"Sounds like a great class. By the way, six of them came and sat by me during church last week. I felt really welcomed."

Ernie stepped inside and immediately saw Callie. "Come on, Ernie, let's grab a seat." They made their way to the same pew they occupied the previous Sunday.

"So, how did your class end up with the opportunity of being greeters every week?"

"No one else seemed to notice the need," she answered. "A lot of the members have been here so long that they forgot what it's like to be a visitor. Somebody needed to keep new people from feeling lost."

"You're doing a great job," said Ernie.

"We're the future of the church," Callie replied. "If nobody welcomes the visitors, there might not be a church in the future."

He could tell by the music that worship would be beginning soon. More young adults came to sit in the pew Ernie and Callie occupied, plus the pew immediately in front of them.

Frank, another of the young adults Ernie had met last week, came in with Cindy Martin. "Good morning, Ernie. I'm glad you're back. I found this pretty lady looking for you."

"Just like you said, Ernie," Cindy remarked as she sat down next to him. "You're here in the midst of the young adults."

"We consider him one of us," said Kate. "Actually, we'd like to claim you as part of the gang too. Okay?"

Cindy smiled. "Sure. It's always nice to have a place to belong."

Ernie whispered, "See the lady at this end of the second pew? That's the young adult Sunday school teacher, Jana."

Cindy's eyes grew big. The woman looked to be in her eighties.

From Ernie's other side, Callie whispered, "Jana's going to retire from teaching us in less than two weeks. She's moving to Florida."

Ernie had no trouble following the order of worship during the first half of the service, but Cindy had no church background. "What's an offertory? How do we know when to stand? What is children's church? Is a dollar enough to give?' He patiently answered all her whispered questions. Still he was glad when Dan stood up to preach, knowing that Cindy would settle in for the morning message.

Dan led the congregation in a short responsive reading then stepped away from the pulpit and began to slowly pace.

"I don't remember my dreams anymore. I guess they aren't all that memorable. When I wake up from a dream, it takes only a minute or two for it to slip from my memory. Is that normal?

"But when I was a kid, two themes kept coming up in my dreams. In one, I'd be trying to get someplace, but something would always keep me from getting there. Maybe I'd lose my ticket, or I'd take a wrong turn, or it would be farther away than I had originally thought. I couldn't reach my destination.

"And in the other kind of dream, I'd get too close to a drop-off of some kind and fall off a cliff. When I'd wake up from that kind of dream, I'd find that I had fallen out of bed and onto the floor.

"Those two kinds of dreams were more like nightmares, I guess. They didn't have happy endings. What was lacking was a bridge in both cases. I needed something to get me from where I was to a safe destination.

"Many people live out those nightmares today, wide awake. They can't get to where they want to be, or they sense a cliff coming up. The answer to both is Jesus.

"Let me read to you from the book of John, chapter 14."

Ernie was enthralled with Dan's way of weaving the plan of salvation into Jesus's farewell message to his disciples. The pastor equated the words, "I am the way, the truth, and the life" to Jesus's proclaiming himself to be a bridge to eternal life. Glancing to his left, Ernie could see that Cindy was hanging on every word.

"Jesus is the truth people want to find. He's the one standard for good and right that doesn't have to be adjusted to different situations. We are the ones that have to adjust. There is a rock-solid standard of truth.

"And I find that the more I change to fit the Bible's pattern of commandments and statutes and rules, the more I find life. I don't always understand why the Bible says to do what it does, but when I follow it, my life is better.

"The Bible is from God, and Jesus and God are one with the Holy Spirit. Do you see how Jesus could say that he is the truth and the life?" Dan paused to let people consider that question.

"And Jesus is the way, the bridge, to God. To be justified, after all our mistakes and undone deeds with God, we need more than to give our whole lives to God. It would not be enough. God is holy, and we are impure, so even giving our whole selves to God would not justify us.

"But God's policy is that he would take Jesus's death on the cross as payment for our sins. We only have to accept that plan. It seems too good to be true, but many of us have found that it *is* true. If you'll accept God's offer of Jesus as the bridge to being justified in God's eyes, your life will change immediately, and you will know that you are accepted by the creator of the universe."

Cindy was deep in thought. Ernie wondered if she was thinking about Dan's message, or whether her concentration was on what she would do later today or tomorrow.

The song leader was now at the podium. "As we sing our closing hymn, if you are ready today to take God up on his incredible deal, please come forward as we sing, and pastor Dan or I will pray with you. Friends, nothing will ever compare with getting into a right relationship with God."

As the congregation sang "What a Friend We Have in Jesus," three people came forward. Ernie looked at Cindy, who was not singing but was intensely watching those at the front of the church. He touched her arm and asked, "Would you like me to walk down front with you?"

She glanced his way and shook her head. "Not today."

၆

Cindy excused herself immediately after the closing prayer with, "I think I see somebody I know. I'll see you in the morning, Ernie. Cinnamon Blueberry."

He turned to Callie and the young adults beside her. "You should all come by my store sometime. I've got some great coffee."

"Callie said you've got juggling supplies," said Frank. "That's kind of crazy. Maybe I could learn to juggle."

"You can't hang onto money," said Callie. "I don't know how you'd learn how to handle Indian clubs and balls."

"It might help him with a lot of things, even money," said Kate.

Ernie's eyes brightened. "Are y'all busy today, say seven o'clock? I need some help rearranging furniture. Come on down, and I'll treat you to free coffee and muffins."

"As long as you have some decaf too," said Liz.

Arnie clapped his hands together. "Sounds like a party."

❧

"You took a mighty big chance, driving all the way up here without calling first," said Opal Carrollton. "I might have been out shopping or playing golf."

"I suppose it was a risk," responded Ernie. "Is it usually hard to find you at home on Sunday afternoon?"

"Actually, I'm always here on Sunday afternoon. You're just lucky I had finished my nap." Opal opened the door wide for Ernie to enter. He followed her to a small room with four flowered upholstered chairs.

"Betty had this picked out for my sister's sitting room. She figured an old bird like Mavis needed a nest, a little room that was her private space. Now it's my nest. It's even got room for a friend or two to visit."

Jesus was there. Everywhere he turned, Ernie saw a picture or plaque with the Savior in it. A picture of Jesus laughing was centered over one bookshelf. "I am the way, the truth, and the life" was on a sign over the door. Another picture showed Jesus with a child in his lap and children all around. Another plaque proclaimed "There is only one right way. The Jesus way."

It was obvious which chair Opal usually sat in. It showed more wear than the other three. On a little table next to it were a well-worn Bible, a devotional book, and a pair of reading glasses. Directly across the room from that chair was the most striking picture of all.

"Opal, that is just an amazing image. It looks so real, and yet I know it can't be."

"Ernie, that is as real as anything in here. I walk hand in hand with Jesus every day I live. But I know what you mean.

"I was at a craft fair a few months ago with Betty. She had to stop and rest, so, just out of curiosity, I went on to a corner booth we had skipped earlier. An artist displayed photographs he had made by combining a photograph with a painting. By posing a person just right, he could cut out their image, place it in front of a painting, and take a photograph that made it look like the present-day customer was actually in the picture."

Ernie gazed at the picture for a long time. Opal sat down in her chair and opened the front cover of her Bible. She copied a name and telephone number from a business card onto a scrap of paper and handed to Ernie.

"What's this?" he said.

"It's the name and phone number of the artist. You need a picture just like that. Just mention my name, and he'll know the kind of picture you're talking about."

Ernie smiled and put the slip into his wallet. He sat in a chair opposite his host.

"I'm back in church, Opal."

"Of course you are. That's what I told you to do, and I wouldn't expect you to be here if you weren't back in church. Is it the church we went to on Easter? That was a little modern for me."

"No. I would have loved to go back there. It was a lot like the last church I was a member of without the controversy. But God encouraged me to go to Northside."

The elderly lady laughed. "Trust in the Lord with all your heart. Don't lean on your own understanding. Do you know why you're there?"

"It's pretty obvious, but kind of scary. A group of young adults has claimed me as one of their own. I recognized this as one of those situations God engineers. And now they tell me that they will need a new Sunday school teacher in two weeks. Everything I hear from God confirms that I should volunteer to be their new teacher."

"So why does that frighten you? Surely you've taught a class before."

Ernie fidgeted in his chair. "It happened so suddenly. For years I've worshiped on my own. Now I'm the leader of a mob."

"Peter wrote that we should always be ready to share the hope that is in us. Maybe you're a little rusty. Step up to the plate, Ernie. You'll do fine."

Ernie smiled and nodded. Opal could see that he turned to another page in his mind, ready to talk about something else.

He sat quietly, stroking his moustache a few times and focusing his eyes on something far away.

"Opal, when you visited my store, you remarked that nothing in there told a customer that the proprietor loved the Lord. I've been mulling that over. I've developed a little space near the left end. God spoke to me that this space was to be used for ministry. I've decided to have a special Christian sharing time two Fridays a month, maybe call it 'Coffee with Jesus.' I'll encourage people to share songs, poetry, short stories, all with a Christian perspective."

"Kind of an open-mike night, or Christian karaoke?"

"Yes. That's right."

"Do you have a karaoke machine, or some kind of audio equipment?"

"I probably won't need it. The space isn't that big. I wouldn't expect to have more than ten people at least at the start."

"Ernie, what will the space look like during the rest of the month? Just an empty spot?"

He didn't answer right away. This little lady was sharp, and about a half-step ahead of him in her thinking.

"I want something to sell that is for ministry, some Christian item that encourages spiritual growth. I'm not sure what it will be yet."

"You've got some praying to do. And let me pray for you right now, then I'll go make us some coffee. Do you drink instant?"

Ernie laughed. "If you pray over it, I'll be okay."

On the way home, he called the telephone number Opal had jotted down. He recognized that it was a Barkley number.

"Don Jarvis. Can I help you?"

Ernie paused. The name sounded familiar.

"Hello?"

Ernie found his voice. "Hello, my name is Ernie Bostwick. I've just seen a picture you did for a lady named Opal Carrollton, and I'm really impressed with it. It depicts Opal walking hand in hand with Jesus. I'm wondering if you can do one like that for me."

"I surely can. But it doesn't have to be just like that. Ernie, I don't suppose you could stop by this afternoon, could you? I'd be glad to show you the pictures we could put you in, and let you see what kind of photograph I'd need of you. Actually, I do best when I can pose you and take the photo myself. I live at the corner of Maple and Main in Barkley."

Ernie glanced at his watch. "Yes, I can be there in about ten minutes."

"That's great. By the way, Teddy never stops talking about how great a juggler you are."

CHAPTER 28

Glen picked up the roll of *Wall Street Journals* on his way in the door and headed for the coffee urns.

Something was different. First, Erie was not sitting in his favorite chair. Second, and more important, lamps and tables to his left were all out of place.

"Ernie, what's going on? Are you in here?"

"Over here, Glen, behind the lamps." Glen saw a waving hand appear.

Tall floor lamps, spaced three or four feet apart, formed a large quarter circle that centered on the back left corner of the room. Between the lamps were four-foot-high bookshelves or white folding chairs.

Other chairs sat in a row between the outer ring and a platform, about four feet by eight feet, in the corner of the room.

On this makeshift stage was a chair, occupied by the night-and-day resident of the store, Henry.

"Glen, welcome to my coffeehouse." Ernie chuckled. "You are the first to see the changes we made last night."

Glen stepped into the cordoned-off area and looked slowly in all directions. Table lamps stood as a border in front of the stage. To Henry's left was the bamboo thingamajig that had become Melissa's idea of a decorative light source.

"What do you think? You're not saying much." Ernie stood up from a folding chair near the wall.

"I don't know what to say. It sure is different. Are you going to have some kind of show this morning? Or is this one of those beatnik coffeehouses from the sixties?"

"I think I'm going to call it 'Coffee with Jesus.' I had a little extra space, so I'm going to let people come in on Friday nights and sing Christian songs they wrote, or read Christian poems they put together, that kind of thing. Kind of like a Christian talent show."

"Christian juggling?"

"Sure," said Ernie. "Anything that has a Christian message to it. God told me to use the space for ministry."

"And coffee, right? 'Coffee with Jesus' has got to serve coffee."

"Three kinds of coffee. Two decaf and one regular."

"Hey, Ernie, what did you do with the books?"

Ernie smiled and stepped up on the stage. "They're here, behind Henry. He distracted you from noticing the shelves on the two walls behind him. I knew I shouldn't have let him wear that pink shirt."

❧

The jingling bell announced the day's second customer.

"I remembered you'd want Cinnamon Blueberry today. Was I right?"

Cindy beamed. "Perfect!" She accepted the blue No Better Day than Today mug from Ernie's hand and eagerly took a sip.

"I'm sorry I ran off after church yesterday. I wanted to say hi to Gloria. I saw her in the choir."

Cindy's eyes caught the rearranged part of the store. She stood motionless, eyes moving back and forth. Her gaze stopped at the stage. Gradually a smile began, growing by the second. "A coffeehouse!" she gasped.

She sat her coffee mug on the counter and dashed out the door to her car. Judging by the bobbing of her head, Cindy was looking for something in the glove compartment. After a minute, she emerged from the car, dashed back into Ernie's with a piece of yellow paper in her hand, and made her way to Henry's side.

"I'm going to try out your stage, Henry." She unfolded the paper and started reading:

The Hesitating Foot, by Cynthia Martin.

I've happened on a forest path,

Slightly hidden, hard to see.

I cannot pass it by. It's now

Somehow calling out to me.

I'd heard of this trail, times before,

But it never caught my eye.

Had I been seeking something more,

Or just looking at the sky?

Some, I knew, had strode that path,

And never were the same.

They had a glow, that would ever last,

A life force they had tamed.

I thought it not much more than fable.

I did not try to search.

I built a road, and made it stable,

With money, stone and earth.

Why should I try to find a way

That promised little might?

Upon my self-built road I'd stay,

Not hidden, in plain sight.

But now the path is square before me.

I know God called me here.

The path is Jesus, surely, only.

Do I dare, or do I fear?"

Ernie stood and applauded, as did Gloria, who had quietly slipped in.

"Well done," he exclaimed. "Can you read it again Friday night?"

"This Friday? Wow, you're really going to do the coffee shop thing that quick? Yes, I'd like to read it again. Who helped you move things?"

Gloria said, "I recognize some of this furniture, but it certainly didn't look like this the last time I was in here."

"The young adults from Northside Church came down last night and helped me move things. Gloria, the stage was here when I moved in three years ago, but I had disassembled it and had it in my storeroom."

"Do I recognize these chairs?" said Cindy. "They look just like the ones my cousin rented for her wedding last month."

"The white wood folding chairs were in my garage. I got them at an estate sale last year, forty of them. Everything else was here. Just in different order."

"I've got to run, Ernie," said Cindy. "But where are the books?"

Gloria echoed, "Yes, where are the books?"

❧

Thirty minutes later, after a dozen customers had gotten newspapers and coffee (and a few muffins), Gloria and Ernie sat with their cups of Seattle Sunrise.

"The stage looks great, Ernie. Is it going to stay like this all the time?"

"I'm not sure. There's a little something missing."

"Can you add more books? You used to have more."

He shook his head. "They really weren't pulling their weight as far as sales go. And that thing my friend, Opal, said sticks with me. There ought to be something in this store that plainly says I'm a Christian. I never meant for it to be a secret."

They sat in silence for a few minutes. Gloria liked how her friend was changing. It was more than just church attendance. He was listening for God's guidance and actually hearing it. He had always been a good Christian man from the first day she met him. Now he was a growing Christian, emerging from stagnation, and that was so much better.

Not only was Ernie more attractive, he had a renewed interest in dating. Somewhere in his past, he had been deeply hurt in a relationship, she could tell.

On the other hand, perhaps she had recovered from her husband's untimely death. Maybe she seemed datable.

"There's a space, maybe four feet square, that needs something Christian," said Ernie. "I just don't know what it is yet. I'll ask Jack when I see him again. He has connections."

❧

The early morning eight-thirty-to-nine-thirty crowd was his favorite. Even the grumpy customers transformed with a good cup of coffee. The pause for filling new urns of coffee was inevitably a time of great fellowship, including encouragement for the proprietor.

"Man! Look at him go!"

"I'm timing you, Ernie. Thirty-one, thirty-two, th… done! New record!"

"Oh yeah! He made that American in Paris today. Good stuff!"

"I know he'll always have Seattle Sunrise. Ernie drinks that."

Depending on his route for the day, Jack Rhodes sometimes beat this crowd. Other times, like today, he caught the tail end of it.

"Short trip today, Ernie. I've just got a dozen stops around Columbus then up to West Point. Whoa, looks like you made the changes you were talking about."

Jack walked over to shake Henry's hand and rub his head. "Hope you can sing, Henry. Hey, Ernie. I've got something in the trunk for you. It's just what you need for this empty spot over here."

Ernie looked over at Jack. "More books?"

"I thought you were cutting back on books."

Ernie responded, "That was my intent. It seems like everybody is asking today, 'Where are the books?'"

"Maybe this will make them forget the books. Just a minute, I'll go get it." Jack went out the door to his car.

Maybe books could sell if Ernie specialized a little. He needed to appeal to a niche market. Ernie decided he would think through what sold best and try to carry more of that and less of other books.

Jack came back in with a long, narrow box and a smaller, square box.

"This, my friend, will make you the only source in town for a growing product line. You might even become your own best customer."

Ernie watched quietly as Jack removed pieces of metal tubing from the narrow box. In less than two minutes, Jack had put together a five-foot-tall rotating rack. He moved it to the empty space just outside the cordoned-off entertainment area.

"Fits the spot, Jack. You sure know your empty spaces. Maybe all I need is an empty rack."

Jack smiled at Ernie. "Empty racks don't make money. You wanted something that labeled this a Christian store, right? There's a growing market for contemporary Christian CDs, and there really is no place in Barkley to buy them. You'll even have some of those eighties praise songs you love so much, buddy."

"Hey, I'm not that far behind the times. Jack, you know the market better than me. How big an investment are we talking about?"

"Believe me, you can handle this. The rack has sixty-four slots, sixteen on a side. You'll want to start with two hundred CDs. That's about three per slot. I own the rack, and you only pay for what you sell."

Ernie stroked his moustache a few times. Jack knew how to sell. "So you're saying I pay you nothing today?"

"That's right. So the only downside is you'd be labeled a Christian business from now on. You pretty much know the pluses and minuses of that."

"Sold. Jack, if this doesn't work out, do you have any other ideas?"

"Books. Christian books."

Ernie wondered if there might be room for both.

❧

It had been a great Monday. Was this National Coffee Day? He'd better get a coffee order together now that Melissa was here. Then he'd have to give Friday night's coffeehouse some thought.

This really needed a flyer. Callie and Arnie and the young adults said they would invite friends for this Friday's Christian talent show. Ernie needed to put together an information sheet of some kind that they could hand out.

Time, place, invited participants, all that could fit on an index card. What he needed was a picture.

"Mr. B, phone's for you."

"Thank you, Melissa." Ernie picked up the telephone by the cash register.

"Ernie? Don Jarvis. Look, I've about got your picture ready. Just need to frame it. Do you suppose you could stop by and take a look at the proof? I think you'll love it, so if you don't have time, I'll just go ahead."

Ernie looked around the store. He had three clock orders that had to be finished by tomorrow noon, but that would take no more than an hour. Melissa had the coffee urns caught up. There were two customers in the store.

"Tell you what, Don. Give me fifteen minutes. If I don't get there, just go ahead. I don't want to hold you up."

"Okay. That'll work. See you soon."

Melissa spoke up, "Mr. B, if you need to run an errand, just go ahead. I'll be all right."

He turned, bowed low, and slipped out the door.

❧

The picture was stunning. Jesus sat on a boulder, speaking casually. There were no crowds, just a close friend sitting on another boulder. The other man was dressed in blue jeans and a white polo shirt.

"Ernie, you're not saying anything. Do you approve?"

Ernie Bostwick only continued to stare at the photo of Jesus, amazed at how natural it was to see his own likeness in the picture.

"Don, can I ask you a favor? Can you make me a dozen copies of the proof on your copier?"

❧

It looked like a party.

When Ernie returned to his store, all the seats in the area near the coffee urns were occupied, plus a folding chair. Everybody had a mug of coffee and a cookie or muffin.

"Hey, Ernie," called out Sarah. "Great coffee!"

"You didn't have any American in Paris brewed yesterday," said Frank. "It's tremendous."

"Just thought we'd stop by," said Callie. "What have people said about the room arrangement?"

Ernie smiled. "At first, they're stunned. It's a big change. Then they're curious about Friday night. And nearly everybody asks where the books are."

"Have you got any flyers we can post around town?" asked Kate.

Ernie produced the copies of the proof Don Jarvis had made. "Almost. If we could just write in the time and place around the border of this picture, I think it would make a great advertisement."

Ernie passed the pictures out to the seven young adults around him.

"Wow!" said Callie. "That's perfect! The picture looks so…real. How did you do that?"

"It's a combination of a photo of me and a picture of Jesus. The dad of my juggling student makes these. He'll have a framed picture of this, full color, before Friday."

Arnie made a point of clearing his throat very loudly, and Callie caught the hint.

"Ernie, there is another purpose to our visiting you today. Here, sit down in this chair." She promptly got up from the green recliner, and Ernie dutifully sat down.

Callie continued, "We love our Sunday school class. It has been kind of the glue to keep us and our lives together. We'd like you to be part of our class." Callie paused. She seemed to be searching for her next words.

Liz jumped in. "What we're getting at is, we're losing our teacher soon. If we don't find a replacement, the church may just take the first volunteer for the job."

Callie found her voice. "Ernie, would you be our teacher?"

The other young adults all looked at him and indicated their assent with a nod.

Ernie felt honored but also ganged up on. "Let me ask your pastor. After all, I've only attended twice. He may say that's too little to test my commitment."

CHAPTER 29

"I'm excited about tonight. Aren't you?" said Cindy.

"You're always excited about Friday night since you cut back your hours at French's. I understand."

"Ernie, you know what I mean. And I'm ready for the first 'Coffee with Jesus' with two more poems."

"Great! You know I'm expecting the one you recited last Monday too. Is our friend from the sandwich shop coming?"

"I think so. I told him about it, and he's supposed to be off," said Cindy.

Ernie thought through a list of performers for tonight's coffeehouse. Teddy was coming to juggle. Sandra had written a short story. Kate and Arnie were singing a duet with CD accompaniment. Besides Cindy's poetry and the song Clint sang to them at the sandwich shop, that was all that was planned. Of course, anyone would be allowed to perform without prior notice. Callie mentioned putting some clean jokes together for a monologue, but Ernie wasn't counting on her; it was probably a bigger job than she thought it would be.

"What do you think of the CD display I put in this week?" Ernie walked over to the rotating rack Jack had installed on Monday and looked back at Cindy.

"To tell the truth, Ernie, I don't recognize any of these singers. All this church stuff is new to me. I did see one song title I recognized on one of those karaoke CDs. They sang it in church last Sunday."

Ernie slowly turned the rack. Some of the artists he was very familiar with from his days at the River. Most he had at least heard of. Until Cindy mentioned it, he had not even noticed the karaoke CDs at the bottom of one panel.

"Somebody could sing along with a karaoke CD if you had any way to play it," said Cindy.

"What do I need? Kate and Arnie are bringing a CD player for their song tonight. Would that do?"

"No, you need the words displayed for the singer too. A karaoke machine has a CD player, a big speaker, and a screen for the words."

"Cindy, do I sense that you've done a little karaoke singing?"

"Maybe."

෴

The new picture drew several remarks since Ernie put it on display Wednesday.

"That's just unbelievable," said Glen. "Jesus and you both sitting with a cup of coffee. It looks as natural as you and me on a morning in your store. You owe Don Jarvis a lot more than whatever you paid him for that picture."

Ernie smiled with pride. "It wasn't cheap, but you're right. It's priceless. It was the inspiration for what I'm calling our Friday night Christian coffeehouse gatherings, 'Coffee with Jesus.'"

"Hmm." Glen walked around a little, looking at the picture from several angles. He looked at Ernie and raised his right index finger ready to make a point. Glen opened his mouth to speak but thought better of it. He stared at the picture a few more seconds.

Ernie ventured, "You were going to tell me what you would name the picture, weren't you?"

"How did you know?"

Ernie smiled. "I'll bet I had the same thought when I first looked at it. The name Don gave it is on the back. I totally agree."

Glen walked over to the picture and tilted it enough to read the plate on the back. "That's it. No other name would do. What else would you call having a talk with Jesus but 'prayer'?"

Glen gathered up his newspaper and headed for the door. "Hey, I'll be here for the coffeehouse. Anything to support a friend."

∂◦

After lunch Friday, Ernie made a final check on supplies. He expected at least ten people for Coffee with Jesus, but what if twenty showed up? "Sometimes curiosity brings in more than direct invitation," he spoke aloud to Henry. The mannequin did not disagree.

There was plenty of coffee. Two urns would contain his two decaffeinated varieties, and the other would have Reggae Blend, a flavor he hadn't brewed since Callie and friends had discovered his store. There was an adequate amount of cookies and muffins. On the other hand, what if people were especially hungry? What if a few extra people came? He decided he was succumbing to first-time jitters and did his best to put the scenario out of his head.

He checked the seating in the coffeehouse area. In total, there were fifteen chairs. Other guests could carry a chair or two over from the usual coffee area. Of course, there were two chairs on stage.

Unless an unusually large crowd came, everything was ready. There really was no reason to expect more than a dozen people this first time. No reason at all.

The jingle of a bell announced the arrival of another customer.

"Gloria, so good to see you. What's in the box?" Ernie stepped over to help her with her package.

"It's cookies for tonight. I thought perhaps a different flavor just for the coffeehouse nights, might encourage people to come back. It's peanut butter cookies with crunchy peanut butter made from my grandmother's recipe."

"Are they the same size and price as the other two varieties?" the proprietor inquired.

"Yes, I did that to make it easier for you. I've got to warn you though. Once you try one, you'll beg me to raise the price!"

Ernie opened the box to retrieve a peanut butter cookie. "Hmm."

He finished the cookie in four bites. He looked at the ceiling and stroked his moustache a couple times.

"Well?" Gloria watched Ernie intensely, eager to hear his verdict on the cookie.

"I'm not sure," he said. He got a second cookie, finishing it in three bites this time.

"So tell me if you like them."

Ernie reached for another cookie, and Gloria slapped his hand. "I can tell you like them. Stop."

He grinned and closed the container of cookies.

"I hope church is like those cookies," Gloria added. She served herself a mug of Cinnamon Blueberry and sat down.

Ernie did his best not to ask her to explain her last statement. He knew she wanted him to inquire, but he would wait her out this time.

Gloria picked up a newspaper and glanced at the headlines on the front page. She slowly read from top to bottom then turned the page.

"Why?" said Ernie.

"Why what? Were we talking about something?"

"You said that you hope church is like those cookies."

"Did I say that?"

Ernie nodded.

Gloria folded the newspaper and put it down. "I just meant that since you've tried my church twice, I hope you'll keep coming."

Ernie said, "It seems God wants me at Northside. I think I'm finding my niche."

"So does that mean you're ready to join? I saw you talking to Dan for a long time yesterday."

Ernie wouldn't say.

∾

After closing, Ernie drove straight to the Dairy Barn. He needed to be back at the store no later than six thirty.

"Hey, Mr. B. Looking forward to tonight," said Teddy as he placed a napkin and silverware on the table in front of Ernie. "I'll be getting off at seven thirty, then I'll go home and change and get my juggling bag."

"Have I seen everything, or will you surprise me with something new in your act?"

"I've got one little addition as long as I don't forget the peanut butter. What can I get for you, sir?"

Ernie laughed. "I'd like a chicken sandwich with a side salad, please, Teddy. Ranch dressing will be good, and a glass of water."

"Coming right up. Gloria told me about the special cookies she made. It's going to be great!"

∾

"All the coffee's ready, Mr. B," called out Melissa. "Are the peanut butter cookies two for a dollar, same as the others?"

"Gloria charged me the same price, so yes they are," Ernie replied. "Put them in that spare glass jar behind the counter."

"Already done. There are about a dozen of both kinds of muffins. Do we have any more?"

"No, but I'm sure that will be enough. What time is it?"

"Mr. B, there are clocks all over the store. It's quarter 'til eight. Everything is ready with fifteen minutes to spare."

There was a tap on the front door. A senior citizen stood outside with a large cardboard box in her arms. Ernie unlocked the door and said, "We're almost ready. We'll open the coffeehouse at eight o'clock."

"Mr. Bostwick, it's Betty. Remember me? I'm Opal's niece. I've got a present from Opal for opening night."

Ernie opened the door wide. "Thank you! Come on in. What in the world is in the box?"

Betty Carollton stepped into the store and put the box down on the floor. "Opal said you didn't have any kind of sound system, so she bought you this karaoke machine. It's all put together."

"Did you try it out?"

"Mr. Bostwick, Opal has been singing praise songs all afternoon. She had all the cats hiding under the furniture. I know that it works! I'll come back in a few minutes. Opal is up the street, finishing a game of billiards."

"What?" Ernie exclaimed, but Betty had already exited.

He pulled the karaoke machine out of its box and carried it to the stage. Henry had found a seat in the audience, leaving two empty stools for performers.

"Melissa, do you know how to operate this?"

"No, but sounds like Miss Opal can show us."

And they kept coming through the door.

Callie and seven of her Sunday school friends were the first to arrive. Sandra had her story in hand, neatly typed on three sheets, and Kate and Arnie had their accompaniment CD.

"Callie, did you have any luck putting together a comedy routine?" asked Ernie.

"It's short, but I think it's pretty good."

"Everything's good tonight. We want to support anyone who is willing to stand up front."

"Hey, Ernie," called Sandra. "I didn't know you had karaoke."

"I do. Since about twenty minutes ago."

Opal and Betty came next and held the door for Teddy and his father. Clint was close behind, carrying his guitar case. "Hey, Ernie, good to see you again. I'm supposed to have a few friends coming."

"Great," said the proprietor. "Did you finish the second verse of the song you were working on?"

"Sure did. Three verses and a bridge."

Opal clustered around the karaoke machine with Callie and friends, pointing out the different features on the appliance. Melissa was kept busy, filling orders for coffee, cookies, and muffins.

By ten after eight, Cindy and Gloria had arrived. Glen came in with an envelope in hand.

Ernie stepped up to the stage at eight fifteen. "Welcome to Coffee with Jesus. Tonight, we are here to share our talents, glorify God, and support each other in our artistic efforts. I hope we can do this every other Friday night, or maybe the first and third Friday of each month. I have two rules for Coffee with Jesus. Number one: everything performed has to be about our relationship with God. This will be a Christian event.

"Number two: no matter how well anybody does, every effort is worthy of applause. It's never easy getting up in front of people. We don't have to perform in any particular order. If you have more than two songs or poems or whatever, split them up."

It was an incredible night. Cindy practically ran to the stage to start things off, reading the poem Ernie had heard on Monday.

Clint followed. His skill on the guitar was better than Ernie remembered. Even though verse 3 of his song had a rhyming problem near the end, applause was abundant.

Teddy's juggling wowed the audience. Near the end of his act, he asked someone to bring a small table to the stage. Teddy opened a jar of peanut butter, placed a table knife next to it, and laid out two slices of bread. With only one dropped ball, he was able to make and eat a peanut butter sandwich with his right hand while juggling three balls in his left hand.

There was a pause after Teddy finished. No one seemed willing to follow Teddy's splendid performance.

Callie was the first to get up. She took her seat on one of the two stools on stage.

"Where does a Christian girl find a guy? I asked my mom. She didn't know. She said she only knew to go to a bar. I said, 'Mom, a bar is no place for a Christian.'

"And she said, 'There's more than one kind of bar.'

"I decided to try it. You know, listen to your elders. I tried it, but it didn't work. Do you know I didn't find a single cute guy at the salad bar?

"My motto used to be, 'Men are snakes.' I even got a snake tattoo. See? But I was wrong. They don't crawl on their bellies. They love their bellies too much.

"They say the way to a man's heart is through his stomach. Doctors know better. They go through the chest.

"I like men. They're nice to have around. I also like iguanas, fruit flies, and overripe bananas. I think there's a pattern there.

"What goes thump, thump, swish, crash? A man trying to be quiet by walking through the living room without turning on the lights.

"When God made humans, He didn't say it was *good* until after He made both man and woman. After He made man, He said, 'Oops.'

"I hope you understand that all of this is said in fun. God loves both men and women. If God didn't mean for us to laugh at ourselves, He wouldn't have allowed us to create mirrors.

"God made men to be bold, brave, and aggressive. They are built to walk into danger first. But no! They get around that by being polite. 'Here, I'll hold the door for you, so you go in first.' I don't want to go in first!

"No joke though. Whether you're a girl or a guy, the first thing to do when looking for your lifelong companion is pray. God has the right person in mind for you, and we are notoriously faulty when we try to choose by ourselves. Be patient. And remember, we look on the outside, but God looks on the heart.

"Thank you."

When Callie sat down, people all around patted her on the back and whispered, "Good job!"

Glen strode to the stage and opened the envelope he had kept in his lap all night.

"I've kept this envelope in a safety deposit box at the bank for many years. My mother, now deceased, wrote me this little note and hid it in my suitcase when I went off to my first job. It was the first time I had ever lived away from home. It's precious to me as you might guess."

He unfolded the letter and began to read. "Dear son, you have grown up now. Your father and I have always done our best to provide a good Christian home for you, but now everything is up to you.

"Remember that we love you. More importantly, remember that God loves you and always will.

"I long to give you all sorts of advice and rules for you to live by, but it all boils down to this one thing: love God with all you heart, soul, mind, and strength, and love your neighbor as yourself. Love, Mom.

"P.S. Stay in church."

Glen quietly folded the letter, returned it to its envelope, and returned to his chair in the audience. People stood and softly applauded.

After everyone had shared who wanted to, people hung around, drinking coffee and eating. Ernie made a decent profit that night, but it could not compare to the spiritual gain experienced by all who attended.

∽

Mike looked at his watch. It was just after ten on Saturday morning.

"Melissa, I haven't seen Ernie for an hour. Do you know what he's up to? I've never seen him stay in his workroom for this long without taking a break."

"I'll check." She walked back to the workroom, knocked softly, and walked in.

Ernie sat on a stool, eyes closed, with his hands in his lap.

"Oops, sorry. I didn't know you were taking a nap."

He opened his eyes and smiled. Melissa could see wet streaks on Ernie's face.

"No, I just needed to spend some extra time in prayer this morning."

"God really blessed us last night, didn't He, Mr. B?"

"Yes, Melissa, God certainly did."

CHAPTER 30

Ernie stepped quickly over to meet the elderly couple entering the church.

"Good morning! It's a great day at Northside Church. I'm Ernie Bostwick." He handed each of them the day's worship bulletin.

"Thank you," the sturdy white-haired lady responded.

Her slim husband added, "You're new here, aren't you? It's nice to see people get involved instead of waiting for someone to beg them to serve the Lord."

"My husband has served as an usher for, what is it, sixty-four years, Clinton?"

"Sixty-five now, Elise. I started when I was fourteen."

"Nice to meet you, Clinton and Elise. I'll be here every Sunday."

Ernie moved to intercept the next attenders, a couple in their thirties with a little boy carrying a toy truck.

"So glad you're here. Say, I've got a truck like that in my store. Yours looks nicer though."

The little boy smiled up at Ernie, who reached in his pocket and produced a peppermint candy. Ernie handed it to the young mother. "Here's something for emergencies."

"Why, thank you. When I was a child, we had a Mr. Johnson who always had a peppermint for the children. We really looked forward to it. Johnny, say thank you."

"Thank you, sir," said the blond little boy.

Arnie wandered over to speak to Ernie. "Say, you're really good at this. You really make people feel welcome."

"I'm glad our Sunday school class greets people. I want everybody to see the love of Jesus as soon as they enter the door. Some of them have probably had a hard week."

Arnie nodded. He moved back to his place near another entrance.

Ernie noticed that each member of the young adult class seemed enthusiastic about their self-appointed role as greeter. They smiled warmly, and their body language showed a really open, friendly attitude. Even the coldest response didn't affect their zeal for the job.

At a minute or two before eleven, the greeters headed for their customary seats in the sanctuary. "My turn to stay out here for the late arrivers," said Callie. "I'll be in at five after."

Cindy caught up with Ernie just as he was going into the church sanctuary. "Sorry I'm late." He extended his arm to escort her in. They sat at the end of one of the pews with the young adult class, leaving a space between Sarah and Ernie for Callie.

After his welcome and a few announcements, Dan said, "We have the special privilege today of accepting three people into membership at Northside. I ask these to come forward at this time. Let's all turn to the liturgy on page 35 in our hymnal."

Across the church, a middle-aged couple rose and came forward. Ernie Bostwick also made his way to the front.

The pastor continued, "Ernie Bostwick comes to our church by transfer from the River Church in Perry. Millie Harnett is transferring from Trinity Methodist across town, and Douglas Harnett is joining by profession of faith and will be receiving the sacrament of baptism."

Dan asked any special friends of those joining the church to come stand with them in support of their friend. Another couple came up to stand with Douglas and Millie, and the entire two rows of young adults emptied to stand with Ernie. Cindy also came. Gloria came down from the choir loft.

Pastor Dan worked through the sprinkling baptism ritual with Douglas, with congregational responses and assent, then joined the three to the church. He asked the congregation to please extend a welcoming handshake or hug to the new members after the worship service. Everyone returned to their seats.

As the worship service progressed, Ernie noticed that today's sermon was titled "What Are You Doing Here?" He smiled as he contemplated how a visitor might respond when seeing that in the bulletin.

Dan announced as his scripture text 1 Kings 19 and proceeded to read all twenty-one verses of the chapter. "Especially notice," he said, "those words in verse nine, repeated in verse nineteen. God asks, 'What are you doing here, Elijah?'

"Elijah had won a great victory for God on Mount Carmel. You remember the story. Elijah challenged all the prophets of Baal to a simple duel. They set up a burnt offering to Baal, and Elijah set up a similar sacrifice to God. They did not light any fire. The real god would respond to his followers by sending fire from heaven to burn up the offering. The prophets of Baal called on their god for six hours. No response. Elijah called on our God, the one true God, and He acted immediately. Fire came down from heaven and burned up Elijah's offering.

It even burned up the rocks of the altar. I'm not calling it lightning, because there wasn't a cloud in the sky. It was fire from heaven. What a dramatic victory.

"But now Elijah is running for his life. He's ready to quit. He feels like he's done enough and tells God he's ready for heaven.

"That's when God says, 'What are you doing here, Elijah?'

"Isn't it funny how a question like that from another time and place can reverberate in our souls today?

"Maybe those words are for you. You've done great things in the past. You've led your children and several others to Christ. You've served your church and your community. But you've reached a point in your life where you've declared to God and everyone else that you've done enough.

"God says to you, 'What are you doing here?'

"He told Elijah several more things He had for him to do. He was even giving him a disciple to train, and that would take years.

"God told Elijah, 'Stand here and take a look at my glory.' And Elijah was reenergized.

"So what are you doing here? Have you wrapped your life up into a little ball and told God that it's all the territory you want to serve in from now on? Have you quit looking for new challenges?

"Maybe it's time for you to take a look at God's glory. It's not just for us. It's bigger than that. God wants the whole world to see His glory and respond to it. It's not time to quit.

"If you are tempted to take a break, or to stop reaching out for God altogether, maybe those words are for you today: what are you doing here?"

Ernie felt uncomfortable with the sermon but in a good way. He had been like Elijah, doing great things for God, but giving up when the challenges got tougher. Today he felt like he was back on track.

During the last hymn, Ernie felt a nudge from Cindy. He leaned over so that she could speak in his ear.

"Will you go down front with me? I'm ready to be a Christian."

He looked at her and nodded. "Do you want to be baptized today?" he whispered.

Cindy quickly nodded.

He whispered again, "Do you want to join the church?"

She stared at him. Three seconds passed.

"Yes," she said quietly.

Ernie took her hand, and they both stood up. People around them turned to look as they walked down the aisle. Ernie saw Gloria stop singing, smile, and start crying. She put down her hymnal and came down to meet them at the front.

Dan walked forward to meet Cindy and Ernie. Ernie whispered a few words to the pastor, who nodded and continued singing to the end of the verse. He turned to the pianist, who brought the hymn to a gentle stop.

"Friends," said Dan, "Cindy Martin comes this morning to give her life to Christ, to be baptized, and to join our church. What a glorious moment for her and for all of us! As before, I ask any friends to come forward in support of this precious one. I see Gloria and Ernie are already here."

All the young adults came streaming forward again.

Dan said, "Cindy, let's you and I kneel and pray for you to accept Jesus as your savior. Do you want me to pray, and you repeat after me?"

Cindy said, "No, I know what I want to pray."

She and Dan knelt as did Ernie and Gloria.

"God," Cindy began, "I want to follow you the rest of my life. Thank you for giving me Christian friends like Ernie and Gloria, who show me what a difference you can make. I accept Jesus's death on the cross as payment for my sins, and I give you control now. Amen."

The entire congregation heard Cindy's prayer through Dan's lapel mike. One by one and in groups, they all stood and clapped their hands in praise to God.

Dan led them again through the baptismal ritual. Dan couldn't help but laugh when Cindy whispered, "Feel free to use a whole handful of water!"

As the service ended, people lined up to welcome the Harnetts, Ernie, and Cindy. Gloria was smiling from ear to ear, happy for her friends. The young adult class was especially proud.

Their Sunday school teacher shook Ernie's hand and gave him a big hug. "Dan just told me some good news. I'll be leaving for Florida on Tuesday, and he told me you volunteered to take over as teacher of my class. Thank you, from the bottom of my heart."

"God supplies all our needs, according to his riches in glory, the Bible says. I hope they'll love me as much as they do you." Ernie gave her another hug.

"Cindy, that was amazing," said Callie. "You're going to love being a Christian. If you need to know anything, just ask me."

"The first thing I want to know," said Cindy, "is if I can join your Sunday school class. I'm not exactly a young adult."

"You are now," said Frankie. "Consider yourself one of us."

❧

Ernie dialed Jack Rhodes on his cell phone. "Jack, mind if I bring Gloria to join us for lunch today? We're having a little homecoming celebration."

"Sure," answered Jack. "I'll pull up an extra chair. Say, should we plan on Gloria joining us every Sunday?"

Ernie smiled at Gloria. She matched his smile with a bigger one.

"Yes, Jack, you can plan on it."